CARE GIVE OR TAKE

a novel

ROB BROWNELL

SYLLABALLISTICS PUBLISHING · DECATUR, GEORGIA · 2025

ISBN: 979-8-9859264-3-9 (Paperback)
ISBN: 979-8-9859264-4-6 (E-book)

Library of Congress Control Number: 2024919007

Alessandor Earnest, developmental editing, www.theimpofediting.com
Ariel Anderson, copyediting, www.arieledits.com
Dick Margulis, interior design and composition, www.dmargulis.com
Maddie Cohen, proofreading, www.maddiecohen.com

Published by Syllaballistics Publishing
info@syllaballistics.com
www.syllaballistics.com

For those who cared for me

CLAGETT LAY FLAT ON the floor, his bony shoulder blades pressed painfully against the hardwood. Overhead, the ceiling bore the scar of his shoddy repair work. He well knew the framed wildflowers arranged on the walls to either side—Akimbo's collection. The landmarks placed him in the downstairs hallway. He felt dazed but was fairly sure he had not lost consciousness.

Though he had been walking cautiously, when the toes of his right foot snagged on the floor, he lurched sideways and struck his shoulder against the wall. His useless arms and weak legs were unfit to regain his balance. He tipped backward. He leaned into the wall in a futile effort to brake as his body traced an arc to the floor. The experience registered as a blur of motion followed by two thumps—his rump and then his head meeting wood.

His body did the sensible thing and panicked. He felt his blood pressure drop, his face drain of color, his thoughts bog down under a white snow of desperation. Once the ringing in his ears subsided, he focused on whether he could feel blood pooling behind his head. Apparently neither bleeding nor broken, he was, regrettably, marooned in his own hallway.

The rippled ceiling repair lurked overhead, distracting him from his predicament. Working with spackle, he had turned barely noticeable plaster cracks into a 3D relief map of new homeowner overconfidence. How cruel to be reminded of a long-ago failing when embarking on an entirely new one.

He yelled for help. To no avail, he shouted at the smartphone in his pocket. He knew exactly where Akimbo was at this hour, yet…abandonment still struck him as the most likely explanation for her absence. He imagined she had skipped town and left him—for good reason. She was tired of taking care of him, worrying about him, watching ALS debilitate him. She resented that most of the words out of his mouth were requests for assistance.

She was a caring, nurturing woman who deserved better than to be saddled with his care. She tended her plants and livestock with tenderness and devotion. She raised her chickens from eggs and kept her dairy goats in neat pens, milking them and feeding them unfailingly. True, she slaughtered and cooked the young males, the roosters and goat bucklings, before they toughened up into leathery masculine sinew. But she did it mercifully, flushed with righteous barnyard antipatriarchyism.

Her abandonment seemed inevitable, but to disappear like this, without saying goodbye, was unlike her. Maybe something awful happened to her too? Maybe she lay on the barn floor, wounded, bleeding, Gracie and Zoey—the goats—bleating at her from their pen…

Zoey: Why's she just lying there?

Gracie: I knocked her down. I never really cared for her. Cold hands.

Zoey: The good news is her fingers won't be freezing our hooters; the bad news is we'll starve without her.

Gracie: Hooters? Really? That's degrading.

Zoey: Can we agree that starvation is the bigger concern?

Gracie: Even in the face of starvation, hold on to your self-respect. You're more than the milk you produce!

Zoey: I will miss her empowerment talks. She wasn't all bad.

The tragic coincidence that he and Akimbo both lay helpless was such a horrible possibility that it seemed all the more likely. Fate was cruel like that in his book.

Fate had seemingly left *him* shackled to discomforts—imagination run amok, wife missing, bony backside throbbing, vision fixed on the ceiling's shrine to his incompetence.

———

A gangly figure dressed in loose black clothing, bamboo scythe in gloved hands, face obscured by a wire mask, stood over him.

"What's going on?" his vision of death inquired. The figure removed the mask to reveal itself as his wife, Akimbo, looking down on him with a frown.

"I thought you were the Grim Reaper for a second there." Not a good start. "A gracefully aging Grim Reaper, mind you."

"I gather you're okay?" She looked annoyed, interrupted, not terribly relieved to find him alert. Gracefully aging, but still grim.

"I need help."

"I can't take care of you anymore," she said. The certainty of her statement was undeniable, not a hint of hyperbole.

"Am I bleeding?"

"I don't see blood this time. Anything broken?"

"I don't think so."

"I'll be back in a few minutes," she said.

She pushed her way through the screen door, its metal

spring groaning. He heard the whispers of her bare feet retreat down the porch steps.

She reappeared with six students and a skittish mother on carpool duty. The students still wore their sparring garb and wire-grill face protection. They were small, like bonsai samurai. Scrunchied ponytails sprouting from the backs of their heads gave the only clue that they were middle-school-aged girls. The mother wore an expression of nervousness pasted over with good manners.

"Joan, you remember my husband, Clagett," Akimbo said politely. She tiptoed along the wall until she stood over his head.

"Yes, of course, we met at last year's barbecue. How have you been?"

"I've been doing just fine, thank you. Taking a little rest here, that's all."

"I'm glad," Joan said.

Akimbo barked stern commands in a martial arts pidgin. "Three each side of him, facing opponent. Take position!"

"Hai!" the girls shouted in acknowledgment.

The children scrambled to line up along Clagett's sides. Joan knelt to support his ankles.

Once positioned and instructed, the group readied themselves to lift Clagett to his feet.

"On three," Akimbo barked. "Ichi, ni, san…hajime!"

They strained together.

The rescuers dragged Clagett to the safe harbor of his wheelchair. Akimbo arranged his limbs and cinched his seatbelt. She saw to the departure of her students and reappeared in her uniform. She didn't sit, and Clagett knew she was still wired, as was he, in the aftermath of his fall.

Since his ALS diagnosis nearly two years prior, she had progressively taken over his care. First he lost strength in his arms, then his hands, and within a year all he had left was a twitch in one thumb. His ability to walk followed suit. Stairs went, then walking on uneven ground, then on carpet. She compensated for him, filling in for his missing abilities. With each task she assumed, the more she disliked all the tasks.

She never wanted children or any responsibility resembling childcare. Her parents had prioritized ministering to those in need and often left their daughter under the watchful eye of the good Lord Himself, which is to say alone. She adopted the view that childhood was a cruelty imposed by adults.

As her husband's needs approached those of a toddler, she grew resentful of even his smallest requests. His life, or what was left of it, was an ongoing emergency, always demanding attention. She considered possibilities like hiring caregivers, running away, and putting him in a facility, but they smacked of her parents' neglect and brought on waves of guilt. She carried on, suffering for her love.

She deteriorated along with him, her identity disappearing as his care reduced her to merely an extension of him. She came to believe that devoted caregiving by a loved one was at best a wishful ideal, and at worst a punishment for both of them.

"You have to talk with me about this," Akimbo said. "I can't do this anymore. I'm sorry if you think I'm a bad person or a bad wife. I'm not cut out for caregiving."

"I knew this was coming eventually. I don't think you're bad. I think I'm bad at disability."

"The disease isn't your fault," she said.

He'd heard that so many times that it barely carried

meaning. At this point he only wondered why people so frequently considered the *possibility* it was his fault, before assuring him it wasn't.

"It sure does feel like it," he sighed.

"You could've arranged care sooner, before I became desperate. *That* is your fault. We need to prepare for what's in front of us. You need to prepare. You need to make care arrangements. I don't want to do it for you. I won't do it for you. I can't do it for you. Can you do that for me?"

"I'll start looking for help."

"You need to finish looking. Soon. The time to start is in the past."

"I promise."

"Not just a little help. I'm out of the game."

"You're leaving me?"

"No, I'm not leaving. Why would you think that? I'm hurt you would think that. Do you believe I'm the kind of person capable of leaving?"

"Are you that kind of person? There's a lot happening to me that seemed only remotely possible until recently. I could use assurance."

"I'm not leaving," she said adamantly. "I could leave, but I'm not."

He wasn't completely assured.

"You need to stay in your wheelchair. I don't want you walking. Even with my assistance, I can't stop you from falling. Will you do that?"

He thought he was bravely prolonging his mobility. She saw it differently.

"I can do that."

This is how it happens with ALS, he thought. *One day you can barely walk and the next day you can't. One day you're alive...*

His mind reeled in defense of his actions…He didn't *like* imposing on her, but if he had to use the bathroom or there was a mosquito sucking on his ear, what was he to do? Be stoic and suffer? He loved being with her; he loved receiving her care. Was that wrong? He knew he was an enormous burden, but his care was temporary—she would live on. Didn't that imbalance factor in somehow?

A surge of panicky confusion sapped his energy and spun him into a funk. He reclined his chair and started to nod off.

"Call Geldine!" she yelled. A slam of the screen door punctuated her exit.

His wheelchair's souped-up computer tablet menaced him with possibilities, daring him to do other than search for caregivers. The tablet's cameras forever spied on his eyes and moved the cursor according to his focal point. It *knew* what he read, when his attention wandered, when he glanced at clickbait.

But…the clever eye-gaze technology didn't deliver him from the stultifying clicks through internet sludge. The very thought of wading into a caregiver search was almost more than he could bear. On the other hand, if he didn't at least attempt progress, he faced a truly unbearable conversation with Akimbo.

He searched broadly for caregiving agencies within range of their farm. His tablet rewarded him with listings bristling with possibilities: childcare, after-school care, private nurses, nonprofits, home care, memory care, respite care, adult care, caregiver care—everything right up through hospice care. He was mildly surprised that funeral directors didn't turn up, *cadaver care* or some such, eager to get their foot in the door, their hand in the wallet.

He decided to only contact businesses without a hospice division, just so there was no misunderstanding—telling himself that he had to start somewhere to get anywhere.

Another surge of panic swept him away as the implications of *hospice* settled into his psyche. He couldn't escape the fact he was dying, but he didn't want hospice workers telling him he was *dying* dying. The thought of mortality bled dry his willpower.

When he awoke from his second nap, he committed himself to progress. But first, he looked up *hysterical napping*, which sucked out through his eyeballs half an hour of what was left of his life. Disappointed by his distraction, he decided calling Geldine was the thing to do. Calling her was easy and was Akimbo's recommendation, a two-for-one win.

Geldine was a neighbor, but by no means did he think of her as a friend. They didn't invite Geldine and Langford for Christmas eggnog—they called when a distempered fox wandered into their barn or they harvested more zucchini than they could eat.

His computer's microphone and speakers served as his telephone. Using eye-gaze control he picked out Geldine's mobile phone from his contact list. He reached her at her day job, caregiving at a nursing home, where she was persuading her old lady to eat another bite of peaches.

He jumped right in and told her that his ALS had progressed to where he needed assistance and so was calling to see if she had recommendations.

"I thought you'd had a stroke," she said. Her patient became audibly agitated, thinking she was the stroke victim, and it took Geldine's renewed persuasion to turn attention back to the peaches.

"No. ALS," he corrected and left it at that.

"That's a shame," she said. Her voice carried the fore-knowledge of someone who had seen his future and sincerely felt for his situation.

She asked about his health and his current care. She asked perfunctory questions about blood pressure and medications. Her enthusiasm peaked with close questioning about bowel movements and incontinence.

She buoyed him with positivity and assured him that a home care agency would best meet his needs. As if it was reason alone to hire them, she promised he would develop a close relationship with his loving caregivers. That wouldn't apply to Akimbo, who might grow to hate them. Or vice versa.

He heard her patient grunt and say, "Don't buy it!" before Geldine poked another spoonful into her mouth.

"She's talking about nursing-home care. Don't mind her."

"Is she okay?"

"She's fine. It's all good. Nursing-home caregivers are stuck with six, maybe eight people, and none get the attention they deserve. You don't want that." Without missing a beat, she said, "Caregiving is a job that's more than just a paycheck. Do caregivers do it for money? Yes, we've got bills, but we care about your well-being and the money too. I've asked for loans from families long after the patient is out of the picture—that's the sort of special bond I'm talking about. They still feel guilty about the stuff they said."

She said she got to know caregiving clients so well that they were like family except they paid her money, unlike her own family, who were all about taking. Also, clients tended to have better food in the refrigerator and bigger televisions than her own family, bigger even than the television Langford bought in the supercenter parking lot before the lightning fried it.

"I'll have to call back on my break," she said calmly. "I need to deal with a breathing obstruction."

———————————

They spoke again late in the afternoon—"bedtime for her patients," as she called it. This go-around she was noticeably interested to discuss personally working with him.

"I've thought this over," she said. "I called an agency I've run up against before. They're not as high as some of those expensive agencies that won't hire me. They bring in cheap out-of-town labor. I think they would do the job and would put me on your case for some hours, since I recommended you."

"Okay…" He was stuck back on what she meant by *not as high*. He was almost certain she meant *not as expensive*, but he had to wonder if caregivers were the true beneficiaries of medical marijuana.

"I can bring the care coordinator with me tomorrow morning. She'd like to give you a taste of your own care," she said.

Clagett responded with an uncertain grunt that she took as acceptance.

He had once been a man of accuracy, rigor, and uncompromising effort. He had believed in foresight and planning and meticulous execution. That was now gone, replaced by a willingness to let the universe go about its business, provided it kept him loosely informed. He had secured a caregiver visit, and he had no energy to make another call—he assumed the universe had spoken.

So began his third nap of the day.

While Clagett slept, Akimbo moved upstairs to the bed-room he once used as his office. She left his work detritus where he had left it, even though only she used the desk now. He had made a decent living, financially speaking, programming machinery that didn't hold her interest. Over the last year he'd extracted himself from his consulting contracts and with that went his income.

Amazingly, the only evidence left of his technical life was a stack of notes scribbled onto grid paper, a wind-up robot toy, and his trusty binoculars.

Behind the desk hung a caution sign he'd come across in Asia someplace. It graphically warned of a factory hazard, but, for someone about to be dismembered, the stick-man victim wore a comical expression—according to Clagett anyway. When he first hung the sign he asked if she was worried about what would become of the workers, seeing as how he had their sign. No, she had said, the workers didn't even occur to me. You're right, he had said, fuck 'em.

She sat at the desk and pulled up a months-old account-ing of their savings. Her first glance at the numbers brought on intense hopelessness, knowing as she did that the total was destined to only fall unless she took better-paying work. The upkeep of the farm was a constant financial drain, but she gained a measure of satisfaction from the physical effort. The upkeep of Clagett brought less satisfaction, she was ashamed to admit.

She quickly calculated the cost of caregivers, assuming they worked twelve hours a day, every day, for 30 percent over minimum wage…But for how long? How long did she think Clagett would live? The question was excruciating to consider even without tying it to money. She averted her eyes from the computer only to have them land on the stick-man caught in a machine. *I'm right there with you, buddy,* she thought.

Two years, according to the doctors. Probably less. The total caregiver cost popped onto the screen and her stomach dropped. She checked her numbers for accuracy. They had *some* runway with their savings, but two years of caregiving was a scary big number. Should she hope for one year? Or was his life worth any sacrifice, including her financial future?

She emailed her friend Gia, a financial planner, writing that she wanted to discuss her future.

2

THEY MET IN JAPAN.

Akimbo lived there, tutoring English, traveling aimlessly when she could afford to. Before, back in the States, she'd given the working life a fair shake for three entire months, all the while troubled that she would be laboring over variations of the same tasks for the rest of her life—like Sisyphus, but with the added headache of management oversight. She abandoned her wispy career ambitions and her boyfriend and all interest in a traditional lifestyle and lit out for…someplace different. Why she chose Japan—whether for adventure or misguided notions of Eastern meaning or sheer distance from her current self— she couldn't say.

She rented a room from elderly Tomoe, a maddeningly pleasant widow who giggled even while reprimanding Akimbo for the heavy footfalls of antic midnight dancing. When her sleep was disturbed one night too many, the widow invited Akimbo to a park and introduced her to the business end of a naginata, a long wooden pole out-fitted with a flexible bamboo tip. In the samurai days, she explained with a smile, the end of the pole was fitted with a short, curved sword.

Tomoe made the introduction by playfully parrying and slashing and spearing Akimbo in a mock battle. Akimbo stood close to six feet tall, towering over Tomoe's five-two aspirations, but the long-handled weapon more than compensated for reach. Tomoe laughed as she tagged Akimbo's vital organs and major arteries, leaving Akimbo unsure whether Tomoe giggled for the joy of wholesome exercise or for the pleasure of punishing her. Regardless, Tomoe's delight was infectious and Akimbo envisioned the joy of someday whacking Tomoe in return.

They settled into a cycle of aggravation—Akimbo antagonized Tomoe with late-night dancing, and Tomoe continued to beat sense into her—until the routine became the foundation of rigorous practice and friendship.

Clagett came to Kyoto on a business trip, his first to the headquarters of the robotics behemoth that swallowed him out of college. He stayed for a few tourist days, and while wandering the city he chanced upon Akimbo and Tomoe in the park.

They were practicing in full protective gear, heads covered, shoulders and chests padded, shins girded. A ponytail of auburn hair lashed Akimbo's back as she lunged and twisted in combat.

She had been in Japan for nearly two years by then. Her naginata skill had surpassed Tomoe's, and their sparring looked lopsided, which could have left the impression the up-and-comer was abusing her elder if not for their laughter and celebratory dance moves.

Clagett made his approach after she removed her helmet and stepped over to a water fountain.

"What did that old lady do to deserve your thrashing?" he asked.

She wiped water from her mouth with the back of her hand but showed no inclination to answer.

"What is that weapon? I've never seen it before."

"Naginata," she said. "It's traditional. It's been around forever."

She wrung sweat out of her ponytail and gave him a once-over. Men rarely left a good first impression, but after two years in Japan, his wavy blond hair and effortless English slipped unexpectedly past her defenses. He was her height—rounding up slightly—with Nordic features. His sneakers, baggy clothes, and accent said American.

"Can I buy you something cold to drink? You must be thirsty," he said.

"I don't think so."

"Can I buy you dinner tonight? I don't know anyone here."

"I'm sorry, would you speak slower? My impertinence is rusty."

He took his proposition up another notch, undeterred by her reticence. "Can we fall in love?"

"Oh, is *that* what you said? I don't think I have it in me."

"I suppose not," he agreed.

"Oh? Why?" She insisted on knowing.

"You laughed maniacally while hitting that lady. Cruelty is a red flag for me."

"And yet here you are." She twisted her face, suggesting he *should* keep his distance, but rather liked that he wasn't intimidated.

"I shouldn't have said *maniacal*. You laughed in a happy, delirious sort of way," he corrected.

"Seriously?"

"You sounded positively ecstatic."

"What if I took off my mask and was ugly?"

"I saw beauty in your movement."

"I find that hard to believe."

"Actually, you hooked me when you shouted, 'And there goes your other kidney!'"

"I didn't say that, did I?"

"You shouted, like I said. I couldn't help but laugh. Best moment of my trip."

"Better than what? Business meetings? High praise."

Later, over shabu-shabu at her favorite restaurant she couldn't afford, the one she saved for visitors with credit history, she asked if he made a habit of approaching dangerous women.

She returned to the States several months after they met, moving within striking distance of Clagett, a couple of hours away. There, a respected Japanese expat ran a small naginata club where she continued her practice. Soon enough, Clagett was making regular weekend trips to visit her.

Clagett came to know her circle of fellow students, teachers, and competitors. He came to know that *interesting* was the polite way to describe them. They weren't more eccentric than average adults. In most ways they seemed rather benign, but he couldn't reconcile that with their shared enjoyment of hacking imaginary enemies to death.

Akimbo seemed happiest when she held a naginata. Clagett teased that she preferred it over him, which she didn't deny, but rather deflected, saying that a comparison wasn't possible. He floated theories about its power—security object, comfort object, fetish—but she would only ever admit that it felt right.

Her teacher faulted Akimbo for her inability to conjure the essence of a steely killer, to face her opponents with unwavering resolve. He went so far as to mention the problem to Clagett after they were into their cups of sake, saying he worried she wouldn't have survived the samurai days. "The battlefield is no place for laughter," he grimly pronounced.

At naginata tournaments, Clagett watched her jog onto the floor, a happy bounce in her step, eagerness in every move. The judges openly blanched at her playful demeanor. She looked no more serious as the matches unfolded. Even as she overwhelmed opponents with body blows like bolts of lightning out of a clear sky, head strikes that cracked like thunder, she seemed to lack a winner's resolve—she seemed momentarily lucky.

Up close, those who repeatedly suffered under her blows heard laughter they interpreted as nervous titters or sadistic satisfaction. Behind her mask, though, she smiled gleefully, giggling with unbridled joy.

Clagett believed that she was expressing her true self, channeling the absurdity of competition and violence into movement. The other competitors put on ferocious faces and posed as warriors, the artifice of which only clouded their minds and slowed their weapons. Akimbo dismissed this theory as well.

———————

Six years later, under the watchful eyes of family and friends and whatever gods the guests brought with them, Akimbo and Clagett vowed to stay together in sickness and in health. Whether out of youthful optimism or lack of imagination, he naively assumed he would never be on the sickness end of the bargain. He romantically interpreted the promise as: he would do anything necessary for Akimbo if she fell ill. He pictured himself doing so lovingly, patiently, and empathetically.

"I can't be your everything," she said.

Early in their marriage, Akimbo had bluntly stated this

simple truth. At the time, they were discussing a pimple on his back, one she was reluctant to squeeze, but they both understood that her statement had broader implications. He said that made sense and reciprocated that he could not be her everything either, though up until that point he had been willing to try and would have, in fact, squeezed a pimple on her back had she not been blessed with perfect skin.

Over the years, on a case-by-case basis, they refined what they were and what they were not to one another, creating a jagged line of expectations.

Akimbo's thoughts on providing sustained care remained unexplored territory; he never had occasion to idly ask, "If I were paralyzed, would you help me wash my hair?" The question, when finally asked out of necessity, opened frank discussions about the muscular shutdown that his future held in store. The answer was both yes and no.

Yes, they readily agreed that his basic needs, like food and cleanliness, would be seen to and that he would be made as comfortable as possible. As gratified as he was to easily settle that initial point, he was disturbed to discover his basic needs were up for discussion.

But no, Akimbo would not be the only one attending to those needs. Eventually his care would be more demanding than she could manage alone. It was only a matter of time until his comfort would be placed in the hands of paid caregivers.

Throughout their discussions, he regularly polled his feelings about the reverse situation, caring for Akimbo if she were the one in need. He was forced to reconsider his youthful ideal of personally providing Akimbo with loving care. He humbly accepted it as an egregious lack of imagination.

3

GELDINE AND LANGFORD WERE their closest neighbors, proximity-wise. They lived about half a mile away, just off the county road, in a sprawling family compound made up of a once-stately-now-decrepit farmhouse, three prefab ranch homes (two standing, one burned to the ground), a double-wide, and a travel trailer on cinder blocks, all populated by complexly related generations of the Shiflett family and their hunting dogs.

The Shifletts descended from God-fearing Protestant gentry whose ill-gotten riches greased the skids for their descendants' slide into idleness and good-natured decadence, and eventually poverty.

Geldine came into the Shiflett fold in her early thirties, at an age when her pool of marriageable prospects was depleted by drug use, jail time, and paychecks garnished of child support. She met Langford in the ER waiting room. He waited for stitches in his chin after his step-cousin's wedding devolved into divorce proceedings. She waited for her client's release after the old lady fell. Geldine, a descendant of Caribbean cultures, was an unlikely addition to Langford's life—unlikely not because of the racial difference but because she was employed.

Their chemistry was a mystery to family and community, and yet it had persisted for two decades, long after the failures of marriages with definable attractions like family money or a nice rack. Geldine's lasting commitment to the Shiflett life was testimony to the redemptive powers of helping others.

———————————

When Clagett called to ask about caregivers, Geldine was at a low point in the ongoing cash-strapped, legal-imperiled predicament known as her life.

Langford's twin nephews had borrowed her car, without her knowledge, the night prior, on their fifteenth birthday. Their joyride ended abruptly in a culvert, leaving a twin with a lacerated forehead and her car inoperable.

The healthier twin roused Geldine because, by common agreement, she was the competent family member called to deal with medical emergencies. Geldine set out in Langford's car, a Swedish beater bequeathed by one of her formerly living clients. Langford had sworn he would take care of the car, but predictably he let the registration lapse, giving cause for a jittery cop to ticket her along the way.

She retrieved the nephews from the hospital. The wounded one set up camp on her couch to recuperate under her care. From the comfort of Langford's lounger, the other nephew strategized market opportunities for his brother's pain medications.

The citation was no small thing. If she left Langford to update the registration and pay the ticket, past behavior suggested he would rail against the injustice but ultimately ignore the whole problem, leading to additional fines and eventually an arrest warrant. Paying off the ticket fell to her.

Her car had been towed and impounded. She needed that car to get to work, but she needed to work to pay the repair costs and the impound fees.

This is how it happens, she recognized. *One minute you're keeping up with your bills, and the next you're bankrupt.*

On Clagett's behalf, she reached out to Care Less, an agency she knew to kickback a finder's bounty for new clientele. Her past interaction with the agency had been nothing short of combative, prompting her to swear she would never deal with them, but that was before she needed quick cash. She wouldn't say anything to Clagett about that because, to be fair, she had nothing nice to say about any of the agencies she worked for.

The coordinator at Care Less, Ariola, eagerly agreed to the referral fee if Geldine could get Clagett on board. Ariola promised Geldine would get hours on the case, too, which, as she rationalized her choices, seemed like a real blessing. She could get to Clagett's farm on foot, she'd be close to home to look after the concussed nephew, and the referral money would pay off the ticket. She'd deal with the cars after the next paycheck.

She felt a pang of guilt for involving her neighbors in her troubles, but she had to take care of herself—no one else was going to do it.

4

ELDINE AND AN AGENCY rep were scheduled to visit late morning, but at the crack of dawn, for Christ's sake, a vehicle pulled up in a commotion of grinding gears and leaking muffler and thumping bass. Although the driveway stopped at the side of the house, in her waking disorientation Akimbo swore the racket came from above and settled onto her painstakingly landscaped backyard.

She pulled on sweatpants and groped her way along the banister, feeling her way down from her second-floor lair. With the stairs impassable to Clagett, the upstairs and its precious closet space were entirely of her dominion.

She passed by Clagett in his living room bed, his eyes wide open, brow knit with concern. He was agitated leading up to this caregiver visit. She didn't know why. Caregivers would provide more attention than she cared to give. He said he was struggling with the nudity part of receiving care, but who knew for sure.

"Go back to sleep," she said. "I'll see what this is all about."

He mumbled panicky gibberish.

She brewed her tea, sipped, and surveilled. There were no signs of life, but there was definitely a vehicle of sorts parked in her backyard, backed right up to the porch like it was a loading dock.

She was not given to conspiracy theories and wild speculation, but it seemed apparent that the vehicle was a boxy delivery-van-sized spacecraft perched on four shock-absorbing landing legs. Given the dents in the hull and the tape holding together a landing light, the clunker of a craft had seen hard service. She surmised that an alien visitation was in progress, though not your high-quality saucer variety people enthused about in the news.

She wasn't shocked by their arrival—Clagett's diagnosis had reset her capacity for shock and aliens barely moved the needle off of *numb*. Primarily, she resented their disruption of the atmosphere of calm she so carefully cultivated. Their arrival was an intrusion, a violation of their sanity safe space.

Unquestionably, the science minded would find interest in an actual alien encounter. Not them. She and Clagett had abandoned all pretense of fascination with science when they wandered into the treatment desert separating him from an ALS cure. A new dinosaur? Wow. Explore space? Great. *How about a little more focus on exploring our own bodies?*

This was so like Clagett to assure her that he had arranged care with Geldine. He said she was now freed of his unrelenting burden (his choice of words). A widowed friend advised her that *burden* wasn't the socially correct description for spousal care, even though completely accurate. What should she call it? Labor of love? Unrelenting *obligation*? Unrelenting *privilege*? Now she was *privileged* to have an alien spacecraft in the backyard, depriving her of rest.

That something dangerous was afoot didn't concern her; the worst that could happen in their lives already was. She doubted that a vehicle of that caliber could mount a full-on planetary invasion. If Clagett got himself abducted, it would serve him right—not really, it wouldn't serve him right, she didn't mean that.

As long as they were competent caregivers, she guessed it didn't matter where they came from. Although, she had a premonition that an interplanetary commute would mess with their reliability, creating still more work and frustration for her.

She simmered over the crushed purple coneflowers and the landing-gear indentations marring her sustainable mint. She pictured her wheelbarrow forevermore dropping into the divots, jarring her shoulders. The thought of the vehicle crushing her plants angered her as if she herself had been squooshed.

Who do you even call in a situation like this? Doubtful the sheriff would show up unless they had meth on board. The farm extension agent might be interested if she framed the aliens as an invasive species. Langford was rumored to jacklight deer with automatic weapons, but she doubted he would come over and hunt down his wife's employer. But you never knew.

Akimbo returned to the living room and updated Clagett on the space van's arrival. "I couldn't make this stuff up if I tried," she concluded.

"Aliens today, of all days? Why does everything get so complicated?" he griped.

"It's incredibly disruptive," she agreed.

"What should we do? Call for help?" Clagett asked.

"Technically you invited them."

"Call the press?" he tried again.

"Like the concerns of a middle-aged white couple would be of human interest?" she said skeptically.

"What if I slept with a celebrity? That makes for surefire news interest."

"I wasn't aware you had."

"Not *yet*. I like my chances, though. I applied to the Grant-a-Wish Foundation."

"Did you now? Let's keep that option on the back burner."

"I *am* disabled, you know," he insisted. "That should earn viewer interest points."

"You're not *permanently* disabled," she said. "It's temporary, more of a transitional state. But…we could make a case that you're working through mental health issues—that's quite popular these days."

"I am?"

She raised her eyebrows at his naiveté. "Let's concentrate on your care for now. We'll keep the press at bay. How does that sound?"

He thought that over. "Should you save yourself?"

"Let's at least give them a listen," she said with finality.

She caught sight of Geldine strolling down the driveway and around the side of the house. Someone emerged from the van and joined her on the back porch. They rapped on the door.

"Can't they even trouble themselves to wait for the appointment time?" Akimbo said sharply, as if Clagett had engineered their inconsiderate arrival exclusively to torment her.

She hefted an umbrella and gave it a waggle, gauging its suitability as a weapon, and made her way to the back of the house. She opened the door so they could converse but stood her ground and blocked the entry.

With the morning sun behind them, she could make out the silhouettes of two women—one noticeably heavy, the other Geldine, angular and skinny.

"My, aren't you a tall specimen," the heavy woman said appreciatively. Akimbo heard a lifelong smoker's rattle of moist phlegm coating the woman's voice. Her lips moved troublingly out of sync with her voice, like seeing lightning before a thunderclap.

"Good morning," Geldine said. "This is Ariola."

"Ariella?" Akimbo asked.

"Ariola! It's a beautiful morning!" said the heavy silhouette.

"Spelled with an eye, not a nipple." Geldine twitched her head toward her companion.

Akimbo glowered at the women, trying to make sense of their words without the benefit of feeling the least bit sociable. "What?"

"The letter *i*," said Geldine.

"We're your new caretaking team," said Ariola. "We're with Care Less."

"That's two words," whispered Geldine.

"And you must be Akimbo!"

Akimbo managed the briefest of smiles to confirm her identity. Ariola's pep was more than she could handle at this hour.

"Important day!" Ariola exclaimed. "We made sure to arrive early."

"No kidding," Akimbo said under her breath.

Geldine, seeing Akimbo's irritation, ushered them along, saying, "How about we see to Clagett?"

"He's in bed, in the living room."

Ariola asked excitedly. "Is he ready for his big day?"

"Is anyone ever ready for this?" Akimbo asked.

"Well, we are! We are pumped up—as you say—to join his final journey," Ariola enthused.

"Right. I guess you'd better come in then."

Akimbo led them to Clagett's bed. He fixed his eyes on the stranger as he reconciled his preconceptions of aliens to her actual appearance. She was not the freakish limbs-like-spaghetti, bug-eyed extraterrestrial he expected, nor did she present reptilian features.

Akimbo rested her hand gently on his shin as she made introductions.

"We'll be taking care of you this morning and later we can all discuss schedules and fees and such," Ariola explained. "We want you to feel comfortable in our hands when you make your decision. Does that sound good, Mr. Clagett?"

A question from an alien squelched even his rudimentary yes/no response. He looked to Akimbo for hints how he should react. In her subtle eye roll, he read hope, resignation, and an urge to flee. Primarily he read the suggestion that he should chill the fuck out.

"Sure, I suppose so," he replied without conviction.

Ariola was remarkably humanoid, indistinguishable really. She had exotic aquamarine eyes and golden Mediterranean skin. Her hair was nearly black, short and lush, with multi-toned highlights that brought to mind the fur of a tortoiseshell cat and an accompanying urge to stroke it. Otherwise, she gave the impression of an average American in her thirties. She sounded wheezy and out of shape, was overweight, her shoulders stooped, and her skin pleaded for moisturizer. On second look her skin revealed green undertones, as if the yellow of someone with jaundice combined with the blue of someone choking—in other words, unhealthy in a multi-systemic way. She seemed surprisingly eager to be there for someone looking so starved of oxygen. If she were human, Clagett would have guessed she was a lifelong smoker.

Ariola came decked out in an outfit that landed some-where between hospital scrubs and men's formal wear. Her pants and top were gloss black and featured all manner of pockets to misplace her possessions. The top was cut like a dinner jacket with a deep V that revealed a white shirt with delicate ruffles running down her chest.

Geldine, of course, he knew, though he'd never seen her gussied up in work clothes. Her scrubs were the traditional shapeless cut, in beige, and printed with teddy bears. She looked fit and ageless even though she was at least push-ing fifty. She bundled her locks out of sight in a decorative bag on top of her head. Sunlight played on the chocolate brown skin of her face and forearms, her tattoos rippling as she drummed her fingers against her thighs. Trim and alert, she projected a readiness to get down to business.

Akimbo started the visitors on a tour of the medical sup-plies collected around the living room and the downstairs bathroom.

He closed his eyes and receded into himself. There, he found shame for his thought about choking a jaundice suf-ferer. Odds seemed good that people with jaundice were too burdened with the medical establishment to complain about his thoughts, but, to be safe, he pictured writing an open letter apologizing for his imagined mistreatment.

"We've taken a minimalist approach to supplies," Akimbo said. "The doctors want to stick us with cure-all gizmos for every problem."

"Oh yes, so true, so true," Geldine said knowingly.

She pointed out his care essentials—his bed controls, Hoyer lift, shower chair, adaptive clothing, nitrile gloves/ hand sanitizer/antibacterial soap/alcohol wipes, wheel-chair joystick, wheelchair charger, eyedrops, lip balm, body lotions, face lotion, cortisone cream, razor, clippers, toothbrush, mouth rinse—just the visible supplies.

Breathing machines perched on small mobile tables were parked in the corner, next to the couch. "He's still getting used to the ventilator. We use the cough-assist machine when he can't get the mucus up on his own," she said.

She opened a drawer of a repurposed filing cabinet to point out his catheter supplies. The other drawer, she explained, collected the odds and ends—beeswax salves, heel warmers, far-fetched remedies—he insisted on ordering online. To complete the inventory, she mentioned that the hall closet held stockpiles of consumable goods and the attic stored boxes of barely used ankle supports and shoulder contraptions.

As Akimbo talked, Ariola kept up parallel chatter selling the many virtues of caregivers. She painted a rosy picture of their experience and the depth of their sensitivity to Clagett's needs. Geldine supported her with a hype-man's rhythmic "Oh yes" or "So very true."

Akimbo gave a top-to-bottom rundown of his physical condition, areas of sensitivity, range of mobility, skin status, and nose hair length—currently unacceptable, boogers visibly gestating.

His nasal passages called Geldine to action. She snapped on gloves and went to work with tissues and cotton swabs. When the extraction became dicey, the hairs on the verge of being wrested from his nose, him whining at a girlish pitch, she called for hydrogen peroxide with all the authority of a surgeon. He felt a childlike thrill to have generated so much attention. Seeing Geldine's grace at tackling an unpleasant chore, Akimbo relaxed noticeably and edged closer to the door.

"With a steadfast caregiver at your bedside, the tragic journey of illness can be a beautiful thing," Ariola promised. "All the way to the bitter end."

Geldine whispered a heartfelt, "Amen."

"Great, have at it," Akimbo said. "Don't let them smell fear," she whispered to Clagett. "Call me if you really need me."

———————————————

Geldine moved with efficiency and surprising strength as she wriggled Clagett's clothes off and tugged on clean replacements. His nude audition—a moment he had instinctively dreaded—and the caregivers' total lack of interest caught him completely by surprise. And yet, it passed with neither shame nor caregiver laughter...nor, sadly, exclamation. Their utter disinterest made him wonder why he had spent his life assiduously wearing clothing.

"People say that you know you're disabled when your private parts aren't" was the only commentary Geldine offered.

Statistically speaking, this was only the second time in his life that a woman had wrestled clothing from his body. Having two women simultaneously participate in the act was a first. While the facts of his encounter were notable, mutual disinterest demanded an asterisk in the record book of his life. Of course, he didn't *actually* keep a lifetime record book; the notable details were easily held in memory, saved to think about when the present wasn't to his liking, like that moment.

He kept his eyes closed, playing grown-up peekaboo, wishing he was invisible, pretending their chatter was about someone else.

Seeing him stretched out on the bed, Ariola commented, "He's a tall one, like his wife. Bony, though."

"He was a good-looking fellow in his prime. He looked like one of those beautiful Aryan Nazis, except he was harmless," Geldine said.

"What's wrong with him anyway?" Ariola wondered aloud.

"He's got the ALS," Geldine said. "He can feel everything; he just can't move much. It kills you eventually."

"I guess that's good. He deserves an end to it."

"Amen," Geldine agreed.

Geldine continued to prep him for the day while Ariola foraged around the room. He was still on his back, his worldview narrowed to the ceiling, but from what he could tell she was placing items into a large canvas bag. When caught straining to see her, she calmly explained, "A little rearranging to keep things efficient." She rooted through piles of his folded clothing.

Within an hour of their introduction, Geldine had Clagett dressed, bathroomed, and plopped into his wheelchair. He made his way to the kitchen for his customary breakfast. He found the back door open and saw Ariola tossing canvas bags into the ship's cargo area.

Geldine came up behind him and seized control of the wheelchair, overriding his eye-gaze control with the attendant joystick. She navigated him out the back door and parked him at the top of the porch steps.

Ariola dragged a loading ramp from the back of the ship and extended it across the divide between the ship and the porch.

Clagett yelled, "At-home care! I said at-home care! I made that perfectly clear." He feared Akimbo had blindsided him and was shipping him off to a nursing facility.

"Everything will be fine. This is our job. This is what caregivers do, take patients out of the house. It's all good, it's all good," Geldine assured him.

"Where's Akimbo? Does she know what's happening?" he shouted.

"It's fine. She's coming along too," Geldine said.

In nervous anticipation of needing caregivers, Clagett had thoroughly worried for his privacy, his modesty, his dignity, the few breakable items strewn around the house. Now, confronted with their power, he quickly grasped that his paranoia was undersized—the original concerns were proving to be virtually inconsequential compared to the real problems.

———————————————

While Clagett got his first taste of professional caregivers, Akimbo sought refuge in her chores and the companionship of her animals. Her chickens generally had little of substance to say, unlike Gracie and Zoey, her goat confidants. Sometimes when she milked them, she sought their advice. She found that having teats in her hands encouraged conversation and honesty. Why men had the opposite reaction, she didn't understand.

"Clagett is with caregivers today. I'm fearful but I'm also relieved," she confessed. "I hope we made the right decision."

Akimbo's powerful grip shot spurts of milk that rang the metal collection bowl.

Gracie: Caregivers are the best! We love the way you take care of us!

"Doesn't everyone want to be taken care of, at least to some degree? He might find comfort with them."

Zoey: Absolutely! What's not to like? We have our pen and our pasture and regular meals. We get to visit with you every day while you yank on our hooters with those ice-cold hands. No freedom, but that's a minor complaint.

Gracie: There's the tedium of routine too. That really grinds me down.

Zoey: Yeah, that's huge. But aside from that we love captivity!

Gracie: Of course we love it! We worry you'll kill us if we say otherwise—ha ha, that's a joke.

Zoey: She's joking! But maybe sometime we could discuss the power dynamic at play here—

"I'm still thinking about escaping my husband's care," Akimbo confided.

Zoey: We hear you, sister, we think about escape all the time. The gate has us baffled or else—

"What do you think *I* should do?"

Gracie: Open the gate—you can trust us!

"Should I abandon my husband in his moment of need? Put him out to pasture at a care facility, so to speak?"

Zoey: Would he be better cared for there?

"No, probably not."

Zoey: Would he be happier there?

"Definitely not. He would miss me. He would be lonely."

Zoey: Would you be happier without him, without the care responsibility?

"No, if I'm honest, I suppose not," she admitted.

Gracie: Then absolutely send him away! You both should suffer!

Her goats were terrible with advice. They held on to petty resentments for their captivity. They threatened HR complaints for inappropriate touching. They couldn't forgive her for eating their children.

Akimbo heard shouting from outside the house. She released the goats into their pasture and speed-walked toward the house.

———————————————

Geldine nudged the wheelchair onto the ramp. She drove an unnerving serpentine path to mid-span with the ramp bowing noticeably under their combined weight. High-pitched whines escaped Clagett.

"What's going on here?" Akimbo called, bustling onto the scene, her rubber barn boots slapping the ground. "Where are you off to?"

"I'm not *trying* to go anywhere, I'm being taken to a care facility! You did this!"

"I don't know anything about it," Akimbo said.

"It's just a little outing. It's fine," Ariola assured. "It's all part of our introductory process. I told you earlier that we'd all get together and talk about the details."

"They're kidnapping me!"

"Don't be ridiculous, we're not kidnapping," Ariola said dismissively. "Technically this would be an abduction, but we're not doing that either."

"Where are you taking him exactly?" Akimbo asked.

"Our short-term care facility. It's just for a quick health check and some questions. Standard intake procedure. We need you to come along, too, to sign forms and such."

"Me?" Akimbo was caught off guard.

"It's best if you come along to keep him calm. He seems like he needs it."

"Um..." Akimbo wasn't keen on the suggestion.

The wheelchair reached the cargo hold and Geldine parked it alongside a pallet of cheese puffs and gummy bears. Clagett still faced forward, aimed at the metal bulkhead door to the driver compartment, unable to see the women now behind him. She began strapping his chair to the floor.

"This isn't how it's supposed to happen!" Clagett cried out.

"Can you get in there and try to quiet him down?" Ariola beseeched Akimbo.

"Keep an open mind," Akimbo called to Clagett. "They're caregiving experts. They know what's best for you."

"You'll get used to it," Geldine said. "Transitions are difficult."

"Why are you doing this to me?" he anguished.

"You called me, remember?" Geldine said. "We're doing this *for* you, not *to* you."

Ariola was losing patience. "Are you coming along or not?" She glared at Akimbo.

Akimbo looked longingly at the barn. She glanced at her stained jeans and blood-drive freebie T-shirt and mucked-up boots and had no inclination to tidy up. She had chores to finish, animals to feed.

"Geldine, can you keep him calm during the visit? He knows you...sort of."

"Hell no. I'm not going along," Geldine said. "I mean, it's all fine. I have work this afternoon. That's all."

With an "alright then" of resignation, Akimbo climbed into the van and situated herself on the floor next to Clagett.

"This seems strange because it's new territory for us. I'm a little scared too. Can we think of this as an adventure?" Akimbo sympathized.

Clagett went quiet, sullenly accepting he was stripped of veto power.

"Geldine, is Langford home?" Akimbo asked. "Can he feed my livestock until I get back?"

"He's there," Geldine said with a note of regret—for herself and the animals. "I'll tell him."

Ariola shrugged and pulled the doors closed.

5

AKIMBO GRABBED CARGO STRAPS where they anchored pallets to the floor. She braced her back against the wall and her boots against Clagett's drive wheel.

The vehicle lurched and metal squealed. They felt a slowing down like they had never experienced, something beyond what they associated with the stoppage of motion, like a complete stop plus more stopping.

It was like they had been living on a freight train, so numb to noise and vibration that they took it for peace and quiet until the train finally came to a stop.

"What the—" Akimbo whispered.

They glimpsed the earth through finger-graffiti scratched into the dust-coated back door windows. The graffiti artist had written *WASH ME* and sketched a coital tableau with striking avocado-sized balls. With the earth superimposed behind the graphic message, it resonated with environmental meaning for Akimbo, something like "Have the balls to clean up your earthly mess."

Clagett deciphered the view literally. "We're deeply screwed," he said, "and I don't think we're even close to rock-bottom penetration."

The earth receded until they could make out entire cloud formations and continents and then the outline of the earth itself.

"Something is very wrong!" he hissed to Akimbo.

"They're giving you a medical exam, some paperwork, that's all."

"In space!"

"You don't need to yell. This process is strange to me, too, but I'm trying to accept it."

Clagett was way off routine and separated from all the equipment that made his life comfortable. He felt increasingly vulnerable, stripped of his security blankets. He cut loose, shrieking, "I don't want to leave home!"

"You're going to be fine," Akimbo reassured. "It's just a quick visit. They promised." She looked in a canvas bag and rooted out an apple and dinner rolls to share with Clagett. "You're hangry," she said. "Eat something."

They ate in silence while admiring their planet. At this remove it looked pristine, unspoiled.

Ariola emerged from the driver's compartment. "Ahoy there!" she greeted. "Let's get to know one another."

She pulled boxes of supplies in front of Clagett, took a seat on one, and beckoned Akimbo to join her. She waited expectantly for them to give her their attention.

"Ahoy!" Ariola said again, in a frightening outburst. "I'm Ariola, and welcome to your onboarding orientation. Our aim is to put you at ease and set expectations for your out-of-this-world customer experience. We will take the next few minutes to answer visitors' most frequent and troubling questions. Sit back and enjoy!

"Where are we going? A great question, thank you. You will be orbiting Earth in our state-of-the-art hospitality center. In addition to standard amenities like floors and air, we offer contemporary conveniences, all free! You'll find furniture and windows. Our synthetic gravity is a full 23 percent less than Earth's. Quick weight loss? No problem!"

Ariola put on a serious expression and said as an aside,

"Always use caution when moving about. Don't get the idea you can fly. You can't. To repeat: you will not be in *zero*-g." She touched her forehead as if in remembrance of someone who didn't get the message.

Her tone of voice reminded Clagett of the smarmy cautions at amusement parks. With his parents' conditioning, he had lived in constant fear of abduction at those happy places, though by a carny, not by aliens. The paranoia his parents instilled was a gift he parlayed into a career; it was a curse that made him ever fearful.

"Many first-time visitors ask if they are about to die. Thank you, that's another great question. My people adhere to the science of rebirth, so the short answer is no, *we* are not going to die. Unfortunately for *you*, however, if during your visit we accidentally release your eternal essence from its current bodily form…well, you're a goner. I guess the even shorter answer is: maybe."

Her mention of death brought to mind dying on a roller coaster, another formative phobia. The janky space vehicle made the old fears—decapitation, fatal motion sickness, heart attack—seem remarkably prescient.

"Be sure to reserve an afternoon massage to soothe your kinks! You'll need one after your morning interrogation"— she lowered her voice to a fine-print whisper—"which might be followed by, or conducted simultaneously with, vigorous rectal reconnaissance."

Clagett had never considered dying of a ruptured colon. Though obviously alarmed by the possibility, he found professional interest in the discovery of an unexpected edge case for injury.

"Excuse me, Ariola, may I ask a question?" Akimbo said.

"Okay, but I'm sure I'll answer it in due course." Ariola looked flustered by the interruption.

Akimbo chose not to wait. "If your ship is orbiting Earth, how come no one on Earth has noticed it?"

"I was getting to that. Now it's not a great question. You turned it into a half-decent question at best. Anyway, we hide in plain sight, fully cloaked as an economy hotel. Have astronomers noticed our hotel? Certainly. Ask yourself what you would do if you discovered a hotel in space."

"I'd say, 'Holy shit, a hotel orbiting Earth!'" Clagett said softly, momentarily distracted from his morbid thoughts. The question mercifully hooked his attention.

"You'd say, 'Oh, that makes sense. The space tourists will have to stay somewhere,'" Ariola said.

"She's got you there," Akimbo said. "That's what I would say."

"I find this hard to believe," Clagett mumbled. "How did you even get a hotel here?"

"We use only the most advanced space-age technology outsourced from other cultures. We have a saying: 'If you understand how something works, it's time to upgrade!'"

"She's got another point there," Akimbo said. "That's how I operate too."

"*Technology*, what a great word," Ariola said proudly. "Can I hear some kudos?"

"Kudos!" they called back, mustering more enthusiasm than seemed proper.

Ariola launched into her big finale: "I hope you are reassured that your experience will be a safe and memorable one. We welcome you on board and say again, 'Ahoy there, sailor!'"

"Wait." Clagett was reluctant to let go of rationality. "What about this van flying around? You can't hide that. People must notice."

"The van is disguised as a flying delivery truck. In your

haste to get loaded you obviously overlooked the side panels, which read, *Aerial Delivery.*"

"But it *is* a flying delivery truck." He struggled with her explanation, if it could be called that.

"Exactly, it's the perfect disguise!" Ariola clapped. "People see it and say—"

Akimbo modulated her voice to sound Midwestern chipper. "I heard that airborne delivery was coming. I guess it's here!"

Clagett had to laugh. Ariola gave Akimbo a well-deserved kudo.

"Why don't we do a quick icebreaker?" Ariola continued. "I want to learn a little about you. I'll go first. My name is Ariola—you know that already—I'm your new care coordinator, and I'm grateful for this opportunity to befriend you both. That's the right word, isn't it? *Befriend* means give friendship? Am I right?"

"You got it right," Akimbo said. "Kudos."

"I get it confused with *behead*, which *doesn't* mean give head," Ariola explained.

The Earthlings did not respond.

Ariola smiled at Akimbo to pass the conversational baton.

"I accept that you want to help my husband," Akimbo said. "But honestly, this is more disruption than I expected. My peace of mind is in shambles. I'm not grateful for your help yet. Should I be?"

"Say your name."

"I'm Akimbo."

"Wonderful! Yes, Akimbo, we want you to act grateful. Now we need to hear from Mr. Clagett. What about you? What are you grateful for?"

"I'm grateful that you haven't harmed us, not much else."

"Why would we harm you? We are emissaries from a peaceful planet. We mean you no harm, just a brief medical procedure, followed by an interview. Now it's your turn to pick a question, Clagett," Ariola instructed.

"Okay. So...where are *you* from?"

"You wouldn't know it," Ariola said. "It's nicer than Earth. Not so humid there and no insects at all. My home is quite beautiful. White clouds drift close to the ground. We live together harmoniously. You folks might want to take a shot at that instead of shooting at each other." Ariola clapped her hands together. "Let's hear from our guests. Tell us where you're from."

"We're from Earth. That farm," Akimbo said. "Where you nabbed us."

"Have you traveled anywhere else?"

"Does Japan count? Or are you asking about other planets?"

"Planets."

"Then no. How about you, Clagett, honey, did you ever visit another planet?"

"No, first time in space."

"Wonderful! We have first-timers," Ariola cheered.

They watched with fascination as the space van backed toward the mother ship's loading dock. They were treated to a view of the entire alien vessel, which, as Ariola had mentioned, resembled a mid-range hotel. A marquee blinking *Space Hotel* and a toll-free phone number completed the disguise. The van ground to a halt with a scraping of metal.

"Step lively through to the double doors. Our seal is wonky and I don't want anybody getting sucked into space." Ariola touched her forehead in remembrance.

They opened the cargo doors amid a piercing whistle of escaping air and hurried Clagett down the ramp into a bleak entryway that looked and smelled like a parking garage elevator vestibule.

They packed into an elevator car with Ariola. Clagett sat facing the control panel. Oddly, it was an accurate replica of what he was accustomed to, with push buttons for each floor. Likewise, a red emergency button protruded from the bottom of the panel. A sticker next to it read, *In case of* (Here there was an unrecognizable symbol he equated to a ravenous space squid/spider. The creature's scale was difficult to gauge, but given its expression, he gathered it had appetite for an entire crew if it bided its time and picked them off one by one.) *don't use the elevator.*

They stopped at the sixth floor, the top. The elevator opened onto a carpeted hallway rife with the vibe of a bygone hotel chain. The homey touches looked outdated and worn, like most of their decor back on the farm. Pillow-sized white clouds drifted here and there in the hallway, the only indication that they were someplace more than ordinary.

Ariola directed them to the last door down the hallway. "Watch your step, take it slow," she said. Akimbo walked oddly, seeming unsure if her feet were touching the floor. "Gravity," Ariola said with a shake of her head.

"Gravity," Clagett agreed.

Freed from the clench of Earth's gravity, Ariola had transformed from a hunched-over heavyset woman to an elegantly straight-backed, wrinkle-free version of herself. She walked with grace and breathed without the sputtering sounds of phlegm.

She ushered them into a three-room suite fashioned with furnishings from the 1970s, back when the future looked inexcusably ugly. A cloud entrained behind Akimbo followed her into the room.

"What's with the little clouds?" Clagett asked.

"A touch from back home. Our atmosphere is mostly safe for you to breathe. Some abductees report temporary side effects like lightheadedness, confusion, and memory loss. Permanent damage isn't a worry for your short visit."

Akimbo waved her hands frantically to drive away an encroaching cloud. "Did you call us *abductees*?" she asked angrily.

"Sorry, I meant *clients*. No kudos for me! Wait here for a little bit while I go see if Adnoydd is ready for you. He'll be briefing you on our services." Ariola darted out of the room.

Their living area featured a large curtainless window obscured by a layer of frost. The in-room temperature control unit whined and rattled beneath the window and with its gasping breath managed only to thaw a small view port through which they made out the black emptiness of space.

Akimbo braved the plains of burnt-orange shag carpeting in stocking feet and poked through the kitchenette's cabinets and refrigerator, the bathroom soap selection and toilet paper supply. The bathroom, she noted, was not equipped for wheelchair access. More importantly, the full-length mirror revealed the wonders of the ship's lower gravity, which miraculously elevated certain aspects of her figure.

She did a model's turn in front of Clagett.

"Notice anything different?" she asked.

He took in her familiar lanky shape, admired her subtle curves, studied her face. The sagging skin under her chin, which he knew to be a focus of her self-image's discontent, had levitated to its youthful position.

"You look younger. Perkier."

"Why thank you! I almost wish I had been abducted years sooner."

She settled onto a sofa and Clagett wheeled to her side. They conferred about their predicament with the intensity of long-married couples—in other words, they quibbled.

"Is the heat on? There's a terrible draft coming off the window. We need more heat," Akimbo said.

"It sounds like the heater is running. That tiny area is defrosted."

"You tell me to turn on the air conditioner when the car window fogs up. Maybe they turned on the air conditioner."

"The air conditioner removes moisture, dries the air. That's why it helps with car window fog. What we need is heat."

"That's what I said," she reminded him.

"I'm trying to help."

"Oh God! How did I end up here?" she moaned. "You should have come alone."

"Until death do us part. Remember?"

"Death is *already* prying us apart," she insisted. "We were like 30 percent apart starting the day."

"That's an exaggeration."

"I'm a prisoner!" she moaned.

"We're both prisoners."

"But I'm inside a prison that's inside a prison." She glared at him.

"What's the first prison?"

"Taking care of you is the first. This room feels like the second."

"I'm a prisoner in my own body, inside another prison."

"What's your second prison, the room or the wheelchair? Don't start claiming you're in three prisons either."

"Which is worse, room or chair?" he mused.

"Why, so you can say you're worse off than me? That by comparison I'm super happy and free?"

"The room! Okay? We're in the same prison together."

"You'd be fine without me."

"I'm better with you," he said.

Akimbo went silent.

He likened her coping process to casting off the chaff that clung to her convictions. In this instance, she vented fear and anger and confusion and left behind an unspoken belief that they were better off together. The thought gave him comfort even when offset by the marital peril of presuming to understand his wife's thoughts.

His own mental machinery ran in the opposite direction. He argued dispassionately and what remained in his head was the chaff—uncertainty and fear.

Two rapid knocks and the door opened. Ariola backed into the room carrying canvas bags filled with basic necessities from their own home.

"There's one more down the hall by the elevator. Grab it, would you, Akimbo?" Ariola said. "I'll put your food away."

Akimbo stepped warily into the hall and made her way back to the elevator, feeling watched from each peephole. She hefted the bag and froze, seized by an impulse to leave her husband in their care. She need only push the elevator button and stow away back to an unencumbered life of her own design. The idea was selfish and opportunistic—spur-of-the-moment madness—but not without temptation. She reappraised the corridor leading back to Clagett. For all her fleeting thoughts of leaving him, she knew she couldn't. They were better off together, for however long he lasted.

6

ROLLING INTO TOWN WITH superior intelligence and technology had seemed like an unbeatable plan, what with knowledge being equated to power. Adnoydd's planet, a small regional outfit looking for a foot in the door, had leased the rights to exploit a mostly rural county in the Southeast. The brochures showed enticing images of corn-fed rubes, ripe pawpaws, virgin expanses of honeysuckle vines.

They discovered big problems.

The people had a lot of guns. Like, a lot. The people were mean and uncooperative, too, especially the people with the guns.

They brought along petty cash but came to find the ATM machine wouldn't accept the card they jerry-rigged. In fact, the machine ate the card and he had to schedule an appointment to retrieve it, but the manager was out with a root canal until Wednesday, at which point the manager told him he didn't have proper identification to retrieve the card. Oh, the relentlessly inhospitable environment! Consequently, they struggled to buy provisions—their own guns, for example, had they been predisposed toward vio-lence, which they were not.

Then there was the matter of the insects. They were in the air, in the water, on the ground, *under* the ground—every-where! All those legs! And the humans' guns weren't meant for the bugs! How stupid was that? It seemed pretty clear who was winning that evolutionary competition, despite the humans' showy firepower.

Despite the many dangers, Adnoydd lived among humans, suffered in their oppressive gravity and thin atmosphere, learned their ways, interrogated them, looked deep into their dark side. What he couldn't work out was how to cash in on Earth's abundant supply of Earthlings.

During rotations back to the home planet, the higher-ups floated numerous and embarrassingly far-afield ideas, then left it for the crew to evaluate. Pressed to generate profits, they committed to exportation of human-flavored beef jerky: exotic, vacuum-sealed, long-lasting, lightweight—seemed like a can't-miss product when they were sitting around the conference table. They made seven delivery runs to the home planet before beef toxicity started killing customers! Not to minimize all the collateral rebirths among his people—he admitted that was regrettable—but still...*he* suffered through seven interminable trips to screw a pooch!

(One of his favorite pithy human expressions. Pooch screwing was often referred to, but they never *fucked* the pooch, which struck him as odd, because they seemed to fuck everything else. A crackpot once claimed to have screwed the *fucking* pooch and that was, frankly, a logistical conundrum.)

From the first scouting missions to abducting crackpots and cattle, he had witnessed his planet's lame scattershot exploitation efforts...and where had it got them? To his way of thinking, they had learned only one core lesson: knowledge had its merits, but knowledge can't compete with a wad of cash when you're at the checkout counter buying bulletproof vests.

Desperate for capital to support their aimless search for exploitation opportunities, they were reduced to menial work. They eked by, taking thankless remote jobs—telemedicine, legal advice, technical support—jobs that made clear who was exploiting whom.

Adrift in this atmosphere of subsistence, Adnoydd happened upon Geldine and stumbled onto the financial promise of caregiving.

His encounter with Geldine occurred not long after the beef jerky cluster of fuckery, while he was still assigned to the Abductions and Admissions Department. They'd given up on nabbing crackpots and cattle, but still grabbed random humans—though on a strictly catch-and-release basis. The *why* of it went unexplained. On the orders of his higher-up, he targeted a human warehouse known to be reliably stocked with easily snatched specimens. This wasn't his first visit there; he had plucked more than a few withered prunes from the warehouse and had no reason to anticipate difficulties on this outing.

He parked the space van in a visitor's spot near the front door. Under the portico, right there in the open, on benches and rollators and wheelchairs, sat a fresh selection of targets lined up like sausages in a deli case. They chatted and dozed. They watched hopefully as a car pulled up to escort a lucky person to a family brunch.

Adnoydd assessed the offerings and decided on a man at the end of the line, closest to the van. He approached casually but with purpose. He released the man's wheelchair brake and gripped the handles.

"Are we ready to go?" he asked the man.

"God yes. Where are we going?" the man asked in turn.

"I thought we could go for a ride. See some sights. How does that sound?"

"Beats the hell out of watching cars come and go," he said.

They arrived at the van. He parked the chair, opened the doors, and situated the ramp.

"Full disclosure," Adnoydd said. "There's a good chance you won't be returning."

"About time. Let's get a move on."

Refreshingly, the man's reaction was as positive as they came. Crackpots usually felt obligated to unspool criticisms of his abduction methods, somehow convinced they were the experts. Cattle were maddeningly indifferent to the whole affair.

Adnoydd had the man strapped into the cargo hold when a slight woman dressed like a nurse came bustling across the lot, her twisted locks swinging in front of her face, waving her hands, calling, "Hold on! Hold on there!"

He packed up the ramp and waited for her to catch her breath.

"I think there's a mistake," she huffed. "Mister B isn't supposed to go anywhere today."

"Geldine, is that you?" the man called from the truck.

"Everything okay in there?" Geldine called back.

"Never been better!"

"My boss said to bring him in for an examination. That's all I know," Adnoydd responded.

"You're not our usual driver," she said guardedly. "This isn't the usual van."

"I'm new," Adnoydd said. "What can I say?" He shrugged.

"Actually," the man called out, "I've never been worse.

Can we pick up the pace? I don't want to keel over in the back of a taxicab."

"Let's go back to the home, Mister B," Geldine coaxed.

"Not a chance in hell! This is my big break! I'm getting out of here for good!"

"He wants to come with me." Adnoydd shrugged again.

"I'm responsible for him," she said. "I can't let him go unattended."

"Marry me, Geldine. Let's run away together! I want to spend the time I have left with you!" the man said with desperation.

"He wants you to come too," Adnoydd said.

She let out a long sigh as if it were the beginning of a curse word that never fully arrived. "Alright, I'm coming. But this is not a *yes* to your marriage disposal," she called.

"That's fine," the man said. "We can just shack up together."

"You see what I have to put up with?" She shook her head in amazement.

"Hop in," Adnoydd said. "It's a quick trip."

———

Adnoydd kept Geldine captive for nearly a week.

She begged him to tell her husband that she was okay. She said Langford would worry terribly for her and that would be bad for Adnoydd. He delighted in thoughts of her husband's anguish.

Mister B was the original target, but, predictably, he discovered he was able to walk in the lighter gravity. From there it was a short step to believing he could fly and then it was a long fall off the mezzanine. Geldine was heartbroken that her charge had not survived the outing and was little consoled by the flicker of joy Mister B experienced on his maiden flight. Adnoydd couldn't care less about Mister B; he settled for Geldine and got down to business.

He inspected her shoes, which were of a novel one-piece molded-plastic construction, and he pestered her about their comfort and durability. With traits shared by loafers, flip-flops, and galoshes, her shoes bedeviled him with the question of whether socks were an appropriate undergarment.

"There are those who go without, but I can't on account of my sweaty feet," she said.

With that cleared up, Adnoydd slipped on her shoes and minced in front of her, to provoke outrage. She had the audacity to laugh.

He took his browbeating up a notch and blamed Mister B's death on her irresponsible care.

"I always tell my old people that falling is their number-one thing to worry about," she rebutted. "I'm not allowed to restrain them to the chair, so there you go. What are you hassling me for anyway?" she asked defiantly. "What did I ever do to you?"

"It's my job to interrogate—"

"Just because I'm human? Help! Help! I'm being profiled! Bring me something to drink, dammit!" she demanded.

She sipped menacingly. Why *was* he interrogating her? Adnoydd sat quietly while he failed to come up with an inspired reason to break her spirit. Their looks of terror had once been reason enough, but that got old. These days he could barely bring himself to elicit anything more than looks of mild discomfort.

While he sulked, she prattled nervously about her saintly work, caring for elderly people and family members.

Adnoydd found himself listening with interest—her stories were much juicier than his flaccid intimidations.

Her attitude shifted toward fear the more she talked, as it dawned on her that she was facing someone of staggering intelligence. She whimpered and stomped her feet. She prayed to her God. She asked for mercy. She begged Adnoydd for a loan to cover new tires for her car, painting such a picture of tragic circumstances that he might have helped her if he had access to that kind of cash.

Geldine's head slumped in defeat, chin rested on chest, eyes on the floor. "I'm humiliated to have asked for money," she said softly. "I've got a big payday coming in, going to be rolling in dough, but I'll miss out on the opportunity without at least one new tire. There's enough for everyone to strike it rich. I could have shared it with you."

The goldmine of which she spoke intrigued him. To secure her cooperation without putting himself through another round of intimidation, he gave her cash to replace the one tire she had to inflate by hand, with a bicycle pump, before every drive. He threw in for the installation and balancing and the replacement insurance, which she said was absolutely essential. Taxes too.

He casually asked about striking it rich.

She whispered that there was an upcoming baby boom-ageddon with unlimited caregiving hours available for the taking. She said her golden goose's gravy train was pulling into Easy Street Station and it would be like picking money from a money tree.

"Hold on a second," Adnoydd interrupted her confession. "What's this caregiving thing?"

He wanted one of those money trees. He saw himself on his home planet tending orchards of money trees, nowhere near this hellhole Earth.

"I get paid to aid people." She took a deep breath and tried to steady her voice. "People who can't take care of themselves. Old folks. Sick people. People like that man you took with me, God rest Mister B's soul."

He knew about the human tradition of letting age and infirmity overtake them, but he wasn't aware that they willingly *paid* to prolong the experience. He had only heard of families taking care of their own for free, and it sure hadn't sounded a hundred percent willing.

"And they *pay* you for that?"

"I'm sure not working for nothing," she said adamantly.

He'd encountered plenty of human follies, but this took the cake. He loved the inhumanity of forcing people in need, those perhaps unable to work, to *pay* care workers. Where he came from, they rebirthed the needy so they could start over in better circumstances. The concept of profiting from barbarity was...alluring.

"There's big money trees in that?"

"Lots," she said.

The pause in Adnoydd's interrogation and his interest in her work put her at ease.

"If there's money in it, there must be a catch," he said skeptically.

"Keeping people comfortable is a challenge, that's for sure. When a sickness gets worse and a patient dies, that's very difficult. Sometimes the family will show thanks by giving you old clothes or maybe a beater car that hasn't been driven in twenty years. I prefer cash."

"You must need a degree...or some kind of medical training."

"Nuh-uh. I'm a *certified* assistant, but most aides aren't. Heck, I can train people."

"You must be shitting me," he said in disbelief.

(He loved this expression. Contrary to expectation, it wasn't an accusation that someone was shitting *on* him, it was an accusation that he was being shat. Headfirst, he visualized.)

"There is plenty of that involved with the job, but you get used to it," she said offhandedly. "My first client was a tall man, still could walk but his memory was shot. The very first night I worked, he got up to use the bathroom. I was in a chair in the corner."

"You were just sitting there?" he asked.

"Most of the time, watching him sleep. Sometimes I'd stretch my legs and look through drawers."

"And that's the job?"

"For the most part. Anyway, he was a big man, as I said, and he had a healthy appetite—plenty of fiber, I come to learn. As he's walking across the carpet, a turd shaped like a fat cottonmouth snake slid right out the leg of his pajamas. The thing was in one piece, and that's a challenge even when you're sitting still. To do it while walking…that's truly a feat. Right then and there I thought I'd made a horrible career choice. I gagged and nearly walked out the door."

"What happened?" he asked, fully engrossed in the tale. This was memorable stuff. *Like a fat cottonmouth snake* was definitely going into his collection.

"What do you think happened? My patient took me for an intruder and tried to bash my head in. When people wake up confused and find a person of color in the room, they can make rash assumptions—maybe you've noticed. I said, 'Don't threaten me, put down the lamp, and for the love of God watch your step.' I told him nothing to worry about and go back to bed. Eventually he settled down and fell asleep. Then, I suited up and got to work on the floor.

That episode taught me I can handle anything. You'd never know it to look at me, but I'm like a superhero cleaning up shitty situations that ordinary folk can't even imagine!"

Heck, Adnoydd realized, sneaking around houses in the dark and watching people sleep was already their bread-and-butter prelude to abduction. Watching humans die was not what he would call entertainment, but there wouldn't be tears either. Caregiving! Now that suited their temperament.

He'd stumbled onto a jackpot—more than just money to stay afloat, this sounded like the scheme they'd been searching for.

"Tell me everything," he said.

With each passing day, the ship's atmosphere soaked into her system, fogging her memory, leaving her confused and vulnerable. He slowly extracted everything she knew about the business of caregiving.

7

Y NAME IS ADNOYDD, and I'll be examining you today. I trust your abduction has been pleasant so far." Damn! He shouldn't have said *abduction*. "Visit," he mumbled, trying to override his error, thereby drawing attention to it. There he was riding the pooch again.

In his role as director of rebirth and sales, the job most adjacent to medic, he had the duty to assess Clagett and Akimbo's physical condition. "How are you feeling today?" Adnoydd asked.

"Terrible, depressed," Clagett said.

He could tell at first glance that Clagett was in terrible shape. From a sales standpoint, terrible health was excellent news. As a long-term source of income...not so excellent.

"I'm old school when it comes to physicals," he said. "I think the thing to do here is an anal probe." Adnoydd smiled. "Or, as I once heard said, 'take an odyssey to your ileum.'"

A classics professor once blurted that out mid-probe. Adnoydd asked what that was supposed to mean, and the prof lamented that people had lost their taste for the classics. After they boiled him down to jerky flavor extract, he proved right.

"You may experience a little discomfort, but we find that a surprisingly large population of...visitors...report they enjoy the experience."

He hadn't exactly invented anal sex—there were plenty

of cultural precedents; gay men and clerics had done the heavy lifting—but he felt like reports of alien probes had captured human imagination in a positive way. He had helped bring anus awareness to the forefront, and from there it gained acceptance in conventional lifestyles. He clung to that belief as one of his identifiable accomplishments, his gift to humankind.

"What is it with you aliens and butt play? What do you expect to find up there? Polyps? I just don't get it." Clagett raised his eyebrows quizzically.

Usually he got a gasp or a scream, not a procedural question. Adnoydd didn't have an answer. He felt the power dynamic shift in his victim's favor. *Victim* was freighted with so much meaning these days. What was the new lingo? *Client*?

When did torture and sales grow so far apart? The old days had been carefree and ruthless.

"We want to make you comfortable. Let's just forget about the probe for now. I was hasty with that recommendation. We'll save that in case you fail to cooperate."

"I appreciate that."

"We appreciate *you*," Adnoydd reassured.

"There's something else I'd really like to ask."

He had an idea where this was leading. The deep questions were so freaking repetitive and inevitably sidetracked the intimidation. "I know what you're thinking," Adnoydd said with a dismissive wave of a hand. "Isn't it an incredible coincidence that you and I, your species and my species, share the same features—arms, legs, eyes, and whatnot? You want to know if we are related."

He needed to add that question to the onboarding presentation so he wouldn't have to face it ever again. That presentation was the smartest thing he'd ever done, which, he acknowledged, didn't say much for his non-anal accomplishments.

"We're not so alike, you and I." Adnoydd unbuttoned the top buttons of his scrubs. He lifted up his undershirt to reveal gills—three horizontal slits with fleshy flaps running across his sternum. Dark chest hair sprouted from the flaps like unkempt mustaches. With each exhale the flaps lifted to reveal spongy green tissue.

"Oh Jesus!"

He usually ventriloquized for customers, lip-synched, but he let his mouth sit in a fixed grin for the full effect. His louvers flexed like lips as he spoke. "We breathe totally separate from our mouths, a major victory for our evolution. No choking on this ship."

He cherished Clagett's look of disgust—a look more on the curiosity end of disgust than he would have preferred, but it worked.

"Can you breathe underwater?" Clagett asked.

"No."

"Because that would be cool."

Adnoydd snickered. "That *would* be cool."

"How do you talk on a cell phone? Your ears aren't even close to your...gills?" Clagett asked. "Speakerphone?"

"Yep. My only gripe about your phones is the oddly specific microphone placement. Private conversations are tricky."

Say what you will about human progress, in truth they made a damn fine cell phone.

"I have the same problem since I can't hold the phone," Clagett admitted. "No privacy."

"Your engineers really need to think about accessibility for nonhumans." Adnoydd held out his hand for a brotherly fist-bump of shared experience.

"My arms don't move anymore," Clagett reminded him.

"Oh, right," Adnoydd said with embarrassment. He needed to get back to a position of power. He lifted the front of Clagett's shirt and gently probed the ridges of his emaciated chest. "Nobody knows if we share a common ancestor, but I do know how uncommonly smooth and sexy this is." He grinned.

He preferred his people's women, but with humans, what was the difference? Did gender even count when you're getting handsy with another species?

Adnoydd traced his fingers along the grooves of Clagett's rib cage. "Be thankful that your skin, even as wrinkled and slack as it is, still covers what's under it. Maybe things aren't so good for you, but I could make them much worse. Do you get what I'm saying?"

"Yeah. Consider me threatened. Actually, common ancestry wasn't my question. I was wondering if you could share how your spaceships fly."

Gill shock usually squashed conversation. *Were they getting flabby and sad?* he wondered. "Why? Who cares?" Adnoydd challenged.

"I guess I feel like there's a business opportunity to make flying vehicles or at least to own a key patent."

"That's old knowledge. It's worthless. It's in the public domain, as you might say."

"Great. Could you, like, share a textbook or something with me?"

"No."

"Could you give me a quick explanation of the key details? You know, point me in the right direction?"

"I can't, and even if I could, that would be like me asking you how to hunt a woolly mammoth. Just stop. There's no money in ancient technology. We have bigger plans for you."

———————————————

Akimbo sat in her underwear on his exam table, a robe pulled to her waist, her posture perfect, her chest smooth and unblemished by fleshy gills. She was an excellent physical specimen and thus warranted close inspection.

"Yep. Yep. Yep. Interesting," Adnoydd said. "Interesting indeed."

He acted knowledgeable as his fingertips slowly stroked her sternum. He projected calm. As an alien imitation medical professional, the Hippocratic oath did not bind him, but he found that humans tolerated his predilections longer if he acted morally restrained.

Akimbo ignored his scrutiny with the thoroughness she gave real doctors. "What's this really about?" she asked. "Is this a clinical trial? This really reminds me of his clinical trials."

"No, why do you ask?" He was pleased she took him for a real doctor.

"The situation seems familiar: threateningly medical, I have no idea why I'm also getting examined, and you seem equally clueless."

"All part of our intake program. Nothing to be worried about." Offering reassurances? Times really *had* changed.

"I'm not worried, I'm just wondering. Hoping." There was barely a hint of terror in her voice. "You seem like you have some cool tech here. Can you help my husband? Do you have a cure for ALS? Is that why you chose us?"

Virtually everyone he abducted pleaded for a cure. Arthritis or headaches or eczema. Dandruff—the most popular request. News accounts on Earth never covered his subjects' selfish demands. They always made him out to be the bad guy.

He knew what came next: accusations that advanced cultures like his own were *obligated* to freely share medical expertise.

"Let me stop you right there," he said. "I've never seen a case like your husband's. We don't waste effort on research."

"So I'm really *not* in a study's control group," Akimbo said with disappointment.

"Nope."

"But you're serious about providing care for him?"

"Yes, I promise."

"And no cure?" She pulled up her robe, signaling the end of his inspection and her cooperation.

"Cures are labor-intensive, unfair. You can't cure everything. Look around you: we barely even have a sick bay." He gestured at the sparse supplies on the shelves. "Anything more than minor injuries I take straight to rebirth."

"Rebirth? Rebirth like spiritual rebirth?"

"Officially, it's like a baptism ritual, but you stay fully immersed longer. Much longer. Once the wet work is out of the way, you're reborn into a pristine new body back on the home planet. If I'm in a hurry, I boot them out the airlock."

"Oh."

"Has your husband thought about his end?"

"We talk about the natural kind, if I understand you correctly," she said.

"Our clients—and this will apply to your husband—aren't eligible for rebirth; only my people are blessed with eternal life. It's a perk that comes with our superior intelligence. I'm sure you understand."

"I understand completely."

"It's part of our program to disincentivize client death. When a client dies, so goes a piece of our profits."

"Absolutely. Profit is king."

"But, of course, you could take matters into your own hands."

"What?" She was taken aback.

"Think it over. Think about yourself. Think about what's best for you."

Adnoydd knew the idea of freeing herself from her husband would appeal to her in some capacity. She would recoil from that realization and condemn the idea as morally repugnant. In the backlash, she would prime herself to accept any situation to keep her husband comfortable.

"Would I suffer legal repercussions for his disappearance?" Akimbo asked. "Any downsides I'm not seeing?"

Okay, not the reaction he expected.

"I'm kidding," she said. "I would never hurt him. I love him now as much as ever." She went quiet. "You, on the other hand, I could kill just like that." She snapped her fingers and burst out laughing.

He believed her.

———

Ariola escorted the couple to a dimly lit, starkly appointed room. A figure lurked behind a light pointed directly into their faces. They heard him whispering, "I can do this. I can do this!"

Akimbo sat on a simple kitchen chair with chipped paint and a tulip-shaped cutout in the backrest. She anxiously rocked side to side, tapping the uneven legs against the bare metal floor. Irritated by the light in her eyes, she stood abruptly and wrenched the lamp head until it illuminated their interrogator.

"Do you mind?" she said with hostility.

The lamp revealed their medical examiner, Adnoydd, sitting in a chair with his legs crossed. The bright light brought out the greenish hue of his face and shadowed the hollows of his gaunt cheeks, bringing to mind a coyote with a decent haircut. His scrubs impeccably fit his rangy physique. He noticed Akimbo admiring his footwear, casual white flats he picked up on Earth.

"You like my fucking shoes?" he asked.

She met his gaze with an unnerving expression of disdain but kept silent.

With a sigh, he said, "Alright, let's get this over with." He aimed the lamp head into neutral territory.

"Who are you supposed to be now, the bad cop?" Akimbo ventured to ask. She was unexpectedly giddy given the circumstances.

"No, no." He laughed. "Those days are behind us. It's all good."

Clagett admired Akimbo's flippant approach to dealing with Adnoydd and tried it himself. "Take me to your leader!" he demanded.

"I'm in charge of the ship." Adnoydd prickled at any suggestion otherwise. To secure his cooperation, his higherups made him the ship's ranking officer.

"No, aren't you supposed to say, 'Take me to your leader?'" Clagett explained.

"Excuse me?"

"Leave him be, honey," Akimbo said. "He's just doing his job." She turned to Adnoydd. "Listen, I don't know where this discussion is heading, but I'd like to point out that I composted and recycled all my life, if that counts in my favor."

"Interrogation, not discussion." Adnoydd slipped up,

falling back on old habits. His two prospects didn't notice his implied threat, caught up as they were in their own conversation.

"My husband is a different matter, though," Akimbo said.

Clagett bristled. "I did recycle, I just wasn't a fanatic."

"Allow me to start over again," Adnoydd said calmly. "I'd like to have an honest conversation about how you fit into our care business. You deserve to have enough perspective to decide whether we are the right agency for your needs. You deserve to have your questions answered. Caregiving can be a beautiful partnership when the synergy is right. Do you think you're ready for an honest conversation about your situation?"

Adnoydd tried to inject sincerity into his pitch, but nothing had meaning to him, not really, except for shoes. Early in his career, he had been enthusiastically angry. Now he struggled to dredge up enough animosity to even intimidate. In his career's twilight, he was reduced to hawking caregiver services.

"I'd like to start with a little word-association game so I can get a feel for your attitudes. Some people find giving up control—letting aides into your lives—to be…How do you say it? Hellacious? How does a game sound to you?"

"I'm so relieved to hear you say that." Akimbo relaxed noticeably. "Clagett and I have been grappling with that very topic—relinquishing control."

"Great, I'll say a word and you tell me what your first thoughts are."

"Fire when ready," Akimbo said.

"Enslavement."

"Is that the first word?"

"Yes. Let me clarify. What is your attitude about being enslaved—a complete forfeiture of control?"

"Definitely negative associations," Akimbo answered.

"Would we learn how to build pyramids? I might be up for that," Clagett ventured. "You had your hand in that, didn't you?"

"Ignore that comment, please," she said.

"No problem." Adnoydd tried to muster a smile. "Please try to take this seriously. I know it's difficult to face the reality of your illness, but sooner or later you need to confront it."

Clagett nodded and subdued his grin.

"How about this word: *submission*, more of a voluntary loss of control."

"Seriously, that's the word? Okay…" Akimbo gave a playful wink to her husband. "Makes me think of silk restraints. Remember that time on vacation, honey? Except I don't think it was genuine silk."

"We don't need to bring that up right now," Clagett said.

"Please, feel free to discuss," Adnoydd encouraged. "It sounds like you need to work through something."

"It definitely was real silk," Clagett defended.

"I saw the credit card statement. You didn't pay enough for real silk."

"I bought them used."

"You bought used bondage restraints? Now you tell me! They irritated the skin on my ankles and I couldn't wear sandals for a week."

"Overall, though, it was an excellent vacation," Clagett said.

"It really was. Are you a beach person, Mr. Adnoydd?" she asked politely.

"Not really. The sharks worry me. Let me pursue a different angle…Would you describe your sandals as feminine with delicate leather straps or more like sporty activewear?"

"Flip-flops... I think. Why—"

"It's not important," he acceded. He went quiet and composed himself. "Back on script... Would you feel better about submission if we branded it as colonization? Stern hands taking the reins as your lives careen out of control."

"That's an offensive notion now," Akimbo said.

"Colonization was the Europeans, not us," Clagett explained. "I'm genetically connected, but morally opposed."

"I'll mark that down as a negative association. Here's another concept: *profiteering.* How do you feel about that? Specifically, losing control of your finances."

"That's the American way," Akimbo said, "but I'm strongly against it."

"Let's add a caveat to her answer," Clagett said. "We're against it unless we happen to be the ones left with the profits."

Adnoydd looked at them with interest. "So not a negative reaction?"

"That one is more situational," Clagett said.

Akimbo nodded. "I'll agree to some flexibility on profiteering."

"Let's try one more word: *caregiving.* Think closely about this one."

"Caregiving?" Akimbo asked. "That's a quick change of direction."

"Is it? We see caregiving as a brand of compassionate profiteering enabled by submission," Adnoydd deadpanned. "How do you see it?"

"But caregiving?" Clagett didn't track the connection.

"Not exclusively for your butt, but that's part of it," Adnoydd remarked. "Caregiving is a profession closely related to abducting, so it meshes nicely with our skill set.

They both entail taking care of a hostage, but get this: care-givers are paid by the hour."

Clagett looked alarmed.

"I'm uncomfortable with the direction of this discussion," Akimbo said warily.

"The brutal truth is uncomfortable, I get it," Adnoydd said. "Let's bring the discussion down to a personal level. Imagine that you're old and infirm, maybe a little addled, memory not so crisp, eyes shot, knees ache, UTIs, the works. Clagett, you can just imagine being yourself. Here's the question: What is it worth for a stranger to take care of your needs?"

"Do we have a choice?" she asked.

"Do you have children to look after you?"

"No, I never wanted any. Never wanted the responsibil-ity," she said.

"Even if we did have children, we wouldn't want to sad-dle them with our care," Clagett said.

Adnoydd amended his question: "I forgot to stipulate… Assume your caregivers use your infirmity to quietly drain your assets."

"But they do take care of us?"

"Yes, to the best of their ability…Maybe that's over-selling…They take care of you to the extent that they're willing."

"You paint a dark picture, but I guess I'd pay for the service," Akimbo concluded. "I can't take money into the hereafter."

"How about you, Clagett?"

"In this scenario, do I have a wife willing to take care of me to the exclusion of everything else?"

"Do you?" Adnoydd asked.

Akimbo raised her eyebrows in question.

Clagett answered, "No, I wouldn't wish that on her anyway. I would take the caregiver and give up a good chunk of savings."

"That wasn't so hard, was it?" Adnoydd said with smug satisfaction. He stood and paced the room. "Don't you feel better?"

Akimbo and Clagett smiled politely.

Now for the big finish. "I'm prepared to offer you an exclusive at-home care bundle. If you sign up for our service now, you'll get complete care and you can enjoy your freedom down on Earth. How does that sound?"

"Hold on," Akimbo demanded. "What if we don't sign up?"

"Don't you want to know the cost of our care package?"

"I want to know if we actually have a choice."

"Everything," Adnoydd explained. He'd had enough tiptoeing around. They needed to get on board.

"Everything?" Clagett asked.

"We have no idea what you're saying," Akimbo said flatly.

"That's the cost. Everything. Your savings, your property, your farm."

"Everything!" Clagett blurted.

"It's not as bad as it sounds. We don't take it all at once; we bill biweekly."

"And the alternative?" Akimbo asked insistently.

"You'll remain on the ship locked in your luxurious suite, food will be provided, but you, Akimbo, are exclusively responsible for taking care of your husband's needs."

"What kind of choice is that?"

"That's just playing out the hand fate dealt you. Don't blame me."

Akimbo covered her face with both hands and groaned.

"I see the two of you have a lot to talk about," Adnoydd

said. He made his way to the door and summoned Ariola. "Have a think on it. Enjoy our hospitality for the night and tell me your decision in the morning, when you're rested and relaxed. Sound good?"

8

ARIOLA PREPPED CLAGETT. WITHOUT a lift and other accommodations, he was looking at spending the night in his wheelchair, and she tried to at least start him out in tolerable comfort.

Alone together in the bedroom, both fearful of what they'd gotten themselves into, Akimbo and Clagett struggled to find words.

"I'm restless," Akimbo declared. "Like literally. I feel like I haven't slept for days."

"Get some rest," he suggested.

She glowered at him for recommending the obvious. Rest how? He was fading away, their relationship with it, their money with it, and *her* life was getting sucked into the vortex too. As if that weren't enough, they'd been suckered into an alien *abduction*.

She worried disproportionately for the safety of her chickens, entrusted to Langford, who lived closer to the rotisserie end of the food chain than the animal husbandry end. With everything else going on, what did that consuming worry say about her?

"I didn't think it could get any less believable," Akimbo said.

"I'll tell you about unbelievable," he countered. "Do you know what he told me?"

"No idea."

"He said they went faster than the speed of light to get here."

"Doesn't lots of stuff go faster than light? I've always thought Einstein's law was unnecessarily restrictive," Akimbo commented. "Laws seem like scientific overreach."

"Right, but..." He realized she was goading him. "Anyway, he said this is what the beginning of the future looks like. He said in the future Earthlings will all die while caregivers watch over them."

"That's a chilling prediction," she said.

"I think he's just trying to scare us."

"I tried to scare him back...I threatened to kill him. Putting him on his back foot seemed like the right play."

"Seriously?" He left his mouth agog.

"Yep."

"Wow, you're amazing." His attention took a hard left turn and he excitedly asked, "Hey, what do you make of their skin tone? Did you see a green cast?"

"Yes, I noticed. Green seems a little traditional for aliens today, a little too Martiany. Know what I mean?"

"Hypothetically," he said, "if someone with jaundiced yellow coloring were choked, would they look green instead of blue?"

She concentrated to follow the twists and turns of his imagination. "Why would you choke someone with jaundice? Isn't their life miserable enough already?" she responded.

"Let's say they choked on something like steak, a cruel twist of fate, not a deliberate attack."

"That would be just like fate, wouldn't it?"

"I think they'd turn green," he said.

"Are you sure you're okay?" she asked with concern. "He didn't hurt you, did he?"

"I'm traumatized, but he didn't hurt me," he said. "Are you okay?"

She coughed out a laugh.

He knew she wasn't okay, that he wasn't okay, that there was nothing okay about the day. They were exhausted by the ordeal, disoriented by the strangers and the unfamiliar surroundings, overwhelmed by the tectonic shift in their lives. He felt as if nothing would ever be okay again. Nonetheless, it was polite to ask.

"Are we less okay than the not okay we were this morning?" he asked.

"I think it's fair to say that caregivers haven't eased my mind."

"You need to get home and lead your life," he said emphatically. "I don't care what happens to me. We can't give up everything we worked toward."

"I can't stay here and take care of you," she agreed. "I'm sorry."

"I wouldn't want that."

"We didn't want any of this."

———————————

Alarms awoke them in the dead of night, the deafening volume dulling her ability to think. Akimbo sat up and tried to wrap her head around what was happening. Clagett's eyes went wide with concern, and though he moved his lips, with all the racket she couldn't make out what he said.

The white clouds drifting above the bed predisposed them to think of fire.

"Fire drill?" she asked hopefully.

He offered a thoughtful response that she missed in its entirety except for the caution "Save yourself!" which aligned with her thinking, such as it was.

In light of her husband's self-sacrifice, she decided to flee for a lifeboat. She hoped the aliens believed in patriarchy to the extent that women escaped first; she didn't support that favoritism, but this wasn't the time to dicker or make a statement.

She evaluated the escape appropriateness of her improvised sleepwear: silky black scrubs—compliments of their host and available for purchase—worn without the outfit's ruffled undershirt. She made for the door without her boots.

"I'll find out!" she shouted over her shoulder to keep Clagett succinctly informed.

With hands over ears, she dashed to the elevator through the hallway's pulsing red lights. Her heart pounded from the sprint. She stepped into the elevator and chose the first floor as a likely rallying point, only then remembering to forgo elevators during…Was it just fires or all emergencies? If she were having a heart attack, she would definitely take the elevator.

She descended in relative quiet, suffering through a wave of guilt for leaving Clagett. The elevator deposited her into a mayhem of aliens screaming in clouds throbbing with red alarm beacons.

She skulked along the wall, making her way toward a more open, less chaotic area. There, the screamers gave a wide berth to a dozen or so body-armored aliens standing in a tight circle. Adnoydd paced at the circle's center.

Adnoydd caught sight of Akimbo. The circle turned their helmets to face her and stared. Exposed, she swiveled wildly, looking for a safe path, until ballistic-gloved hands gripped her biceps and pulled her toward the group.

The SWAT team huddle, made up of men and women alike, focused their attention on her chest. Regretting her hasty wardrobe choices, she crossed her arms to communicate her indignation and to conceal her dishabille. She self-consciously checked her appearance and saw only sternum exposed by the deep V-neck of her scrubs. She had suffered a lifetime of stares in the most inappropriate of situations, but always for the presence of breasts—never for the absence of gills.

Adnoydd signaled a woman to relieve herself of armor. The woman eagerly pulled her bulletproof vest over her head and threw it and other equipment at Akimbo's feet. Her chest heaved, revealing she had been suffocating behind the vest's protective layers. Her gills flapped visibly under her shirt's ruffles, opening wide to draw in air. By common assent the rest of the team followed suit, dropping their vests on the floor, grabbing their knees to catch their breath.

"Suit her up," Adnoydd directed, pointing at Akimbo. Apparently, Adnoydd had, without hesitation, elected Akimbo to address the emergency.

"What? Me?"

Her admirers shifted their gaze to watch her lips move in perfect synchrony with her words.

He moved close and shouted from his chest, "Yes, you!"

"I don't think so."

"Put on the protection, you'll need it."

"I don't even know what's happening."

"That's for the best. Invasions aren't our sweet spot. Trust me, you're perfect. You're disposable...barbarically disposed...whatever."

"Invasion? By whom?"

"It's a what."

"What?"

"Give her a weapon," Adnoydd instructed.

His panting, red-faced team looked at one another with collective unwillingness, like he was asking them to give a weapon to a house cat to kill a mouse. By their reckoning, this was not the time to test loyalties.

"Okay then, hand-to-hand combat. One of you take her to the front line." Adnoydd shooed them away.

The equipment woman appeared to accept partial responsibility for Akimbo's welfare, or at least a responsibility to accurately report what became of the armor she loaned. She started walking and twitched her head for Akimbo to follow.

They passed into a kitchen area and snaked around glistening metal cabinets and appliances. Not stainless steel, a rose-gold metal with crystalline flakes glinting like diamonds. They made their way down a staircase to a storage area. The shelves extended into the distance, stocked with food supplies. The pallets from the space van sat ready for unpacking.

Several aisles away, an armored alien lay crumpled on the floor.

"He was keeping guard," the woman said. "Down that aisle." She pointed. She grabbed the fallen alien's ankles and pulled him toward the stairway. He moaned and blinked his eyes as he skidded past Akimbo. She heard the door latch closed behind her.

Akimbo's body went into competition mode without her mind's explicit approval. Her thoughts raced to find a safe avenue of escape but were sucked into her body's fight response. She scanned around for a weapon. Spotting a cache of kitchen and janitorial supplies, she knew what needed doing. She taped a knifelike thing to the end of a mop handle. The handle felt surprisingly light in her hands, and she marveled at the speed with which she was able to slash the knife through drifting clouds.

Her focus narrowed to a single objective; the alarms disappeared from her attention. She gripped her improvised naginata in both hands and deliberately moved to the head of the aisle where the guard had lain.

There was no visible enemy.

She shuffled forward, weight balanced, her back foot cocked with heel lifted, ready to lunge. She kept her eyes focused forward, taking in all the details of her surroundings, the food bins reflecting flashing alarm lights, the occasional cloud drifting into her view. She saw nothing.

A cloud lingering above the top shelf to her left drifted away from her and slowly revealed what she could only assume was her objective: a spider conducting business at the corner of its web, unperturbed by the commotion.

Granted, the spider and web were above average in size, but not gigantic. She recognized it as a Joro spider, a thriving invasive species that had moved into their county in recent years. They were scary, big, black, yellow, and blue, but harmless. The spider had probably hitched a ride from her own property. She laughed at the possibility.

But still, the Joro didn't deserve all this attention. If Clagett were with her, he would be worrying about edge cases, outlandish cinematic possibilities, like a giant mother spider lurking out of sight, maybe overhead, the thought of which made her check the ceiling. She decided she'd better clarify her mission profile; she jogged up the steps and poked her head out of the kitchen. She caught the attention of the equipment woman and discreetly waved her over.

"Hey. Sorry to bother." Akimbo tried to act more apologetic than she felt. "I want to make sure we're all on the same page, threat-wise. Am I after a spider?"

"Yes, obviously. A big one."

"Right. Thank you, that's helpful. Now, when you say big, just how big are we talking? Bigger than my fist or smaller?"

"Smaller than your fist. You have big hands for a woman."

"Perfect. Thank you. I'll be right back."

She trotted back to the web.

Ordinarily she liked to live and let live, except when it came to eating tender young male livestock, but this spider found her in a mood for savagery.

She lunged forward decisively. Without the pull of Earth's gravity, she propelled herself several feet into the air. With a deft slice she precisely delivered a death blow, cleaving the spider in half.

She dismantled the web with a twirl of her weapon and wrapped the spider's corpse in a funeral shroud of its own silk. She held it aloft, presenting evidence of her accomplishment, as she returned to the chaos of the first floor.

She found the SWAT team there, huddled still amid the throng, watching a video replay of her attack. The alarms quieted and the commotion settled. The guard incapacitated in the basement had recovered once stripped of his suffocating protective vest.

As the panic drained from them, the crowd cheered with all the flatulent vibrato their gills could summon. She wanted to mock their fear of spiders, but seeing their awe, she raised her arms in victory.

This was her moment. She aimed the knife end of the mop handle at Adnoydd and shuffled forward. "Listen up, motherfucker! We need to renegotiate your caregiving proposal," she yelled. She had Adnoydd's attention. "This is what's going to happen: we go home tomorrow and you provide caregivers for free as long as my husband needs them."

All eyes turned toward Adnoydd, who cowed in silence.

"Heed me! I am the avenging angel!" she cried, milking her momentary celebrity for everything she could. "If you break this deal, I will hunt you down! I shall visit my wrath upon you all and infect your homes with spiders." Had she taken it too far? The time and logistics of tracking someone across space were daunting. Better to finish with an arresting visual. "I will slice you in half!"

As if expressing fearlessness, when truly it sprang forth from how ridiculous she felt, she laughed.

"You killed a spider and he's setting us free?" Clagett asked, after Akimbo told her story.

"When you say it like that it doesn't sound like much," she said. "I can assure you they were quite impressed."

"That was the emergency?"

"That's what I just said. Why is this hard for you? I saved the ship."

"From a spider."

Well down the road to feeling unappreciated, she ignored his comment. "You can't account for people's fears. Look at me, I've been needlessly terrified of aliens because of that movie you made me watch. What was it?"

"*Alien.*"

"No, the one with the little boy."

"*E.T.?*"

"That's it. Little boys are such monsters. And that creature was like a shriveled penis with feet."

"I never looked at it like that."

She climbed onto the bed and rolled to face his wheelchair.

"A *spider*?" he asked again. "And they'll take care of me for free?"

"There was a little give and take afterward that's hardly worth mentioning. I agreed to twelve hours of care each day, paying 10 percent off their usual fee, and they cover travel expenses."

"Very savvy!" he said.

"We're going home!" she cheered. "Do you think he simply decided I would be an intolerable pain in the ass if I stayed on board?"

"Your ass is anything but—"

"Not the time," she interrupted.

"You seem more at peace, so that's something already," he said. "I'm glad."

"I left myself behind for a moment. I needed the break."

"Maybe there are other spiders to vanquish."

"Not challenging."

"Vanquish some aliens."

"That wouldn't be sporting. Besides, I'm not looking for advice. I wanted you to know how amazing I am."

"You are amazing," he readily agreed. "Kudos on the killing."

"Thank you," she said.

9

CLAGETT HEARD MUFFLED WORDS from the kitchen. He wasn't sure how long he had slept, wasn't even sure he was awake. He gradually ascertained that he wasn't dreaming: he was no longer on a spaceship—he was at home. The memory that he *had* been on a spaceship was so muted that it barely concerned him. Quadriplegia and dying had anesthetized him to the far-fetched...with special thanks to his "mood stabilizing" prescriptions for their supporting role.

He heard voices approaching, a knock at the living room door.

Akimbo, smiling, led Geldine and a stranger into the room. She cheerfully informed him that his caregiving team had arrived.

"Blevadl is today's caregiver," Geldine explained. "She has lots of experience," she amended, as if that would clear up any apprehension.

The trainee's "Hello" arrived with a heavy accent rounded off by phlegmy diction. The greeting showed up sometime after her lips formed their shape.

Clagett couldn't lift his head to greet her eye to eye. His peripheral vision caught her silhouette and he established that she was a big girl, bosomy and thick of waist, cut from the same template as Ariola and crunched by gravity. He didn't retain her name, but it had sounded despotic, so he decided to think of her as Belva until further updates.

"Where are you from?" he asked pleasantly. Accents intrigued him, and this was his canned greeting.

"Caregiving agency," she answered.

"They'll take good care of you." Akimbo moved back, a step closer to the door. Her face was blank; the relief she felt for herself balanced out the empathy she felt for him. She slipped out of the bedroom, pulling the door closed behind her.

They'll take good care of you? Clagett thought with disbelief. That's what gang leaders said when their lackeys dragged you to the prison shower.

Geldine pointed out the supplies and showed how the Hoyer lift went up and down with the push of a button. She and Belva spent time in the bathroom discussing plumbing fixtures and their many controls.

Belva threw the sheets off him. She pulled free the pillows that propped up his feet, his knees, and his head. He sank flat against the mattress, his legs flopped to the left, his head to the right. She stripped off his boxer shorts in one long pull and tossed them to cover his groin. Once again, his nudity elicited no response. He supposed it was quiet professionalism, but it read as brutal indifference.

Clagett closed his eyes. His embarrassment was easier to tolerate if he didn't see them seeing him.

Geldine gave a curated tour of Clagett and described proper care of the natural wonders found at each scenic overlook.

She coached Belva on proper technique to wrestle him onto the Hoyer sling. His comfort and safety were secondary to Geldine's concern that Belva might injure her back with poor mechanics.

Belva rolled him onto his side facing her, stopping his motion with her hips to keep him on the bed. His face pressed into her inner thigh as she leaned across him to position the sling behind his back.

Rolling him away from her, she flipped him nearly onto his belly. His nose twisted painfully sideways against the mattress. He moaned, but it escaped the attention of his caregivers or didn't meet their minimum threshold for complaints.

The sling drew tight, the coarse nylon leg straps abrading his inner thighs as Belva hoisted him off the bed. Airborne in a fetal position, his bottom exposed, he dangled from the lift.

Geldine selected that moment to excuse herself from the room. She congratulated Belva for finishing the hard part of the morning. She was confident Belva could manage for a little while.

"I got it," Belva confirmed.

"You look ready for an ob-gyn exam," Geldine said on her way out. She gave his knee a gentle push to set him swinging, like one might rock a baby's cradle.

***

In the kitchen, Akimbo ambushed Geldine and laid into her about involving them in such a sketchy enterprise.

"Adnoydd was talking about making us slaves!" Akimbo fumed and aimed a finger at Geldine. Not one to forsake politeness, she asked in a calmer register, "Oh, I should have offered, would you like some tea?"

"I could do with some tea." Geldine gave a tired chuckle. "Nobody's becoming a slave," she promised.

"How can you be sure?" Akimbo demanded.

"The way I see it, people needing a caregiver make for a lousy hard-labor workforce—for crop circling or whatever foolishness they get up to."

"But what about me? And you? What about everyone else?"

"Listen, them aliens don't want to stir up the humans who have guns, rightly thinking they would take a dim view of slavery—maybe not in a general sense but in the sense that gun owners don't want to be the slaves, if you get my meaning. I told him, based on personal experience, enslavement comes with a lot of lingering resentment that will taint the whole conquering experience—"

"When was that? When did *you* have the opportunity to talk with Adnoydd?"

"A while back. He abducted me and one of my clients. I'm not up for talking about that right this minute."

"Why not?" Akimbo asked. Her question landed as an accusation, and Geldine scowled.

"I'll say one thing about it. Adnoydd is an easy mark. You should take note. I played scared and got six hundred dollars out of him by telling him I needed one new tire. Just for one! Told him all sort of stories. Wrapped around my finger, he was," Geldine said proudly. "He's a blowhard. He's in it for the money, same as everyone, except he doesn't know what's what."

"He threatened to take everything we own!" Akimbo exclaimed.

"He's not wrong there. That's just the fact of your situation. If it's not him, it'll be somebody else."

Akimbo lingered over Geldine's blunt truth. "That's depressing, to put it mildly."

"You'll get bled dry more slowly with him. They skirt around nettlesome labor issues and give a good rate."

The reminder of caregiver costs and her tenuous financial position deflated Akimbo. She gave in, mumbling, "I guess you're right."

"I'm a good caregiver. I'll do right with your husband. I've got you," Geldine said.

Akimbo got the uncomfortable impression that Geldine's behavior—blurring the line between taking care of them and taking advantage of them—was the nature of the care beast.

"I need to get back." Geldine headed down the hall.

From his elevated position in the sling, Clagett had a clear view of Belva. Her cheeks were squeezed into bulldog wrinkles. Like Ariola, her hair had a fur-like appearance, but hers was mostly white with near-black tips. His instinct was to categorize the aliens by their hair color/pattern, which led him to question whether that was racially insensitive. He made no progress down that road because his low-hanging fruit swinging in the breeze proved to be the enemy of cogent thought.

Belva manhandled the lift away from the bed and lowered him onto the shower chair, a mobile toilet seat, the mongrel offspring of a wheelchair and an outhouse.

"I need to use the bathroom," he said. It was an understatement, a continuation of politeness that he couldn't suppress despite his increasing humiliation. Instinct told him that politeness would earn leniency.

"From the back or from the front?" she asked.

"Back."

She pushed the chair across the hall to the bathroom, lurching over thresholds, and targeted the drain in the newly renovated shower, former site of Akimbo's claw-foot tub Earth-goddess sanctuary.

"Over the toilet," he said, "not in the shower." He nodded toward the toilet.

"I got it," she said and remaneuvered him, then stepped out, leaving the door open.

Parked over the toilet, he breathed deeply and bore down with what little force his abdominal muscles could muster.

He tried to relax his mind and his bowels. He visualized a beach, but going to the bathroom on a beach was gross and the sand burned his feet. He tried frolicking in the surf, but he clenched up in the cold water. He settled on a luxurious resort's beach-side bathroom, but the attendant kept jingling coins, looking for tips. *Is there no happy place left for me?*

He glimpsed Geldine returning with one of their coffee cups and a bran muffin she would regret eating. Chatter, footsteps, then Geldine poked her head into the bathroom.

"Everything good? Is she amazing?"

Caught at a pivotal moment incompatible with speech, he closed his eyes again and gave a quick nod, wanting her to go away.

In the living area, Geldine and Belva struck up a discussion about his bathroom visit, Belva asking whether it was an anomaly or would be a regular occurrence. She spoke with a sense of wonder, as if she had never used the bathroom, which he supposed was entirely possible. He would have to inquire…or maybe not—he didn't really want to know.

Impatient for news, they reentered the bathroom. He nodded to indicate success.

From its holster behind the toilet, Belva retrieved the menacing metal bidet wand—seemingly styled after 1950s asylum chic. She fired troubling warning shots into the shower, revealing raw hydraulic power that could disband a rioting mob or strip paint from a car.

"She's going to clean you now," Geldine warned.

"Low pressure, please," he requested, hoping Belva understood such hydrodynamic nuances.

She squatted and extended the wand into the gap between the shower chair and the toilet seat. She closed one eye and estimated where the target ought to be based on…what? A diagram…her own alien anatomy? The pressure came on in a surge that nearly lifted him from the seat. He yelped.

Belva was a plodding problem-solver, the wand a curious tool. Its complexity fascinated her. She repeatedly cycled the thumb control between off and fully on, with each pressure spike producing a yelp, until she felt comfortable managing his comfort.

"You would never last under torture," she predicted.

She studied the water dripping from his body.

"You still going."

"I'm done," he insisted.

"Take your time," Geldine encouraged.

"Done."

"Do you feel clean?" Geldine asked with hope.

He felt violated, like he had endured a public colonic.

Belva wheeled him into the roomy shower and worked at the knobs until satisfied that the water was painfully hot, but not so hot it would burn. She hosed him down with a shower wand and began a head-to-toe scrubbing. He kept his eyes closed and braced himself to face his fear of getting his nuts scrubbed by a stranger.

Mercifully, she executed the shower with efficiency. With his eyes closed, the steam, the sound of water, and her almost gentle handling of the washcloth, he found the experience pleasurable. He had three insights. First, the thoroughness with which he cleaned himself had been woefully lacking—his own showers, by comparison, were more of a rinse, a quiet moment of reflection. Second, his fear that his body would misinterpret her touch as sexual did not factor in the reality of a sweaty, wheezing stranger. Third, his fear of getting his delicates scrubbed was perfectly justified.

Clagett shivered while Belva splashed cold sink water on her face and mopped her neck sweat. Geldine fetched towels and busied herself drying his lower half. Belva rallied to dry his scalp with a ferocity he could, in all honesty, grow to enjoy.

"Wow," he enthused, "amazing."

She attacked his scalp again, increasing fingernail pressure until he could scarcely tolerate the pain. He was concerned that pain had been her goal all along.

Belva tugged the back of his neck to lean him forward, parking his ear against her substantial belly. He heard the raspy gills and felt her hot breath as she toweled his back. Her innards rumbled and the smell of sweat clung to her clothing. Geldine slipped the sling behind him.

Back in the living room, they transferred him out of the shower chair and onto his bed. Belva draped a towel across his midsection and slathered him with body lotion. As with his shower thoroughness, he realized that his version of moisturizing was amateur patchwork. Mainly he had attacked whatever itched and was within easy reach.

Belva wrangled his body into boxer shorts, a shirt, and socks. She prepared the sling for the transfer to his wheelchair.

Akimbo stepped into the room to make a quick spot check. She called, "Looks like somebody is shiny clean!"

Belva suspiciously eyed Clagett's wheelchair as he drove

out of the living room. She made fearful raspberry noises with her gills.

"She's never seen a robot chair," Geldine explained.

"We don't trust robots," Belva said.

"How do disabled people get around?" he asked.

"We don't have disabled people," she answered. "We don't allow robots."

He had hoped she would tell stories of jet packs and exoskeletons.

"The weak get born into new bodies," Belva said.

Akimbo quickly interjected, "Clagett, honey, I haven't had a chance to talk with you about that."

He was eager to learn more. "Can I get reborn into a new body? Something young and hot?"

Belva scowled. Akimbo shook her head, subtly warning him off his path of inquiry.

"A contemporary model, something androgynous with multi-ethnic appeal," he specified. "I might pay extra for rock-hard abdominals if they're available as an upgrade."

"It doesn't work like that." Belva turned her back to Clagett, visibly offended that he would mock a sacred aspect of life.

Akimbo said, "You and I need to talk about it in private." She made encouraging smiles like he was a child sitting for a portrait. He attempted a smile.

The morning left Clagett questioning if Belva's performance was his own fault. He had responded with complaints, mostly internalized, when he should have offered direct feedback from the outset. His input had been complicated by Geldine, who dominated the instruction with nursing-home learned-on-the-front-lines advice heavy on speed of execution and light on patient comfort.

Geldine went home once he was in his chair, leaving Clagett free to steer Belva in the direction of his comfort. Over lunch, he attempted to clearly present his care goals.

"I used to program factory robots," he said. "I made them safe for humans. What type of work did you do?" He started further afield than simple, direct confrontation usually called for. Partly he feared retaliation if he attacked head-on, partly he was lousy at conversation, and in either case he rationalized he needed to build slowly toward the core issue.

Belva had dozed off in a quiet period between bites, while Clagett slowly worked his food into a safely swallowable mush.

"I said, what type of work did you do back home?"

"I took care of children. Day care, as you call it," Belva said with reluctance. "It's a job and I needed one."

"Oh? That sounds rewarding," Clagett enthused. "What's your job on the ship?"

"This is my job, dealing with you. Do you think this is my vacation?"

"No, I meant—"

Belva shoveled potato salad into Clagett's mouth.

With his mind void of a follow-up question, Clagett abandoned his pretense of conversation. "Since you're interested, making machines safe is tricky," Clagett said. "People know how to protect themselves because if they are doing something that hurts, they will stop. But a machine doesn't know pain."

He hoped his oversimplification would go unnoticed. In his professional experience, humans were damn poor at listening to their bodies. Often, their inner warnings didn't register until they reconsidered an accident under the punishing lights of an ER.

"If *I* am brushing my hair and I push until it hurts, I would just stop. If a *robot* was brushing my hair, it wouldn't know if it was hurting me and it wouldn't care. Do you get my point?"

"No, not really. We don't like robots. They killed many of my kind."

"Right! Industrial accidents! That's what I worked to prevent."

"Robots from space stomped on many of us. We hid in caves until the robots left. That was a long time ago."

"Well, same idea. The robots didn't *know* they were causing pain and injury—that's my point. They followed their programming."

"The robots said, 'Suffer mightily, little creature.' They enjoyed it. They knew."

"Okay, we're converging from different backgrounds." Clagett struggled to remember why he'd started down this road. "You're not a robot, maybe that was my point. When you brush my hair, or wash me, or dress me, or brush my teeth—pretty much everything you do with me—you can tell when I'm in pain and care enough to be gentle, right?"

"Not sure."

"I see. Well, *next time* you'll know to not hurt me. When I yell 'Aaah!' like when you were putting on my deodorant, you'll know that you're ripping hair from my body and will stop right away. You understand what pain is, unlike a robot. Sound like a plan?" Clagett flashed her a confident smile.

"Are you trying to tell me that I hurt you?"

"Yes, in a manner of speaking."

"Geldine didn't stop me."

"I know, and I need to talk with her about that."

"Why didn't you say something to me?"

"I did. Loudly. Repeatedly," Clagett insisted.

"I wondered what that was about. You should have said that I was hurting you. I know your thoughts are simple, but I'm not a mind reader."

"I did say something along those lines."

"You didn't say it so I could understand it. That's on you."

"I was in pain."

"Next time we'll both do better if you get a handle on your pain. I can't do my job with the distractions."

"Understood," said Clagett. "Let's both do better."

———————————

"How was it?" Akimbo asked.

They lay side by side, he in his hospital bed, she on the couch, an uncomfortable gulf between them.

"What's that?" he asked.

"Getting showered by strange women."

"*Strange* doesn't begin to cover it."

"The women or the experience?"

"All of it. The whole day," he said.

"How was our rock star's performance?"

"Low key. He went unrecognized."

"And his two backup singers?" she asked with concern.

"Got roughed up, but they've been through worse."

"I imagine that was quite an uncomfortable experience, being stripped and showered by a strange woman and you're helpless to resist. I'm sorry you had to go through that."

"Your description doesn't account for the sweat dripping off her brow or getting my face pressed into a fold in her belly, among other pleasantries."

"I guess I'm glad to know you're not into that," she said.

They lay in silence, grieving for the humor in their connubial banter. Talk about his condition made their love language dry and brittle. Even so, the attempt relaxed him for the first time that day.

"I'm lousy at being disabled," he complained.

"You're a perfectly good disabled person."

"I don't just blame myself, I'm disappointed in my disability too," he griped. "I thought it would come with personal insight—instead, I get scatological indignity."

"People treat *disabled* like it's a big word to live up to. Don't put that pressure on yourself."

"I don't even deserve to be called disabled."

"You're experiencing impostor syndrome," Akimbo assured. "You'll get the hang of it."

He heard her reach the limit of her tolerance for self-pity and he scrambled to amuse her. He gambled on an anecdote. "Geldine said something interesting about my groin."

"Oh? I can't imagine what."

"She referred to my *groin* as my *groan*…which really does a better job of capturing the potential for pleasure and pain, don't you think? She's like a linguistic savant."

"If you say so."

No laughter. He took a hard conversational turn.

"I just remembered…What was with all the smiles this morning?" he asked. "There was nothing to smile about. You freaked me out."

"We need to be careful around this idea of rebirth. I think it's a code word for something sinister, like euthanasia for the sick, the disabled, and the old. They seem cavalier about death."

"And yet, that doesn't seem like the worst choice on the table."

"I think we need to act cooperative. We should get a lay of the caregiving landscape."

"You're the—"

"Don't say it—"

"You're the lay of my landscape," he said. It was worth a try.

"You had to say it." She smiled.

10

WITHIN DAYS OF BELVA'S start, she failed to show up for work. Ariola called and explained to Akimbo she was running behind on her morning rounds and emphasized the fault was not hers. She said client privacy—one of the agency's top concerns—prevented her from giving a more complete explanation.

"Basically, one of my caregivers messed up on her overnight shift," Ariola said. "But you'll never hear me admit that."

"Right, but—"

"My girl was supposed to tend to an elderly client, but instead she spent the night in the wrong bedroom watching an infant sleep in a crib. Come morning, the old lady's son found the caregiver holding his kid while his mother had fallen and spent the night on the floor. Threats were made, a baseball club appeared, *fucking* was mentioned many, many times. The old lady was fine, I don't know why he made such a big deal of it."

"But what about *our* situation?" Akimbo abruptly asked.

"I've already assigned Geldine to fill in until I arrive with Blevadl. We're still working out a few kinks in our process, but I promise we'll do better," she claimed.

The conversation was their first indication that Ariola's job was a hybrid of care coordinator and unreliable bus driver. They would come to learn that shuttling caregivers around the county was unpredictable and any semblance to coordination with Clagett's agreed-upon schedule was coincidental.

Geldine arrived in short order and set to work getting Clagett out of bed. In Belva's absence, Clagett told Geldine he was struggling to communicate his idea of comfort, especially to Belva, and wondered if she had suggestions. In part, he hoped to backhandedly approach the same issue with Geldine.

"Why do you get to be comfortable?" she asked in seriousness. "The rest of us make do with comfortable *enough*."

"Yeah, I agree, how do I communicate that? That's what I'm asking."

"If you're in pain, then scream. That will get their attention. They'll eventually learn."

"And if I'm not in pain?"

"Then I guess she satisficed you and you're comfortable enough," she said, dismissing the topic.

She showed greater interest in soliciting Clagett's advice about cryptocurrency investing.

"Don't" was his recommendation. He said she might as well play the lottery, which, as it happened, was where she had invested her retirement savings. Her financial consultation happened while he sat over the toilet on the shower chair. Seemingly, those were pensive moments for both of them.

"Just what is kleptocurrency?" she finally asked. He realized she had a fundamental problem, one they shared: when it came to crypto, neither of them knew what they were talking about.

"Um, *crypto* is like online money. I mean, I know what it is, I just don't have the words to describe it. It's blockchain—"

"Let me ask you a question," she said, preempting his floundering. "Let's say our out-of-town friends earn money here. How do they get it home?"

"On their spaceship?" He wasn't up for mental exertion.

"Come on, you act like a smart guy. What do they use for money?"

Clagett snorted. "I don't know what you're asking."

"A checking account? Could he cash a check back home?"

"Seems unlikely."

"How about with that cryptic money?"

"Crypto? That's interesting. But...even if they were able to access it on their home planet, I don't think cryptocurrency has any value there, same as checks, or dollar bills for that matter."

"So how will they take their money home?"

"I don't know. My mind isn't functioning right now."

"Well, if they can't use it, why don't we take it off their hands?"

"You mean steal it?"

"That makes it sound worse than it is. I mean like swindle them, a little trickery, that's all."

"How would that work?" he asked.

"That's what I'm asking you, Mister Smart Guy."

Geldine situated him on the back porch, where he could pass his day admiring nature and ignoring whatever it was caregivers did out of his sight.

In contrast to a life spent mostly doing *something*, he chose to think of his time between diagnosis and death as "a pursuit of nothingness." The plants in bloom, the shapes hidden in the clouds and the swaying oak leaves, birds darting through the trees, subtle shifts in the weather, best of all a thunderstorm...they were incredible to behold.

The eye-gaze-controlled computer affixed to his wheelchair opened a portal to all manner of nothingness. He immersed himself in mystery novels or red carpet fashion—cultural fascinations light on cosmic meaning. Lately he dug into human preconceptions of aliens, on the whole preferring the camp promoting Amazonian-like warriors over the camp endorsing tentacles and slime. Naturally, he stipulated that the Amazonian-like warriors' stomach-baring animal-skin outfits were their *choice*, informed by the tropical climate and the freedom of movement warring demands.

Then there was the dark side of nothingness—boring days, immune to distraction, spent reckoning with his own lack of cosmic meaning, days absent of purpose, days wracked by self-contemplation that left him thankful for only one thing: he hadn't embarked on a career as a monk.

Belva finally showed up, and Geldine skedaddled home without so much as a goodbye. He heard Belva putter around the house for a while before she inquired through the screen door whether he was okay.

His thumb joint rested uncomfortably on an edge of the armrest, causing his hand to throb. He was in pain and, according to Geldine's—dare he think it—rule of thumb, could justifiably ask for help.

"Could you please move my right wrist outward?" he requested.

She approached, gently lifted his knee, and rested it back in place. "Is that good?" she asked in her terse and heavily accented gill-speak.

"My *wrist*," he repeated. He enunciated as well as his shallow breathing allowed.

She adjusted his other knee. "Good?" she asked.

"Wrist."

"Here?" she asked, touching his neck.

He could have tried a different description of the location, referenced a hand or palm, but in the moment, *wrist* so perfectly captured the problem. "Wrist," he insisted.

She moved the process of elimination to his shoulder and onward to his elbow. "Here?" she asked.

"Yes!" he said when she arrived at his hand. "But the other hand. My right hand."

She was standing in front of him, facing him, and held up her right hand. "Right," she said with insistence. He could tell by her look that she was going to tolerate him for only so long.

"My right," he repeated.

She reoriented herself to face the same direction as Clagett. She identified her right hand, clenched it into a fist, and looked over her shoulder to relate it to his.

Meanwhile, he finally reasoned he needed to provide better instructions, but his choice of words only clouded understanding. "Your left," he said.

"Left?" She opened her right fist and re-interrogated herself with this change.

"Your left if you're facing me. Your right if we're facing the same direction." He decided he owed a comprehensive explanation, that by his brief commands he had deprived her of the ability to make a reasoned decision of her own. "It's really the joint at the base of my thumb that hurts, but since the thumb has several joints, I said wrist because it's close to the pain. I was trying to simplify the request, but I see now I've just made it worse. I'm sorry."

She touched the tip of his *left* thumb. "Here?"

"Right!" he said.

"Good," she said.

She moved his left thumb away from his fingers, leaving it more or less in the same uncomfortable position as his right. She handled him forcefully for detaining her with pointless adjustments.

The right thumb throbbing had not subsided, but it was now balanced with fresh throbbing in his left, which miraculously seemed workable even though he might be less comfortable than when he started. He wasn't sure—he had lost perspective as his frustration with Belva rapidly overwhelmed his thumb complaint. He *did* know for certain he was relieved to be done with their discussion. He had a feeling that this was his new life: deciding whether his discomfort was more tolerable than the frustration of asking for help.

———

Akimbo joined them on the porch for lunch, bringing with her several slices of leftover pizza to share with Clagett. She asked Belva how the morning went, and Belva reported, "Good."

He didn't see Akimbo's response, whether it was a raised eyebrow or simply questioning eye contact, but Belva was prompted to elaborate.

"We got him ready just fine, but he struggled to communicate sometimes. *Wrist, wrist, wrist,* he says. Does his condition affect speech?"

"No, he's always been that way," Akimbo said.

"I beg your pardon! I communicate just fine," he protested.

"It comes and goes," Akimbo conceded.

Belva looked at Akimbo with a tenderness she withheld from Clagett. "How are you this morning?" she asked. Something ineffable passed between them, Clagett saw that much, but he couldn't identify what was happening.

"I'm fine," Akimbo replied.

"Are you sure?"

"Why?" Akimbo asked.

Through unspoken agreement, Belva moved next to Akimbo on the porch bench. Tears formed in Belva's eyes and she dabbed them with the hem of her scrub's sleeve.

"It's so much harder for the survivors," Belva whispered. "I know, I know."

Akimbo nodded.

"Grief takes time to process. That's what I tell myself."

"I don't know where this is coming from," Akimbo said. "But thank you for understanding."

They sat quietly, thigh to thigh.

Akimbo and Clagett exchanged a quizzical glance, both surprised by Belva's commiseration.

"I lost one of my children long ago," Belva explained. "I've never been the same. I thought caregiving might reward me like caring for my child, but...no."

Belva unfolded her own story in detail, primarily for Akimbo. Clagett listened and eyed the pizza. Because she labeled most of the players generically as her "cousin," their blood relationships to Belva and one another remained vague. Clagett was on the fence as to whether her son's passing was an innocent childhood accident or a product of incest and abuse, which, for all he knew, were culturally acceptable where she came from. He was reasonably sure of only a few details: her son hurt his leg, was rebirthed on the scene, there were accusations of neglect, and Belva was experiencing her version of grief.

On top of sorting out the story's basic facts, Clagett struggled to attribute emotions to her descriptions. Akimbo, too, looked puzzled. When he felt unsettled by the son's treatment, Belva made noises he associated with laughter. When she described her son's final injustice, she seemed to have lost interest.

"Anyway, that was what happened," she finished.

"I'm so sorry," Akimbo said. She gingerly touched Belva's shoulder. Thinking that Belva was on the rebound, she went directly for a piece of pizza. She casually took a bite.

"Loss is complicated," Belva summarized. In a delayed reaction, she began to wail in earnest. Her tears pulsed into atomized mist, as if pumped from a perfume bottle.

Akimbo paused her chewing to smile and acknowledge Belva. She slid out of range of her tears.

"Sorry to interrupt, but could I get some pizza, please?" Clagett asked. He was hungry, yes, but hunger was only part of his misery. Belva infuriatingly, disrespectfully, used Akimbo's grief as an excuse to relate her own personal trauma, as if she expected Akimbo to find relief in her tale of woe. He was miffed that Belva had unloaded weirdly tragic circumstances, when their own were already more than they could bear. Desperate for the comfort of distraction, for Akimbo and himself, he asked for pizza.

His request was not well received. Clagett puzzled over his pizza question late into the night. He occupied himself with analysis to understand what had happened.

He concluded that, for healthy people, staying comfortable mostly goes unnoticed. If they itch, they scratch. If they are hungry, they eat. Thirsty? They drink. Horny? They do whatever they can get away with and tolerate the shame. With Clagett relying on caregivers, obviously he stayed horny, but hunger and thirst and itchiness were expressed through language. When his subconscious thoughts were verbalized, he sounded selfish. Which, as he learned, was exactly how Akimbo and Belva perceived his pizza request at the time.

"This isn't just about you," Belva had cried out.

"Can't you see she's upset?" Akimbo asked, as if he was blind, as if he had no greater perspective on the situation than thoughts of his own hunger.

Belva scowled at him disapprovingly.

"I know, I'm sorry, that didn't come out right," he back-pedaled. "I just thought I could be chewing on pizza while you were talking…about something different."

With no subtlety, Belva poked pizza into his mouth and turned back to Akimbo.

Before touching the food, she didn't wash her hands or put on gloves, a sanitation practice Geldine emphasized. Believing he needed to advocate for his safety as well as his needs, he said, "Would you please wash your hands before touching my food?"

Later that night, in bed, he wondered if he had really been as rude as they claimed. Had he really implied that Belva was unclean in an all-encompassing sense?

"Why don't we let her settle down for a little while?" Akimbo suggested.

"I need food," he retorted. "It's an essential part of staying alive."

Belva stabbed more pizza into his mouth.

"For fuck's sake, you're going to choke me to death!" Clagett accused after a long bout of chewing intermingled with sips of water.

"You only think of yourself!" Belva accused. "I have feelings too!"

"We're paying *you* to take care of *me*. In my opinion, it's reasonable to expect a caregiver to be more emotionally balanced than the patient," Clagett said calmly. He felt bad that Belva suffered, but he didn't want to witness it or be inconvenienced by it.

"Here, I'll feed Clagett and you take a little break," Akimbo suggested.

Belva made off-putting sniffling noises with her gills as she went inside.

"Please don't tell me I'm selfish," he pleaded.

"I won't. I know you're just trying to stay sane and alive," she soothed.

"I'm not incapable of compassion, you know. I only have so much to give, and I reserve it for you."

She smiled and wiped crumbs from his lips. "I know. If I have to do her job for her again, she'll get a much harsher lesson in the limits of compassion."

11

O N A FRIGID WINTER afternoon, at a temple in Japan, inscribed into a stone, Akimbo stumbled onto weathered kanji that defied her translation skills. The English tourist guide provided: *You have something you don't want, the craving for something you don't have. Stop the craving and you will have everything.*

There were only a handful of characters on the stone, so some Japansplaining was going on in the translation, but still, the message seemed vital to her. She *did* feel like something was missing from her life. In periods of loneliness, she missed her ex-boyfriend—not all of him, heaven knows, just the comfort of companionship. She saw herself as goofy and vivacious, but without a partner to goof with... was she? Was the rock telling her she needed a man in her life to be complete? If so, she had never come across such a sexist rock.

Or...was the rock saying stop expecting to find wisdom on rocks and she would have wisdom? But if the message itself wasn't wisdom, why did the ancients go to the effort to carve it into a rock? Surely they had starvation and oppressive overlords that deserved their attention—marauding bands of disenfranchised samurai or whatever. What enlightened brainiac spent their time immortalizing word puzzles, and why trust someone with such misplaced priorities?

The ancient philosophers were all men, which went a

long way toward explaining her reaction to the rock. Honestly, gender bias called the whole wisdom enterprise into question.

She waded through snow back to the village, emotionally spent from contemplation. Hungry, she stopped in front of a noodle shop to examine the plastic replicas of their menu offerings. Atop the display case she found a placard in English reading, *You have something you don't want: the craving for something you don't have. Musashi soba will fill the emptiness in your life.*

Now *that* made sense.

She ate heartily and enjoyed thimbles of warm sake. Revitalized and pleasantly relaxed, it occurred to her that, compared to a warm bowl of noodles, wisdom offered little nourishment—in fact, wisdom sucked donkey dicks. She giggled at her own irreverence and knocked back more sake. "And that, my friends," she said aloud, addressing the ancient mystics, "was the sound of one goof laughing."

———————————

When they moved to the farm, Akimbo cleared out the hayloft of the old barn, sanded the planks, sealed the big cracks, and declared it fit for naginata classes.

The town's parents gradually came to support her teaching as they heard of other daughters' newfound confidence and glimmers of gratitude. The classes did not generate much in the way of income, but the money helped cover her farm expenses.

She taught girls exclusively. She demanded discipline and aggression and received peals of laughter for her efforts. Her students absorbed her exuberance, even though she did not articulate it.

She refused to teach boys, claiming they were born blessed with aggression...plus the goats didn't need help stinking up the barn. Clagett believed she was laying the foundation for a matriarchy policed by female naginata warriors, which seemed like an attractive idea, but he did wonder what his complicity said about his masculinity.

She promoted a devotion to cleanliness and insisted the students sweep the loft before class, because she herself had little patience for tidiness.

Her Japanese expat teacher had inflexibly required sweeping as an exercise in humility and silent self-reflection. Through *her* reflection, she realized he was simply taking advantage of his students. Despite that experience, as a tradition, she felt it was important to require her own students to sweep—to afford them the same opportunity to question authority.

Akimbo believed that handing a new student her first naginata was potent with meaning and performed the act ritualistically, after several weeks of preparatory classes, with the class bearing witness. As she placed their personal weapon into a new student's hands, she said, "With this instrument of destruction, choose benevolence. The weapon does not think or act on its own. It is controlled by your mind, your body, and your spirit. It is an extension of yourself."

Clagett once commented that her invocation was a metaphor in which the weapon represented men—dangerous tools best controlled by women. His ability to see and accept the truth without feeling threatened was one of the reasons she loved him.

———————————————

For his midafternoon entertainment, Clagett parked himself at a window to watch Akimbo's students arrive. The children's raw vitality was contagious, making him smile.

When he still worked, his office was upstairs in a front bedroom. He could see the length of their gravel driveway and across the road to the downhill corner of the Shiflett property, where now there was only a chimney and the burned husk of a prefab home. Back then, he could see carpool cars turn onto their drive and would call out to Akimbo that "The invasion is starting!" or "Hurry up and put clothes on!" She would yell back to "Save the goats!" or "Head for the keep!" It was a whole comedy routine they enjoyed, except he seriously did want her to put on a shirt.

From his wheelchair-bound vantage point, parked on the first floor, the cars appeared around the final bend without warning, his voice was no longer fit for calling, and if it was a genuine invasion or Akimbo was outside in the buff... how bad would that be, relatively speaking?

On Tuesday and Thursday afternoons, a carpool caravan of SUVs pulled up to the barn and released a torrent of girls dressed in traditional uniforms: white gi tops and black hakama pantaloons.

Middle schoolers comprised most of the class. They were at an age when finding one's place in the world went hand in hand with attacking one's best friends. There were younger girls, too, sisters and the naturally athletic who couldn't find meaning running after one type of ball or another.

High schoolers dwindled to a handful who couldn't rightly explain their devotion. They weren't especially competitive, they enjoyed helping the younger girls, they liked the exercise up to a point, but mostly they came because they left happier than they arrived, which was an anomaly in adult-sanctioned gatherings in general and culture-broadening classes in particular. The older girls were easily identified because some drove, they were allowed to take their weapons home, and they walked calmly while the younger students raced into the loft, greeting the goats, running at the chickens, screaming to be heard over the screaming.

Broom duty began in a mad scurry to find a place in the line—preferably away from the stairs where barn dust reliably collected. The brigade attacked the floor in two waves, young girls at the front, energetic and imprecise, older girls behind, patiently walking with push brooms. The work began boisterously and settled into quiet as they reached the far side. Akimbo waited and watched by the equipment racks.

A high schooler led the class through traditional stretching exercises while Akimbo encouraged the youngest, who were innately flexible and not inclined to exert themselves pointlessly.

Akimbo took the class through basic drills to ingrain footwork, balance, and posture. The students then queued up to collect their practice weapons. More solo drills followed, each teaching a specific strike, stab, or parry. Akimbo loved that nasty tactics survived the adaptation from warfare to art form. They practiced attacks to the legs and stabbing to the throat and so forth. As with life, she felt strongly that fairness did not apply to self-defense.

They shifted to partner exercises, mock conflicts with prearranged attacks and parries. Akimbo refused to interpret the martial art into philosophy, having given up on the value of wisdom long ago. To the younger students, who peeled off and watched as the encounters advanced in complexity, she offered practical advice: "The best way to avoid conflict is to understand and communicate with your opponent. Understanding is also helpful for killing them, should it come to that." She didn't sugarcoat the objective of swinging a pole with a sword on the end of it.

Some days, the advanced students practiced sparring, decked out in the full regalia of samurai-derivative protective gear. Over head and face each competitor wore a metal grilled helmet called, in Japanese, the *men*. Naturally, Akimbo took issue with the gender specificity of the word, no matter that it was a homophone from an unrelated language. To her, the name was a male instructor saying, "Let the men protect that pretty little face of yours." She stuck with *helmet* but pronounced it like a Japanese speaker would, so it came out *hey-ra-meh-ta*. The girls thought she was saying "hair metal," which became the de facto name.

Akimbo expected all students to treat class like a fight for survival and give it the complete attention it deserved. The demands of practice took the girls to a level of concentration that temporarily suspended their worldly concerns. After class, they felt as if they had awakened from a dream— the world looked fresh, their problems surmountable, their fears deflated. Running to waiting parents, they were eager for the next lesson.

Akimbo experienced renewal through teaching. Through concentration on the progress of each individual, she set aside concern for her husband's needs. She reawakened to a clear and uncluttered understanding of her life: Clagett would die, she would survive.

She looked over to the house, where she knew she would find Clagett parked at a window, watching. He smiled at her and she smiled in return. Blevadl's broad outline moved closer behind him, and Akimbo watched his expression collapse into what she took to be despair.

Her clarity was fleeting. The complexities of her situation flooded in. A thunderhead of grief formed above her, sending out exploratory tendrils of anger, seeing Blevadl as an easy target to drain its fury. She was tempted to return to the house with her naginata and offer Clagett comfort by whomping Blevadl.

She acknowledged the thought was a by-product of her years spent thinking about chopping people, but she felt certain any reasonable person would feel similarly murderous, just more inclined to think of a handgun.

She flushed with the urge to hold Blevadl accountable for invading their privacy, for taking up the physical space Akimbo formerly occupied, for taking the place in Clagett's life that was rightly hers, for introducing an entirely new set of aggravations. She wanted to extract confessions of every mistreatment and...

No, she was grateful for Blevadl's assistance, really she was. She regulated her breathing and hoped desperately for another moment of clarity. Without caregivers she would be trapped in the house, and yet, she felt no affection for them.

12

ARIOLA PULLED A CAREGIVER from the van and marched her to the house like she was delivering a hostage. Akimbo led them to Clagett's bedside.

"This is Wobbegong," Ariola introduced. The new caregiver was young, perhaps early twenties in human years, and consequently was in better physical condition than Ariola and Blevadl. Her taut skin resisted disfigurement by Earth's gravity. The sound of her breath was unmarked by phlegm.

"Where's Blevadl?" Akimbo asked.

"She's not feeling good," Ariola explained.

"She has it coming out of both ends," Wobbegong added.

Akimbo reflexively conjured a disgusting vision of Blevadl's condition. She squelched the image and any interest in learning more.

"What exactly is *it*?" Clagett boldly asked.

"Let's leave it at that, please," Akimbo pleaded.

"I mean, is it alive?"

Akimbo frowned. "Welcome," she said to Wobbegong. "You don't need to answer him."

"Geldine will be over in a little bit to help get the day started," Ariola said, eager to put everyone at ease. "Blevadl will be back tomorrow, unless she can't...so don't worry."

Akimbo slapped her hands against her hips in a gesture of frustration.

Wobbegong flinched.

Ariola pulled a phone from one of her scrubs' many pockets. She passed it to Wobbegong and gave strict instructions that it was for business and emergency use only.

"You're in capable hands," Ariola assured.

She didn't specify what Wobbegong's hands were capable of, and out of an abundance of caution, he interpreted the comment as a veiled threat. He said, "Wonderful," to put on a good natured show.

"I'll be feeding the animals," Akimbo said, following Ariola out of the house.

Wobbegong sat on the couch. Clagett lay quietly, refreshing his memory of the ceiling's every detail. They waited for Geldine.

"How's the weather out there this morning?" Clagett asked with interest, hoping to establish a friendly rapport before he was compelled to make demands of Wobbegong.

She was perplexed. "Do you mean outside your house or in space?"

"Space."

"Clear," she said. "Clear and cold."

"It's that time of year, isn't it?" he said pleasantly.

"I guess it is," she agreed.

More silence.

"Your wife is very brave to tame the wild chickens."

"It's either that or chickens are harmless."

She laughed at the absurdity. "I wanted to meet her. She's amazing." She swept her arms through the air, imitating naginata slashing cuts. She laughed with exuberance as she pantomimed the deathblow to the spider.

"Oh, that."

"She's so beautiful."

"Now that we can agree on."

"I wish my hair would grow that long and turn silvery." Wobbegong's hair—really more of an upright fur that brought to mind a cat struck by lightning—was orange with black stripes. "My breathing slits are so ugly. She breathes out of her mouth and nose! Can you imagine?"

He detected a shortfall in her training. "Do you know the Heimlich maneuver by chance? Or mouth-to-mouth resuscitation?" he asked. "Just in case I choke."

"No, I'm not supposed to be a caregiver. I volunteered this morning."

"Oh?"

"I've never seen a disabled person. You must be powerful, like your wife, to live so long."

"I only became disabled a few years ago."

"Some of the crew says a tick ate your legs, some guess it was a leech," she said. "A really big one. The Nosferatu of leeches."

"*Nosferatu?* Kudos!"

"Thank you!"

"But how—"

"I don't believe such things. One tick? No. A horde of mosquitoes maybe. This place scares me."

"What a coincidence, you scare me," he admitted.

"Ha!" She laughed. "Me? I'm not scary."

"You're responsible for keeping me alive today, but you don't have any experience."

"You'll be fine, it's overrated."

"Experience?"

"Staying alive. My people get reborn all the time."

"I guess that's a way to look at it. What's it like getting reborn?" he asked with genuine interest.

"How would I know?"

They fell into silence, still waiting for Geldine to arrive.

At lunch, Geldine put a halt to the first spoonful Wobbegong prepared, saying, "You Hoover up food without pausing to breathe or talk. He needs small bites or he'll choke. Don't let him talk while he's eating either."

After sampling several bites, Clagett took issue with Wobbegong's spoon delivery style, which was dump-and-run, explaining he wanted to press his lips against the utensil and slowly squeegee the food off.

"Just get it to his mouth," Geldine countermanded when Wobbegong looked for clarification. "You'll sit a bad president if you give in to him now."

He admired the creative twist to Geldine's wording but couldn't resist correcting her. "*Set a bad precedent?* I get a say about my care," Clagett insisted.

"Say all you like," she said, "but not while you're eating."

"I feel like I'm being force-fed," he griped.

"You need practice letting people feed you," Geldine said with conviction.

"That's not how I feed myself."

"Chew more, talk less. Don't be dramastic." Geldine shrugged.

During the exercise in futility that followed, Clagett worked to hone Wobbegong's spoon skills through patient coaching, honest feedback, and exaggerated facial expressions intended as landing instructions. Wobbegong showed little aptitude for the improvement part of the process, largely because she was convinced of the superiority of her own technique. Instead, she took the initiative to spear the roof of his mouth in new ways. She smiled pleasantly while spearing and apologized with sincerity, leading him to suspect her attacks were deliberate.

He reconnected with Akimbo in the evening, as she made her way to bed.

He explained his spoon-training episode, believing it was another example of caregiver insensitivity. He expected her to validate that caregivers ought to deliver food according to his preferences.

"I don't know," she said. "They're trying to help. You might need to compromise."

"If they just made the effort to comply with my expressed wishes, everything would be better," he griped.

"Maybe part of the problem is in the way you express yourself," she said.

He looked to see if she was joking, but she wasn't. He looked for understanding and saw an offering rise to the surface.

"But I get it, you're losing control and you want to hold on to it," she said.

"That's not how I see it. I don't want to be in control, I want to be myself."

"You're still you on the inside," she said, "up here." She tapped her temple.

"Up there is getting turned inside out," he disagreed. "You know, Geldine said disability is when your private parts aren't. I think she was referring to our private thoughts."

"I feel confident that isn't what she meant."

"I wasn't looking for a critique, I'm telling you the way I see it."

"Okay, you're right," she said.

"I'm saying I have to live my life out loud, and everyone feels free to judge."

"I get it. You don't need to act cranky."

"When you can describe how to put a spoon in *your* mouth and can find someone who cares enough to do it for you, then we can talk." He wanted to slam a door or stomp his feet. He closed his eyes. "I'm stomping out of the room," he said.

"Don't walk out of the room on me!" she said angrily. "Talk to me."

He remained silent.

"Come back and finish the conversation!" she yelled.

"I'm not acting cranky. Don't dismiss my feelings. It runs much deeper than that."

"Tell me!"

"My inner self is getting aired to you and a bunch of strangers. It's humiliating. I can't take the criticism, the commentary."

"No one is criticizing you. You're just in a sensitive place."

"So I need to suck it up?" he asked.

"No, but replicating your life preferences is expecting too much of them."

"But I want to live *my* life, not their lives."

"I'm sure the feeling is mutual," she said. She winced at her unintentionally snappish comment.

She paused to compose a measured response. "This *is* your life now, and they are a part of it." She stepped closer to his bed and touched his cheek. "I'm still a part of it too. I'm here with you. I wouldn't have it any other way," she promised. She scratched the top of his head until he relaxed.

She quietly walked upstairs to their bedroom. He listened to the floor creak above him.

Wobbegong became his regular caregiver despite her absence of experience. Predictably, Ariola dropped Wobbegong off late or sometimes not at all. Atmospheric traffic—satellite congestion, ballistic missile tests, meteor showers, and whatnot—was a daily concern. There were delays when the van's wonky landing leg lost pressure. On cold mornings in space, sometimes the van altogether refused to start.

Clagett and Akimbo cataloged the excuses and mechanical failures because they were laughable to recount. Also, if the US military ever charged the two of them with interplanetary conspiracy, intel about the aliens' tactical weaknesses was a bargaining chip.

Because of the erratic arrivals, he experienced intense morning anxiety waiting in bed, as the dreams faded and the precariousness of his situation backfilled his mind.

As his anxiety kicked into gear, he worried that Wobbegong wouldn't show up, that she would be late, that he was alone, that he had been forgotten, that he was being ignored, that they were doing it on purpose, that they hated him. He worried that his wife would pull out her hair if she had to fill in for another caregiver. If he was in the mood to torture himself, he imagined drowning on his own snot, which seemed like a genuine looming calamity with his weakening diaphragm pitted against ever more adhesive mucus.

In an exercise of uninhibited self-torture, he debated whose snot would make for a memorable death, were he to drown on snot other than his own. Snot scored from local rheumy alcoholics was plausible and the very idea imprinted an unforgettably vomitous aftertaste. He supposed the pope would have moral reservations if he even entertained a petition, but with the procurement details sorted, an atheist drowning on pope snot made for a riveting obituary.

Showing up late robbed him of precious hours of his life. Having settled on the pursuit of nothingness as an end-of-life lifestyle, and with his caregivers observing his unstructured time, they wrongly concluded all idle time was equal, that waiting in bed—catastrophizing the mucus crawling down his throat—was the same as sitting on the porch admiring clouds. They were unsympathetic to the emotional difference. When he protested, they accepted no responsibility for lateness.

The anxiety of caregiver arrival was an unexpected touch provided by the agency, a gift to color his days with fear. Their erratic lateness was a passive-aggressive reminder that Clagett depended on the agency and should thankfully accept whatever they offered. He and Akimbo received apologetic but defensive responses to their complaints: "We're doing the best we can," or "We prioritize the safety of our staff."

Akimbo suffered with him, spending her valuable time cursing over the phone, juggling her appointments. While not explicitly blaming him, she was in no position to offer comfort. She asked him one stressful morning if caregivers were making their lives better. She probably meant it rhetorically, but he hazarded an answer: "They are making our individual lives possible."

She supposed that was true.

Geldine was their savior. She graciously filled in for a morning or an entire day. She was relief personified, coming as she did on the heels of wondering where the hell the space van was and why couldn't the agency bother to call. She had freed her car from the impound lot and paid off the ticket for Langford's lapsed registration but was still unable to afford repairs for either car. She was grateful for the local work, and Clagett was grateful for her excellent care.

With Geldine, he didn't have to stay vigilant, instruct, and remind. Contrary to the nursing-home callousness she projected to other caregivers, she kept his well-being in mind at all times. She instinctively understood his needs and possessed an essential caregiver quality that seemed paradoxically rare: she cared. There were relaxing mornings when he listened to entire albums or wrote long messages in his head or remembered every detail about first grade, all while his body separately got prepped for the day.

Some mornings he asked Geldine about herself, and she told him how boring her days were taking care of the wounded nephew. "I never worried he would die," she said. "Dying suddenly is out of character for a Shiflett. They're a healthy lot. Vehicle accidents, a regular occurrence when the cars or tractors worked at all, only ever caused facial lacerations, broken bones, an involuntary manslaughter charge or two, and an amputation if you counted off-road vehicles stolen by an elderly diabetic."

She talked about the nephew's friends, like-minded souls if they had souls at all, who were inspired by his prolonged commitment to inactivity and pain medications, a category of pharmaceuticals they used in a broad and exploratory sense. They felt entitled to Geldine's care, too, and asked her advice about aches and pains whose origins were difficult to imagine, given their idleness.

"I told them, 'You need to get a job,' except I used the *f* word with those boys because fucking is the only thing that gets their attention." She asked Clagett about a knotty investment: "If I come into money, where should I put it, because the banks are always stealing from me?"

"How about getting your car repaired? That's a good use," he suggested.

"I'm talking about big money. The car isn't nothing."

"Where are you going to come by big money? Wait, maybe I don't want to know."

"Me and Langford got an idea: when Adnoydd and company go home, you'll invest their money for them—financial adviser like. There's no value in them taking it with them, you know?"

"Yeah…right. But wait, are they leaving?"

"They come and go. I don't know when."

"But what about my caregivers?"

"Don't worry about that," she said in frustration. "I'm talking about their money! We'll promise he'll make a cool fortune on cryo currents. We'll double their money, maybe triple it, we'll say. They'll make more while they're gone than while they're here. All with your expertise!"

"*My* expertise?"

"That's our play, see? We'll keep the money for ourselves, but when Adnoydd returns, we'll tell him that *you* lost it all on bad investments."

"You're going to blame me?"

"Don't worry, nothing bad will happen to you. You'll be dead by then. That's what makes this plan perfect."

———————————

With multiple caregivers in the mix, Clagett uniformly enforced the schedule of tasks developed with Geldine. Repetition helped free him from instruction and left him to imagine other, more interesting circumstances. Unfortunately, repetition also brought a sameness to his days. Time slid past like his wheelchair spun on a treadmill, leaving him stuck midweek. The weekend, with its promise of a break from routine, seemed evermore out of reach. There were no days off from illness.

Wobbegong quickly adapted to his care, faster even than the so-called trained caregivers. Geldine's brief oversight gave her a leg up, but mainly she succeeded by remembering Clagett's routine and addressing his needs up front, heading off DEFCON 3 calls for attention that interrupted her phone use.

Clagett privately attributed Wobbegong's success to his own clever psychological tactic: he contributed positive reinforcement that played on her admiration for Akimbo.

"Akimbo will be amazed when I tell her how gentle you are," he exclaimed as she put him in bed. "You put my socks on so effortlessly! I think you do it better than everyone, even Akimbo!" He complimented her every success.

On occasion he chided her while positioning Akimbo as the enforcer: "Please don't answer your phone while you're working with me. Akimbo expects you to give me your undivided attention."

She had fielded a call, on speaker of course, while he hung naked in the Hoyer sling. That the call included video came to light when he heard the caller ask, "Who's the guy hanging by his ass chaps?"

He had mixed luck getting her to do household chores. "Akimbo appreciates a clean counter!" didn't work, whereas, "Akimbo once killed a man who left a mess on the counter!" did, until Akimbo caught wind of his story.

When he requested she sweep the kitchen, she asked, "How?" When he said to use a broom, she asked, "What's that?"

Wobbegong quickly turned his strategy against him, revealing her superior sense for manipulations. "Akimbo will be so disappointed you didn't..." she said whenever he failed to cooperate to her satisfaction, which was his default behavior. She understood and leveraged the importance he placed on Akimbo's peace of mind.

She took liberties he felt helpless to prevent. "You made me work so hard all afternoon so I'm taking a break," she bluntly informed him. "Don't call for me unless you're choking or something."

Another time: "I read about margaritas, so I made some but decided you shouldn't drink them after I already did," she told them one evening. He and Akimbo were immersed in a movie, an activity they regarded as sacrosanct, requiring a vow of silence. Wobbegong bounced on her toes, eager to unleash an alcohol-fueled talking jag. "I *have* to tell you a funny story about Director Adnoydd!" Wobbegong chortled.

Oblivious to their dismissive reaction, she pressed on energetically, forcing Akimbo to pause the movie—a move only sanctioned for snacks, bathroom breaks, and consultation on dialogue mumbled through the Botox-frozen lips of the actor who hadn't aged well since he'd been in that movie they liked.

"Adnoydd used to work in Abductions and Admissions. One day he's interrogating a crackpot—who knows about what—and the crackpot spits out, 'If you want to understand humans, you need to walk a mile in their fucking shoes!' *Of course* Adnoydd wants to understand humans. He thinks he's the big expert. He figured that *fucking shoes* meant footwear worn during the act—you know, the sex act. Do you know about that?"

"We've read something about it, yes," Akimbo assured.

"He imagines shoes that have grippy soles, are waterproof, and are very fast to put on even in the dark, I guess because you don't have suction cups on the bottom of your feet."

"Athletic slip-ons, I can see that," Clagett said.

"He leads a team to a shoe store and asks to see their fucking shoes. The clerk looks over the shoe displays and says, 'Take your pick.' Adnoydd looks over the offerings—

boots, cleats, flats, stilettos, sneakers—something for every kink. He can't believe the variety, so he says to the clerk, 'These are all fucking shoes?' 'That's right,' the clerk says, 'nothing but.' Adnoydd thinks that over and says, 'You people will fuck anywhere, anytime.'"

"Wow, he arrived at an actual insight. I didn't think he had it in him," Akimbo said.

"Now the clerk is taken aback by Adnoydd's attitude, but still hopes to make the sale. 'Look around. See if something strikes your fancy,' he encourages. Adnoydd doesn't know the first thing about shoes, but he strolls around like he's Captain James T. Footwear—hold your kudos until the end—sometimes closing his eyes to imagine who knows what while caressing a shoe. He settles on a pair of women's white flats that really seem to do it for him, judging by the hip pumps when he closed his eyes." Wobbegong thrust her hips to demonstrate her point. "Like this. Do you know what this means?"

"Does that ring any bells, Clagett?" Akimbo asked.

"Looks vaguely familiar."

"So he tried on the shoes and luckily found a size to fit him."

"I *thought* he was wearing women's shoes on the ship," Akimbo said.

"Those are the ones."

Clagett and Akimbo waited expectantly.

"Funny," Clagett said.

"That's not the funny part," Wobbegong corrected. "He abducted the clerk and used him as a beef jerky flavor. The jerky tasted like shoe leather!"

"Human-flavored jerky?" A pulse of anxiety shot through Clagett's system.

"Yeah, he tasted like leather!"

"Is *that* the funny part?" Akimbo asked.

"Isn't that so crazy?" Wobbegong giggled.

"Unspeakably so," Akimbo said. "I hope that story was nothing more than a bad joke."

Not clued in to her story's reception, Wobbegong plowed onward to clear up an open question about the power of the shoes. "Just so you know, we agree on the ship and nobody fiddles with Adnoydd, even when he wears the shoes. He freaks over humans and that's super gross." She extended her tongue in distaste and inadvertently revealed small pockets dotting its surface. Clagett suppressed a heave, so vile was their textural dissonance.

"You know what I'm talking about." Wobbegong laughed.

Clagett blinked rapidly to clear the nausea tears.

Wobbegong's boldest scheme unfolded soon thereafter. Sha'nona, the most senior of Akimbo's naginata students, showed up at the front door after practice.

Clagett had seen Sha'nona around the farm for years, but knew of her mainly through Akimbo's stories. She lived with her Kenyan mother and her mother's no-account boyfriend in a post-high-school limbo of indecision. Akimbo paid her a token wage to help with classes while encouraging her down the road of education and uncompromising birth control.

"Hello, Mister Akimbo!" Sha'nona said brightly through the screen door. She still wore her naginata uniform. Her dark hair was matted down in the shape of her helmet's straps. Her apple cheeks radiated kindness.

"Hi—"

"Sha'nona."

"Of course. Sha'nona. What—"

"I have an appointment with Wobbegong."

"Wha—"

"Manicure and acrylics."

"I—"

"My mobile nail salon business? She saw the Tooth and Nail sign on my car?"

"Oh—"

"I'm earning money for college."

"I guess—" He was going to grant permission, but apparently permission had already been self-administered. He couldn't very well turn Sha'nona away.

"Hi, you must be Wobbegong," Sha'nona called in greeting.

He fled to the kitchen to escape the chemical odor that quickly engulfed the room. He stewed about paying for caregiver time squandered on a manicure.

The girls chatted easily, bouncing from topic to topic so rapidly that Clagett was hard pressed to eavesdrop effectively. Their conversation narrowed once they hit on a shared passion for their phones. Wobbegong, who had only recently met her paramour, was frightened by her intense longing to have it always in her sight. Sha'nona, who was in a long-term relationship with her phone, having met in middle school, counseled Wobbegong to commit her heart fully, for only through unreserved sharing could she maximize her phone's capacity for distraction. Anyway, that was Clagett's takeaway from their confab.

They dissolved into laughter when Sha'nona uncovered a trove of comical communications left behind by previous users of Wobbegong's phone.

Belva, for instance, had messaged Ariola: *What is a wrist? Dementia patients make more sense than this dud.*

Ariola replied: *LOL a joint. Overmedicate him?*

"Burn!" Sha'nona cried with hilarity after reading that exchange out loud.

Then there was a string of prank messages:

Welcome to Earth! Are you interested in meeting hot married humans in your zip code?

Space Hotel, please reply ASAP. Urgent permitting issue to resolve. —NASA

This is Kenn, asst to Jan Nurb. She wants to reserve six rooms for this Friday if weather permits the launch. Major business synergy to discuss.

Sha'nona read *asst* as *assed*, which prompted gales of laughter and speculation about Kenn's duties.

Busy fighting. Please reschedule your invasion for a time of mutual convenience.

That one supposedly came from the US military.

Sha'nona moved on to the next message.

This is Kenn again. Asst to Jan Nurb? Please respond. This is your only warning.

Boy, you don't mess with Jan, Clagett thought. *What a hothead.*

Hi, this is Jan Nurb. I don't tolerate being gored. May cod have mercy on your soles.

Clagett, of course, knew the name Jan Nurb—she was always in the news. She was the wealthy owner of a massive online marketplace and a partner in a private space consortium. Interest in the Space Hotel and an executive's inattention to clarity gave plausibility to the text author's identity. But for Jan Nurb herself to contact *Wobbegong* with business propositions and threats? Ludicrous.

The women decided to put the Jan impersonator's mind at ease and concocted a polite response: *Jan(?), sorry for the late reply. The Space Hotel is not open for business. We regret that we could not take your party. —Hospitality Managers*

Clagett called to Wobbegong to see about a water refill, but she begged off, declaring she was indisposed by wet nail polish. Sha'nona approached Clagett with polite curiosity and asked if she could help and then gamely refilled his bottle. She said she wondered how he was because she used to see him around the farm but now she only caught glimpses of him through a window, which was creepy.

"It's been a while since I've been in your house," she said, looking around the kitchen. "I thought it would be neater." She slid a shoe across the floor to gauge the grit.

He chatted her up and she said she wasn't sure what to study in college. She'd gotten good grades in math, but hair and nails were her passion and she hoped to follow that path.

"Become a plumber or an electrician," Clagett suggested. "The real money is in the trades these days."

"I was thinking about mortuary science," she said. "I like working with bodies, and being around dead ones doesn't bother me. I think it's interesting."

"Good plan, but...when have you been around dead bodies?" Clagett asked.

"Oh, you know." She shrugged.

Akimbo came in from the barn, catching the end of Clagett's exchange. She looked at Sha'nona and at Clagett. "I don't want to know," she muttered, before disappearing upstairs for a nap.

"Would you like *your* nails done?" Sha'nona asked Clagett.

"Like painted?" he asked.

"If you want. I was thinking you might want a quick trim. No charge."

"Do you do toenails? Mine are ugly."

"I do any nail. I'm sure they're nothing compared to

what I've seen…thick yellow toenails like amber, you could make earrings from the clippings. Would you like to see pictures?" She reached for her phone.

"No, thank you," he demurred.

"I sell necklaces I make from dog toenails."

"Wow," he said.

"I don't do diabetics' nails—you're not diabetic, are you?"

"No."

She set up shop at his wheelchair and attacked his nails with an electric grinder while commenting with genuine fascination about the shape of each toe. "Your toes are lovely, I promise," she assured him. "What do you do all day?" she asked over the grinder's whine.

"What do I do?"

"Yeah. It must get boring sitting around all day."

"No, I'm not bored. I like quiet."

She said she would put him on a regular schedule to prevent skin irritation and infection. "I can trim your hair if you want." She reached out and gently pushed his hair behind his ears. "You still have your hair and it still has some brown color in there—it's a shame it isn't neater."

Brown was a nervy description. His hair had darkened with age but, to maintain equilibrium, had also grayed. In his mind that averaged out to his youthful blond.

"Next time," he said.

Looking pleased with herself, she dropped her business card on his lap, where it sat without purpose until the end of the day.

During his bedtime routine, Clagett asked Wobbegong the question that had nagged him since the afternoon. "Why are you getting those messages on your phone?"

She was awkwardly negotiating the toothpaste tube's cap with her new nails at that moment. She deigned to look up from her work and scowl at his interruption. "The Space Hotel phone number gets routed to my phone. I'm supposed to deal with calls in my spare time. Weren't you supposed to nap or something?"

When it came time to give Clagett his evening medicine, her new nails thwarted her attempts to lift the pills from the pillbox. She tried a one-finger scoop and a finger/thumb pinch and a two-handed chopstick approach before dumping the pills onto her palm. She scooped up the pills with an index fingernail and aimed for his mouth. She grinned like she was Edward Spoonfingers discovering her real purpose in life. He had little time to consider where her nails had been that afternoon and whether they had been properly sanitized. She rested the tip of the nail on his lower lip and slid the pills onto his tongue. Her finger tasted of paint and chocolate chip cookies.

That night, in bed, he defensively stewed, triggered by Sha'nona's question about how he spent his days, as if he wasted his time.

First of all, "day" was considerably narrowed by two chores: his morning routine, preparing him for the day; and his evening routine, decommissioning him for the night. Subtract from that: eating, polite conversation with caregivers, distraction by caregivers, unpredictable health events (depressive days of semi-consciousness, hacking up jellyfish-like blobs of mucus, bowel inconveniences rated on a scale from stoppage to unstoppable), wheelchair breakdowns, untimely software updates, etc.

The remaining time was first allocated to the business of staying alive, which was expected, given its importance, but the time consumption aggravated nonetheless. Via computer he met with doctors and nurses who recorded his decline for medical posterity. In return, they prescribed medications and machinery to make his life tolerable while scantly prolonging it. They assured him that his weakness, anxiety, mucus lung plugs, coughing and hocking, hoarseness, constipation, nightmares, skin breakdown, constant cold, and such were all part of the package and completely normal. They asked about his caregivers, and when he complained about their unreliability, they confirmed his lay observation, saying, "We hear that a lot."

He spoke with his therapist about his depression and anxiety and regrets. Recently, many a valuable therapy minute was invested in venting about caregivers.

Clagett said, "They're arguably worse off than I am, but I don't think I should have to minister to their problems."

She agreed. She asked what would happen if he confronted them with his complaints, which struck Clagett as perfectly logical if the discussion were between two rational adults on equal footing, but failed to capture how vulnerable his position seemed.

When they had a moment alone, he and Akimbo relaxed together and sometimes relived their early days. They professed undying love in ways unintended for others' ears. When anger and angst welled up, they vented about caregivers until the time wasted complaining became as irksome as the caregivers themselves.

***

The next morning, probably—with time passing so unreliably he wasn't sure, but undoubtedly it was soon after she got her acrylics—Wobbegong refused to put gloves over her precious nails before she showered him, reasoning that her nails would just puncture the fingertips.

The sensation of her long nails scrubbing his scalp was delightful, and he politely asked if she could continue for a moment, claiming he felt like his scalp was extra oily.

"Uh-huh," she responded knowingly.

"And really work the conditioner into my scalp with your fingers," he added. "I think I've got dry skin underneath the oiliness."

She humored him with snakes of conditioner smeared around with soft fingertips.

After the shower, she vigorously dried his hair with a warm towel. She used an unpredictable pattern that kept him guessing—hoping—she would hit a particularly sensitive area at the top of his scalp. She followed the towel with delightful strokes of a stiff-bristled brush. To leave it with a natural look, she raked her acrylic fingernails across his head and tousled his forelock with a flick. The dismissive flick was the catalyst.

He developed a near-instantaneous desire to have his scalp scratched with long acrylic nails. His towel covering, physical surrender, and flickers of shame were all ingredients for a good fetish, but there was no sense of eroticism. No, there was only intense fleshly pleasure built on the specificity of acrylic nails, a stiff brush, and an uncaring attitude.

Clagett took to innocently requesting that Wobbegong thoroughly brush the top of his head, saying that his hair took a solid ten minutes before it got to its optimal position. She snorted with her gills in a way that read, *As if.* If he persisted and told her to rake her nails across the crown of his head, to give his hair a lived-in look, she gave him an aggressive claw across the top of his head to discourage further demands.

"What's this I hear about your scalp itching?" Akimbo asked after Wobbegong left one evening. "Do I need to take you to the dermatologist?"

"No, I'm fine, I just like the feel of getting my head scratched," he confessed. "You know how blind people gain acute hearing as compensation? My paralysis has led to scalp hypersensitivity. It's a gift."

"Why are you making up excuses for the girl? You've got her worried she's doing something wrong."

"They're not paid to make me feel good, they're paid to keep me from feeling bad," he explained. "That's how I see it. They shy away from anything more than what's required to keep me alive."

"You can hardly blame them," she said. "People would take advantage of them if they didn't draw a line somewhere."

"Plus they'd have to work harder," he said.

"Their cut is probably less than minimum wage...if they get paid at all," she tossed back. "You can't expect more than minimum cooperation."

"Are you saying we should pay them more?"

"I'm saying you need to expect less," she said.

"If I was healthy, I'd scratch my own head for free."

"I'm sure you would."

"It doesn't seem fair."

"It isn't, not in the least."

"What about them taking advantage of us? Where's our line?"

"What do you mean?"

"Caregivers so distracted that they barely pay attention. I know you've seen it."

"Wobbegong?"

"She's on the phone constantly. She had Sha'nona on speaker while she was putting me in bed. They couldn't stand to hang up. It's an invasion of privacy."

"I didn't know that. I'll speak to both of them."

"I told Wobbegong it was unacceptable."

"What did she say?"

"She said I was being judgmental."

Akimbo put a halt to Wobbegong's phone affair. "You can't devote your attention to the phone and leave only an empty shell to take care of Clagett!" she reprimanded.

"I only use it for business, that's the rule," she said. She shrank away from Akimbo, bruised by her criticism.

"How is talking with Sha'nona business?"

"Well, that's *my* business," she said petulantly.

"What about the other calls you answer?"

"Which ones?"

"Which ones! The 'We're not open for business yet, but we do appreciate your call!' calls," she bellowed.

"Oh that. Those are calls to the Space Hotel. People keep pestering me for reservations. I'm like, *why*?"

"That's not part of Clagett's care! Don't answer those calls while you're here!"

"How about texts? I get a lot of those too."

"No!" Akimbo exclaimed.

"You're being mean!"

"Unlock your phone and give it to me."

"Please! No!"

Akimbo held out her hand to confiscate the object of affection. For insurance, she added her stare of death until

Wobbegong surrendered. As Wobbegong withdrew her hand, her fingertips tenderly caressed the screen.

"Parting is such sweet sorrow," Akimbo observed. "I'll give it back when you leave tonight."

"I'm never coming back! I don't care what happens to your husband!"

"Did you ever?"

Wobbegong glowered and refused to answer. She stalked off to the kitchen to sulk and root for food.

Akimbo had the phone halfway shoved into a back pocket, giving it the view she felt befitted such asinine devices, when she was waylaid by curiosity. She brought up the text thread with the Jan Nurb impersonator, whose messages Clagett had laughingly recounted to her. Like Clagett, she laughed it off as a prank. What self-respecting mogul would write *May God have mercy on your souls* to a business prospect via text message?

Feeling combative, with the phone in her hand as a ready outlet, she took the liberty of impersonating a Space Hotel representative and fired off a text message to Jan: *Who is this really?*

A reply popped up within minutes: *Jan Nurb! Are you stupid or illiterate?*

Akimbo typed: *Stupid. You?*

Jan responded: *Neither!!!*

Akimbo didn't much care for her triple-exclamation-point tone. She wrote: *If you say so. Why are you so PO'ed anyway???*

Jan wrote back: *I want to invest in the Space Hotel and you can't even answer your phone? Do you know how that makes me feel?*

Akimbo guessed: *Unimportant?*

She switched over to the call log and saw a long list of unanswered calls from Jan's number.

Jan replied: *I was thinking along the lines of wrathful, like I am the hand of God about to crush your business.*

Akimbo asked: *You've got grandiosity issues. I don't know who you really are, but you should seek help.*

Jan signed off: *I know exactly who I am. Grab your ankles and brace yourself, honey. Later.*

Thinking she might need to report the Jan impersonator, Akimbo jotted down her number. She felt calmer for having blown off a little steam.

As promised, at shift's end she reunited Wobbegong with her amour. Despite her threat, Wobbegong did return the next day.

13

NEED YOUR HELP," AKIMBO said. "I've put together a list of supplies. There are a few repairs I'd like to make this summer. You know, to spruce up the barn."

"I don't like where this is headed," Clagett said.

"You need to get out of the house and think about something other than your troubles."

"Now you're scaring me."

"A trip to the hardware store is just the thing to rediscover your happy place. Wobbegong will take care of you. Geldine will assist and handle transportation."

Clagett strenuously avoided trips into the public sphere because, frankly, that's where the people were. In his maturity, he was, if anything, not a people person. The hardware store was in a gray area of people intermingled with purposeful objects, which, in the past, made for a pleasant experience, a detail Akimbo now seized.

"Can I lodge a complaint?"

"No. Geldine will be here with an accessible van after you're done with lunch."

"You're not coming?"

"And how would that help me?" she asked with indignation. "I'm dropping off statements and tax returns to Gia. I told you about that."

"Right," he said. He faintly remembered her telling him about Gia and paperwork but suspected he was imagining it just to be agreeable. To *deny* being told was tantamount to asking for honest feedback on his critical listening skills, which he assumed had not improved since his last review.

In short order, she left to run her own errands.

In actuality, Geldine did not appear with an accessible van. Langford, her husband, appeared in her stead, driving a beefy flatbed liftgate truck better suited to delivering appliances or building materials.

Considering the number of years they'd been neighbors, he and Akimbo had rarely interacted with Langford, which was by design. Much of what they knew about the Shifletts was learned from the illuminati who worked the aisles of the grocery store, barbered his hair, or loaded sacks of feed into Akimbo's truck. They learned enough through those channels to know they didn't want to get caught up as coconspirators, so they maintained a distance of plausible unsociability.

Clagett held on to a mental image of Langford, with his knee-high lace-up snake boots and shotgun and gold tooth in front, calmly shooting the diseased fox. He was a big man, over six feet tall, long-legged, narrow of waist, with a barrel chest and soft padding around his belly. His leathery face with a week's worth of stubble and close-cropped scalp brought to mind a well-oiled pelt.

"Where you at?" Langford said after entering the house without so much as a knock or a yoo-hoo. Hearing signs of life, he eased his way to the kitchen, where Clagett was finishing lunch. The floor squeaked under the weight of his steps. He stepped into the room carrying a large black plastic bag slung over one shoulder like the Saint Nick of sanitation. He dropped the bag with a wet squish.

"Langford," Clagett greeted him. "Where's Geldine?"

"Working," he said. "She's back on day shift."

Clagett noticed a change in Langford. "I recall you had a gold tooth up front."

"Got one of those implants." He opened wide to give a full viewing of the tooth in question. He wiggled at the tooth with his finger to show its rock-solid foundation.

"Nice."

"Pricey, though. Still paying it off. What's the world coming to when a person doesn't own their own teeth?"

"Indeed."

"Now who's this here?"

"This is Wobbegong, one of my capable caregivers. Wobbegong, this is Langford, Geldine's husband."

"Hello," Wobbegong said.

"She's one of those aliens, huh?" Langford referred the question to Clagett.

"Yes, it's one of her many fine qualities."

"You know the fellow goes by Adnoydd?" he asked her directly, with menace.

"He's the director. Everybody knows him."

"Is that so? I've got a bone to pick with him over his treatment of my wife."

"We don't have bones. We have something like…what do you call it?"

"Gristle?" Langford guessed.

"I don't know what that is." She scoured her memory. "Spongiosum, I think."

Clagett and Akimbo had been trying to piece together the history of Geldine and Adnoydd. He decided to risk a direct question and asked, "What's your beef with Adnoydd?"

"What's my beef? He took her from me! Left me wondering where she was, imagining the worst. She came back different from when she left—addled, forgetful."

"That's what our air does to humans," Wobbegong said.

Langford gave Wobbegong a hard stare while seeming to weigh whether she was party to Geldine's abduction or perhaps guilty by association.

Clagett couldn't stand the tension. He was already anxious about leaving the house. Langford's anger was too much; it filled the room, pushed aside Clagett's weak attempts to regulate his fear. He tried distraction, asking, "What's with the garbage bag?"

Langford shifted his eyes off Wobbegong and grinned at Clagett. "Laundry. It's clean but wet. Our dryer's broke. I figured I could use yours while we're out on our joyride."

"Um…" Clagett hesitated. "It's there behind me, through the door." Seeing Langford turn his attention to the laundry allowed Clagett to relax.

Langford hefted the bag and disappeared from sight. There followed more theater than one would expect from dryer loading. His heavy fingers drumming on the dryer's lid provided the cadence for a spoken-word meditation on how technology was complicating every damn thing when simple time and temperature were all a body really needed.

He reappeared, the dryer's rumble leaking into the kitchen. He opened the refrigerator and rooted through the top shelf, shoving aside the bottles of goat milk to see what lurked out of sight. "Do you have pickles?"

"We might. Look in the door."

He lifted up glass jars of jam and condiments until he found dill pickle chips. "Naw, I like the sweet gherkins," he said. "The little guys that look like a dill pickle took a dump."

Wobbegong snickered at his remark.

"Well, at least *she's* got a sense of humor. You're so stiff," Langford pronounced. He kicked the fridge door shut to lodge his dissatisfaction with the pickles. "So we're hitting the hardware store, eh?"

"That's what I'm told," Clagett confirmed.

Langford took control of the wheelchair and steered Clagett over the front threshold at a clip that whipped his head forward to his chest and then back again to the headrest.

"Do you know what you're doing?" Clagett asked in a panic.

"Oh yeah, spent lots of time behind a chair. Manual, power…doesn't matter." Langford started backward down the porch ramp. "We used to have night races where Geldine worked, before they fired her for the races. Rally format against the clock."

"You were a caregiver?"

"Ha! Just raced, handled the bets. We took the cup one year, beat the airport in the finals." Langford brute-forced the chair down the cinder path to the truck. "You've got the F3? Sweet ride that. Ever topped out on a flat?"

"Uh, no."

He toggled truck levers and lowered the liftgate to ground level.

"Where's the van? I don't think this is ADA-approved transportation," Clagett said nervously.

"Stiff, what did I tell you?" Langford winked at Wobbegong, and she giggled. "Don't fret, the truck is a loaner. What you lose in safety, you gain in savings."

Clagett's heart pounded. He felt anxiety welling up again, his throat tightened. Leaving the house was stressful enough, but to contemplate riding on a liftgate he knew to be capable of shearing a person in half, operated by none other than Langford? Unspeakable.

Langford drove him onto the lift, putting his shoulder into the backrest to get the chair over the initial hump.

"Come here, I'll show you how to work this." Langford waved Wobbegong to the controls.

Wobbegong at the controls! Clagett desperately estimated whether his toes had safe clearance.

"He's going up!" Wobbegong squealed.

"You're doing good," Langford praised. "Keep us going to the top."

———————————————

The air rushing over the truck's cab peeled at Clagett's hair. The safety goggles, worn at his own insistence, were forced uncomfortably against his brow. The wind in his ears, the retention chains hammering against the truck bed, and the engine's thrum created an outrageous din that undoubtedly exceeded safe decibel standards. Permanent hearing loss was objectively bad, but on his scale of health issues it wasn't that bad, he reasoned.

Chained down as he was on the bed directly behind the truck's cab, his view primarily consisted of the goings-on in the driver's compartment. Langford clutched and shifted his way down the county roads, all the while keeping up a one-sided conversation with Wobbegong, who, by the look of things, was also unnerved. By her good fortune, a touch of motion sickness highlighted her complexion's jewel green undertones.

———————————————

"That solves the mystery of whose laundry I found in the dryer," Akimbo said. "But the more concerning question is... Langford loaded you on a flatbed truck and chained your chair to the deck?"

"Yeah, that's the gist of it."

After dinner, Clagett finally had opportunity to relate his afternoon adventure to Akimbo. They sat in the den, in their official movie-watching positions, chasing away Wobbegong when she presumed to join them.

"Were you okay with that?" Akimbo scrunched her face skeptically.

"I told him I didn't like the idea, but he didn't seem to care. So much is out of my control. I surrender to the universe sometimes, just to see what happens without my involvement. I want to see the shape of the hole I'll leave behind."

Langford parked the truck under the cover of the loading area. He threw off Clagett's chains and spun his wheelchair to face the lift, which at four feet off the pavement deserved a guard rail but was flat like a diving platform and utterly bereft of warning stickers.

As Clagett acclimatized to life as a quadriplegic, his professional training led him to consider how to avoid wheelchair injury. Short of an edge case like stalling the chair on railroad tracks, he figured that a ledge was the primary hazard to watch out for.

In moments of extreme despair, Clagett contemplated how to do a thing he was trained to prevent—using the chair as a means of suicide. Driving off a ledge, he decided, was the workable solution.

Langford raced him full-joystick toward the edge of the lift.

"No, no, NO!" Clagett cried out.

Intense goosebumps swept in waves from Clagett's scalp to his toes, a reaction to fear that in a person with functioning muscles presented as trembling. He closed his eyes to escape the scrutiny of customers drawn to his shout. Langford came to a halt.

"Give me a second," Clagett mumbled.

"Take your time," Langford said. "I didn't mean to scare you."

Clagett collected himself and fought off a surge of embarrassment. "I got confused...I thought I was driving the chair. I couldn't make myself stop," he confessed. "Jesus... What a horrible feeling."

"I've got you. We're okay." Langford patted his shoulder with understanding.

"I was scared too," Wobbegong sympathized. "He's a crazy man."

Langford parked him sideways on the lift so Clagett didn't have to contemplate the edge, all the while assuring they were safe. Wobbegong worked the lift and lowered them to the ground.

———————————————

"You're saying that for a second you thought you were committing suicide? Like you had set the chair in motion but couldn't stop it?" Akimbo asked gingerly.

"Something like that, yes. You know how you can be a passenger in a car and find yourself pressing your foot against the floor as if you have a brake pedal? But when you do, nothing happens? A little like that."

"But when you had the thought, you reacted with fear, like you were making a mistake?"

"Yeah, I suppose so. Look, I'm embarrassed to talk about it."

"Don't be," she said. "If you have those thoughts, we *should* talk about it. I think about it too."

"No...you have so much life left—"

"I worry that *you* might want to."

"Oh."

"In the early stages, when we were socked in by shock, I worried you'd OD on me. It's something of a relief that your accessible options are few now."

"That's absurd, as I'm sure you realize. Feeling relieved I'm less able to kill myself the closer I get to death?"

"Yes," she agreed, "but that's how I feel."

"Don't worry, I don't dwell on it. It crosses my mind."

"That's good. Normal, I imagine," she said. "How would you do it?"

"You mean exactly?"

"Yeah, like what makes driving off a ledge your best option?"

"It's within my control, that's a big reason. It might look accidental. And I don't need an accomplice."

"Logical. Did you ever consider asking me to be your accomplice?"

"No. Never. I don't want that on your conscience."

"A quick lop of the head?"

"Christ no! Now I won't be able to forget that image."

"Who then?"

"Caregivers might slip me pills without pangs of conscience. Langford is a question mark."

"I've discussed this with Gracie and Zoey," she said. "In confidentiality."

"Oh? I'm glad you're able to unburden yourself."

"They are more than willing to help, eager even, if you need a way out. They have motive to kill you, and they have those guilty eyes, but still...I think they would evade police suspicion. If they *did* get picked up, I'm confident they'd stay mum under questioning. The *means*, though, that's the tricky part for them."

"You've put thought into this. More than me."

"They suggested a cat that's rumored to work this area, goes by the name of Tomahawk. He's very discreet, very lethal. A born killer. He'll lull you into false security with seductive purrs until...Whammo! Claws to your carotid. You'll never see it coming."

"Enticing. The only problem is...I'm allergic to cats."

"Rats! And it was such a perfect plan! Just as well, Tomahawk is out of our price range. Best we stick with your DIY approach."

"I guess I appreciate the effort you've gone to on my behalf."

"Anything for you, my love."

"Really, I feel better for having talked about it. Thank you."

"I get it," she said.

Inside the hardware store, a high-ceilinged cathedral to vertical storage, the threesome attracted curious glances and untempered stares. Attention was a new thing for Clagett; in days gone by, he was widely ignored. The store's expert assistance aisle walkers had profiled him as: uptight white guy who thinks he knows best, so forget him. He'd had to ingratiate himself with politeness and feigned ignorance before they would extend the home-repair advice that he ignored...because he knew better.

His physical condition didn't draw attention, of that he was confident. People had largely ignored him as he metamorphosed: from the drooping shoulders, to the noodle arms, to the foot drag, and so on to his chair-bound slack-lipped self. Beauty, chiseled chins, wardrobe atrocities, tight jeans—there were an abundance of reasons to people-gawk, and in terms of popularity, disability was way, way down on that list. Put together a wheelchair, a caregiver with orange tabby hair, and a Shiflett, however, and you have a crowd-pleaser.

A Shiflett alone might have done the trick. The local community prized the family for their Scotch-Irish industriousness as applied to self-destructive pursuits. Their undoings unfolded in ways that gossipers had never contemplated, which encouraged bystander curiosity like they now encountered.

The day manager, with work apron flapping, hotfooted over to greet them.

"Langford! How've you been?"

"Doing good. You?"

"Good, good, good."

Langford was not a man to offer niceties like introductions. The manager took it upon himself to make eye contact with Wobbegong and Clagett.

"I'm Bob," he said with a nod.

"Got a list of supplies, mostly lumber, for my neighbor here. Think you could hook him up?" Langford passed him Akimbo's handwritten list.

Bob wiggled reading glasses onto his face, threading the temples under his headset's structure. "Absolutely! Absolutely! Anything he needs."

"I'm not walking around on a damn scavenger hunt, Bob. This fellow only has so much battery life, so to say."

"Is this a museum of primitive tools?" Wobbegong asked.

"Ha ha!" Bob chuckled. "You guys crack me up!"

"Bob?" Langford prodded.

"Right, right. We'll set you up, no problem. Can you give us an hour to pull this together?"

Langford stood stock-still.

"Thirty minutes, then! Yes, that ought to do it." He called

over his headset and set in motion a search for his "best person," who was probably smoking out back, like always. "Can we get you a coffee or an extension cord or something while you wait?"

———————————+———————

"Hold on, how did Langford know the store manager?" Akimbo wanted to know.

"I wondered that, too, so I asked Langford, 'Who was that stooge?' and he said captain of the Hammerheads softball team. He said he could make a trip to the concession stand in the time it took Bob to jog to first base."

"And?"

"And Langford is the umpire for the league. I got the impression that money changes hands to ensure Langford's fairness. Bob was obliged to help us."

"Langford sure knows how to work the angles."

"He really does."

———————————+———————

"Let's see what you've got under the hood." Langford aimed Clagett's chair down the broad boulevard separating the cashiers from the goods. He violently waved off a customer whose cart blocked the straightaway. "What do you have your speed set to? Two turtles? I'm working with Grandma Moses here!"

"Two tortoises."

"Let's max you out at full rabbit."

"Hare."

Langford punched at the chair controls and dialed up the speed. He situated the rarely used head strap across Clagett's forehead and explained, "This is just in case you come to a sudden stop."

"I don't—"

"I'll make a movie," Wobbegong said. "Where will he crash?"

"Stand down there at the paint aisle and you'll catch everything."

"Wait—"

"If you get the speed wobbles, kill power. Go on now. Let her rip!" Langford cried.

"No—"

"Are you going to make me run behind you?"

"Please, just leave me alone. I don't want to sprint."

"Trying to have a little fun is all. Killing some time."

"I don't want my time killed!" His voice was hoarse, weak, lacking the emphasis he aimed for. He'd gotten worked up, and now his body made him pay. He panted and tried to catch his breath. His tongue felt leaden. "Leave me be," he whispered.

Langford couldn't leave well enough alone and gave the chair max joystick with him running alongside for a couple of aisles.

"I had to," he apologized. "I've got the poor impulse control."

Langford dialed back the speed and drove Clagett out front to the picnic table display, to the shade of a reduced-price awning. Wobbegong stayed inside to wander. Clagett thought she might be keeping a safe distance between her and Langford.

Langford unhinged a bottle of sports drink from its plastic webbing. Where the four-pack came from, Clagett couldn't say. Likewise for the straw that he poked into the bottle before offering it to Clagett.

"Thanks," Clagett said after a delay of careful swallowing.

Langford unhinged a bottle for himself and sucked

down a goodly amount. "I'm glad to see some color in your cheeks. Or is that sunburn?"

"Windburn, I'm guessing," Clagett said.

Langford extended the straw to him again and waited patiently through his swallowing.

"You've got something on your arm there." Langford pointed, but didn't stir from his chair. "What is it? A bug?"

Clagett looked down to see a green spider, probably harmless, but still . . .

Langford watched with amusement, encouraging him to relax and blow at it.

He pleaded for Langford's help in as manly a fashion as he could pull off. He helplessly watched the spider run up his arm, duck under his shirt sleeve, and disappear into an armpit. It tickled a path through his chest hair and found interest in the crater of his belly button.

Clagett wasn't scared of spiders per se, but that attitude was born from a position of power—a broom in his grip. A spider with the upper hand was a different ballgame.

"Don't hurt it." Langford laughed.

"How the fuck am I going to hurt it?" Clagett was stunned by the words that erupted from his mouth.

Langford laughed harder at his outburst.

"What's so funny?" he snarled. He felt the spider scamper across his chest and run down the other arm.

"Whoa! Sorry. I got you." Langford stood and gently plucked the spider from Clagett's arm. He deposited it on the leaf of a nearby potted shrub. "My bad. I shouldn't have laughed." He offered a sip from the straw. "No hard feelings?"

Clagett was embarrassed but lightened by his show of anger. He laughed at his reaction. "It's alright."

"I'll be mindful," Langford said. "You've got some fire inside."

"Sorry, that wasn't like me to go off like that."

"No need to apologize, I was—"

"Oblivious?"

"A jackass," he decided. "Let loose on me anytime. You'll feel better. I deserve whatever you bring at me, if not for what I say to you, then for terrible things I've said to other people. Hurtful stuff. I regret that more than worser things I've done. I had no idea my own words would stick in my craw forever."

"Thank you." Clagett didn't know how else to respond to Langford's self-reproach. He appreciated Langford's offer to be the whipping boy for his discontent.

Without missing a beat, completely unperturbed by Clagett's flare-up, Langford jumped to other things on his mind. "Hey, what do you think about our scheme of 'investing' these aliens' money? Are you in?" He actually air-quoted *investing*, delighting Clagett with the effete gesture.

"Akimbo and I are entertaining it, just for the sake of argument, not for real."

"Hypothetical, got it. It's worth remembering that money problems aren't—they're very real."

"Good point. I guess we'd like to hear your take on something."

"What's on your mind?"

"You seem to be a man who knows his way around the law."

"Spit it out."

"Right…So we're wondering, if a person were to take something of value from aliens, would the cops—or NASA or whoever—have a case for larceny? Would they even care?"

"You're assuming they find out. That sort of negative thinking is dangerously counterproductive. Visualize success." Langford looked him in the eye to impress the importance of positivity in unprincipled pursuits. "As to your query, I think we can safely say there's no legal precedent," he intoned, mimicking an officious prick.

"Legal *president*," Clagett said softly and chuckled, recalling Geldine's use of the word.

"The word is *precedent*," Langford insisted.

"I know, but—"

"Let's bring in an authority, a lethal scholar if you will." Langford grinned playfully. He held aloft the unopened drink bottles and twitched them around like he was fishing and they were the lure.

The security guard—a tall, gimpy-ankled woman who might block the path of a slow-moving shoplifter but wasn't going to be running down anyone on foot—caught sight of Langford and narrowed her eyes. She gingerly shambled her way around lawnmowers to reach their table. Clagett figured they were going to get shooed away—her scowl said she wasn't enduring the walk to welcome them.

"Larson," Langford said. "I hoped I'd find you here."

"Langford," she returned.

"This here is their first baseman," Langford explained to Clagett. "She's got a sure hand and a strong arm. Not many get past first base, though." He winked at Clagett.

"As offensive as ever," she said. "How about one of those drinks you're planning to pay for on your way out?" She peeled off a bottle without waiting for an answer.

"Let me ask you something," Langford said. "We're seeking your professional opinion as an ordained officer of store security."

"Lay it on me."

"It has to do with questions of legality."

"Right up my purview."

"If aliens visited Earth—"

"They're already here. That's a fact. Indisputable. Exhibit A."

"—and had some money on them, if 'a person' took that money, is it stealing?"

Clagett giggled at the second use of air-quotes.

"Uh-huh, wondered that myself. I'd swipe a lightsaber for my kid. Can you imagine a nine-year-old with a real lightsaber? Pure joy. Anyhow. Is it legal? That's like asking if taking honey from a beehive is stealing from the bees. Our laws don't count with them. I figure it's like that."

"Let's say a few bees—aliens—got killed while harvesting the honey."

"Yup, yup." She nodded. "I see where you're going with this." She pulled out a pack of cigarettes and offered one to Langford.

"Nope," Langford said, "don't want to stain my tooth."

She lit a cigarette and ruminated.

"Did you want a smoke?" he checked with Clagett.

"No. Thank you."

"He doesn't look it, but he's on a health kick," Langford remarked. "No offense there, chief," he said to Clagett.

"Up yours," Clagett replied.

"Now you're getting the hang of it," he encouraged.

Larson arrived at a decision. "I don't see a problem killing," she adjudicated. "Worst case they run you up on animal cruelty charges."

"What if they were crying out 'Please don't kill me, I have children'?" Clagett felt the urge to introduce a touch of humanity.

"Whoa now! You're talking *talking* aliens? I'm expecting the tentacle kind. Maybe pincers. Them talking would really mess with your head—all the more reason to kill them quick." She flicked ashes into Langford's upturned bottle cap. "This all assumes they're not the zombie variety."

Langford nodded in agreement. "What if an alien is *already* dead, it doesn't matter how, killed or whatever—"

"Is this like those fresh-killed deer I hear you find at night?" She raised her eyebrows knowingly.

"Anyways, is it okay to eat a dead one?" he asked.

"Uh-huh, uh-huh. Cooked, I suppose? Well, there's no law against it unless they're narcotic aliens, Class One blood or some such. But…I do worry you're barbecuing on biblical ground."

"Leviticus?"

"Bingo. That's the stuff Leviticus warns about, unclean food. There are rules," she said. "You'd have to get a good look at its hooves and work out if it chews its cud or swarms. Even then, ol' Leviticus looked the other way sometimes, like crickets."

"I won't be eating them," Langford said. "I made my peace with God about bacon and crab legs, but I'm not chancing heaven for a taste of alien filet."

"Smart man," she said with a flick of ashes.

Clagett prompted Akimbo, "What do you think about the security guard's authoritative ruling on stealing from aliens? We've got the green light."

"Authoritative?"

"I don't like your tone." He tried to sound peeved. "She and Langford are voices of experience."

"So you say," she said. "I don't feel good about their scheme. Even if it's legal, it's not ethical."

"The aliens admit to eating humans! They talk of colonization! They're unreliable caregivers!"

Even as he tossed out evidence of alien wrongdoing, he knew he willfully contorted his judgment to justify the end—Akimbo's financial security. He *wanted* to believe that stealing from them was deserved.

"Debating this is going to get us nowhere. I need to live with myself. I won't scam their money," she proclaimed. "And I'm not implying you *won't* be living with yourself, so don't go down that rat hole."

"I don't want to scam them either," he admitted. "I'm willing to, for your sake, but I don't want to."

"Good, that's settled," she said.

"It's oddly satisfying to think about sticking it to Adnoydd, though," he admitted. "As the avenging angel you must feel the same way."

She formed a halo with both hands and posed beatifically. "So that's that then?" she asked from her angelic attitude. "You got the supplies and came home?"

"Pretty much."

"Aren't you glad you got out of the house?" she asked.

"That's a leading question. I didn't *enjoy* the experience, but it did reinforce my appreciation for life here with you. Your sanity is a rarity."

"That sounds like a flattering way to say 'Don't make me leave the house again.'"

"You caught me," he admitted.

"So I guess you're not going to join a softball league and become sociable? You've shot my extrovert conversion therapy all to hell."

"Sorry."

"Was Wobbegong helpful?"

"Here and there. She disappeared for a while, got absorbed in plumbing fittings, she claimed. It's just as well—Langford was surprisingly sensitive to my needs. He's an interesting guy, really."

"Go figure."

14

Ariola walked a new caregiver to the house to make introductions. "Wobbegong is sick and is off Clagett's case," she curtly informed Akimbo.

"I'm sorry to hear she's sick. Nothing serious, I hope," Akimbo said.

"She hurt her back."

"Oh?"

Ariola casually explained, "She had it coming out of both ends and slipped in the bathroom—"

"Please stop!" Akimbo held her palm in front of Ariola's face. "That illness is really going around."

"What does that mean?"

"Blevadl came down with the same symptoms, we were told." Akimbo struggled to remember if Ariola had been the one to tell them about Blevadl's case.

"No, she didn't," Ariola denied.

"Oh... Well, I hope Wobbegong doesn't actually have it either."

"I'll tell her you said so," Ariola said.

"Wobbegong has a case of the double-ender," Akimbo called to her husband as she led the new caregiver to his bed. "Ariola is here with a new girl."

The new caregiver, whose name neither Akimbo nor Clagett retained, looked at Clagett smiling up from the bed and said, "Oh, hell no!"

She turned and headed for the space van.

Ariola, at that very moment, decided the woman hadn't been a good fit from the start. "I'll find someone even more suited to your needs," she swore. "I'll get a replacement here shortly."

———————————

Within an hour—shockingly fast in caregiver time—Ariola dropped two caregivers at the house. Blevadl and an unknown woman appeared at the door.

"Welcome back." Akimbo said.

"Thank you. And how are you?" Blevadl asked, looking deeply into Akimbo's eyes.

Hoping to distract Blevadl from another tearful breakdown, Akimbo asked cheerfully, "And who do we have here?"

"This is Smaragdine. She'll be taking over your account. I'll get her going today."

Smaragdine frantically scratched at welts on her head and neck. Coupled with the unkempt punk energy of her spiky calico hair/fur, she made Akimbo think of withdrawal symptoms.

"Thank you. I'm sorry Wobbegong is ill."

"Wobbegong?" Blevadl asked.

"Yes."

"Don't worry about her, you have tragedy enough of your own. She's faking it."

"She is?"

Blevadl shrugged.

Akimbo diagnosed Smaragdine with alien dermatitis. Akimbo reassured her that it was probably just the humidity or pollen. "We have a saying that it's not the heat—it's the humidity—that makes summer unbearable."

"We have a saying too," Blevadl said drolly. "It's not the heat—it's the humans—that makes Earth unbearable."

Akimbo forced a weak grin.

———————————————

While getting Clagett out of bed, the two caregivers lost themselves in conversation about Earth's poor work environment and barely paid attention to the tasks at hand. He listened and interrupted frequently, but politely, to keep them aware of his needs.

Belva railed against the length of their commute as she demonstrated positioning the Hoyer sling under his body. Because of her inattention, he lay woefully off-center. Needing to make a substantial adjustment, she pulled hard at a leg strap and the coarse mesh grated his tailbone.

"Ouch! That scratched my butt," he informed them.

"Sorry, but it had to be done," Belva said, referring to the sling adjustment, not the injury, which she ignored.

Smaragdine complained that physical effort further inflamed the welts on her neck and cheek; consequently, Belva did the lion's share of work. Smaragdine sobbed and moaned quietly and did her best to soldier through her difficult morning, understandably unfocused on learning Clagett's routine.

When he could take care of his own needs, he barely noticed the mundane maintenance routines that consumed hours of every day. He originally thought outsourcing those banalities to caregivers might allow him to live like pampered royalty, but the reality was markedly different. Those routines now demanded his full attention because they were more tedious to his caregivers than they had ever been for him. They, like him, prioritized their own interests.

Smaragdine's skin irritation peaked in the shower steam after watching Belva labor. She clawed at her neck and cheek and a fresh outbreak on her belly.

Simultaneously, the shower steam released a backup in Clagett's clogged nasal passages.

"Could I please blow my nose?" he asked, hoping for the prompt attention he would have afforded himself in an emergency.

Even if Smaragdine's whimpering wasn't already distracting them, he encountered a significant hurdle with his request: Belva and Smaragdine didn't have any experience with nose breathing, sniffling, wiping, or blowing.

"Grab a tissue there and hold it under my nose," he said. He nodded toward a box of facial tissues to spur action. "Kleenex!" he demanded.

Cultural disconnect: they found it impossible to differentiate between boxed tissues, spooled tissue, monogrammed paper hand towels for guests, and the wide variety of cloth towels and washcloths. Belva unwound toilet tissue and held it under his chin. The two women looked horrified, worried about what was going to arrive out of his head, as if the oozing mucus already in evidence was a precursor to something monstrous.

He laughed to himself that he was triggering a fear of creatures incubating in their bodies, à la *Alien*. Monsters popping out of people probably got a lot of press where they came from, probably caused more terror than jihads or epidemics did on Earth, he imagined.

"Hold it right under my nose." He was curt and knew it, but he was embarrassed by his public display of an unseemly body process.

Belva wedged the tissue tight against his nostrils, not to receive his nose's contents, but to block their arrival.

"Hold it more loosely so I can blow."

As he inhaled through his mouth in preparation, she thought better of her participation and withdrew the tissue completely.

"I don't know what to do. What do you want me to do?" Belva asked, masking her reticence with feigned confusion.

Smaragdine moved in with a cold washcloth—the one she had held pressed to her neck rash—and forcibly positioned it under his nose, like one might give chloroform to a bank guard. He'd had enough of explanations. What he took to be an emergency at the outset had worsened into a crisis. He blew, and they gasped in amazement.

Surprisingly, the washcloth gave a superior blowing experience to any tissue he'd ever used. Soft, absorbent, reusable, environmentally friendly, it was the cloth diaper for faces, a supercharged handkerchief.

They studied the contents of the washcloth, wondering what they were dealing with.

"Again," he said.

"There's more?" Belva asked with alarm.

"This is just the beginning," he said.

―――――――――――

Over lunch, his caregivers lapsed into their native tongue, sounding like dolphins with sinus problems complaining bitterly, probably about him, though he had no quarrel with dolphins.

Was *native tongue* even apt? He hoped their gills didn't have tongues.

They showed an amazing talent for multi-tasking, thanks to three gills and a mouth unburdened of breathing. They ate, spoke to him defiantly, and griped to one another all at the same time.

After lunch, with a little remove from the nose emergency and with his antidepressant in full effect, he was able to speak politely and begged pardon for his demanding behavior.

"I let my nose frustrate me," he confessed. "I'm sorry. It's maddening to want something simple done urgently. It takes longer for me to make the request than it would have taken for me to deal with the problem…back when I dealt with problems and wasn't the problem itself."

The two caregivers seemed touched by his admission. They rubbed his shoulder in understanding.

He decided to leaven his sincerity with a little *Alien* humor, thinking they could all share a laugh to break the tension. "Also, I'm sorry if I triggered your anxiety of parasitic creatures," he said. "You must be traumatized by the fear of a monster growing inside your stomach." His playful grin went unnoticed.

Belva and Smaragdine looked to each other for understanding.

"What is this parasite animal you have?" Belva asked.

"Not me, I've heard your people are occasionally plagued by predators gestating in your bellies."

He doubled down on his joke, somehow believing that aliens had *surely* watched their eponymous movie series. If *he* was on a foreign world looking to gauge his safety among the indigenous population, the first thing he would rent on the hotel TV would be the movie titled *Humans*.

Their expressions remained blank.

"I'm surprised I need to explain this to you. It's like this: The monster's larva latches onto someone's face and then burrows down into their stomach. They mutate in a matter of hours and then come bursting out through the abdominal wall in a shower of blood."

Their expressions shifted toward confusion.

"Animals live in our stomachs?" Belva panicked.

"Not now. Not here on Earth. This is a safe haven. You can relax. I meant back at your home—in space. You must have periodic outbreaks."

"Animals don't live in our insides back home," Belva declared.

"Where did you get that idea?" Smaragdine asked. "I don't like what you're suggesting."

"Whoa, I'm making a joke." He gave up trying to make them laugh even though he was finding a measure of satisfaction in their confusion. Were he able, he would have supplemented his defense with arms raised in surrender.

"You've got leeches!" Smaragdine shrieked.

"I do? I feel like a doctor would have mentioned that."

"Leeches and vampire bats. And you're making jokes?" Smaragdine shrieked again.

"Tapeworms, guinea worms, bacteria!" Belva shouted. "Do you know how unwelcoming this planet is? How disgusting your bodies are? Look inside your own stomach! Look at the slime oozing from your nose! That's what I'm afraid of!"

They walked off in a snit. He wasn't sure they would return, but they had nowhere else to go. They stood in the yard and vented. They looped in someone on Belva's cell phone. The sun beat down on them while gnats swarmed around their heads. Belva swatted with the phone. They walked in circles to escape the gnats, exhausting themselves, bringing their desperation to a head.

Clagett knew he ought to be pained by his inattention to the women's feelings. He knew nothing of their history, culture, or views on life—like what constituted humor—and genuinely didn't *want* to be insensitive, but he was at a point at the end of his life when he just wanted help blowing his nose and such. Mounting an anthropological study of an alien civilization was not his idea of peacefully meeting the hereafter.

They trudged toward the barn, and he supposed they were looking for Akimbo to intercede. Akimbo was off having coffee with a friend, or so she had said. She left hints of her comings and goings, but the details remained a mystery to Clagett. She was testing a life without him, trying it on for size. Come to think of it, *coffee with a friend* sounded suspiciously like a euphemism.

The two caregivers cautiously entered the barn, pulling the door closed behind them. The chickens squawked like they'd spotted a fox. The goats trotted into the barn to see if the ruckus was edible. He had time to wonder—*A euphemism for what?*—before the caregivers burst from the barn and stumbled their way down the driveway, away from the house.

Clagett watched expectantly, waiting for a hint about what happened.

Smaragdine clawed at her newly invigorated hives as they spread down her belly and onto her thighs. He made out one word amid their asthmatic whinging: "Spiders."

He took spiders for granted. More of the barn's ceiling was covered by webs than not, some so old they were more dust than web. Akimbo's loft was like a spider suburb, clean and lightly populated, but still, there was no hiding the webs among the rafters.

If his life were an alien horror movie, the barn was the place where the missing crew members would be found mummified in an alien nest...He suppressed that line of thinking lest he speak it aloud and further inflame the situation.

Desperate to escape the out-of-doors, they reluctantly made their way back to the house, pausing every few steps to exchange bickering grunts. Rather than enter the living quarters, they disappeared under the back porch into a basement space where Akimbo stored gardening tools. Clagett called out to them and they remained silent.

He had water in his bottle and was comfortable in his chair. He reasoned that he could survive for a few hours on his own as long as he didn't try anything stupid, which, knowing his limitations, meant he shouldn't try anything. Disturbing Akimbo and stirring up an emergency seemed unnecessary. Geldine answered his call but was occupied. She said she'd come over in a few hours to feed him dinner and get him into bed. He reclined his chair and waited.

———————————

While waiting for their food, Akimbo and Gia—a friend, a financial adviser—exchanged pleasantries, nimbly circling around the circumstances that brought them together. Gia boldly took a step into the center of the ring and asked about Clagett.

"He's okay, all things considered," Akimbo said. "He's in the wheelchair full-time. He seems to enjoy having nothing to do. His breathing is deteriorating and his voice is growing weaker by the day. The disease is attacking his face and tongue, so he's having more trouble swallowing and the words you can hear are slurred. It's horrible. I don't know how much of the change he admits to himself."

Gia listened and tried to relate, an uphill endeavor given how her empathy flinched away from Akimbo's descriptions.

"Caregivers come and go. Sometimes he enjoys their assistance, if not their company. Sometimes they take more than they give and leave him angry. Even if they were absolutely perfect at their job, they're still a presence, a distraction, a person and all that entails. They use our bathroom, load the dishwasher illogically, eat vile-smelling foods, vent their own problems..."

Gia settled on tacitly supporting her friend. She didn't judge or console. She didn't dare extend advice.

"Clagett says that living with caregivers is like having a dental hygienist who plagues you with daily home visits."

Gia nodded and smiled through her absence of understanding. "How's that?" she asked when Akimbo didn't elaborate.

"You have a cordial relationship with your hygienist. She's likeable, dedicated to her craft, concerned for your well-being. Nonetheless, you don't enjoy your time together. You don't enjoy her poking and scraping even though it's in your best interest. That's not how you would prefer to spend your time or your money, and, though she's pleasant, she's not the company you would choose. Still, you thank your hygienist."

"I get that," Gia acknowledged.

"Clagett and I struggle with thankfulness for caregiving. We are thankful, and we say 'Thank you!' out the wazoo. It's just... It's really hard to feel grateful for something that makes you crazy... even though it's less crazy than the crazy you'd be without them."

When the food arrived, the familiar aromas evoked an anticipatory delight that displaced their serious thoughts.

The Number 6 cheeseburger at Lee's Diner was the food you would bait a trap with if you were hunting Akimbo. "Cheeseburger" was a pedestrian description for a dish so refined, she pronounced whenever she proselytized the virtues of the Number 6. The beef was salty, the cheese aged, the roll buttery. A mush of inspired toppings leaked onto the tongue under the squeeze of each bite—sautéed onions, ketchup, brown mustard, a secret sauce—delivering opioid-like transportation to a world wrapped in warm blankets.

She ate slowly to savor every morsel.

Gia sat across the Formica-topped booth looking through Akimbo's financial statements. Her Cobb salad sat picked over and forlorn, unable to compete with the cheese-burger's adoration. At first, Gia thought Akimbo ate at a leisurely pace out of good manners, but as the last vestige of the bun slid out of sight, she felt badgered.

"Screw it," Gia said. "I'm getting one of those burgers and you can watch me eat." She waved at the waitress.

"How are my numbers looking?" Akimbo asked. She licked burger juice from her thumb and gloated.

"So . . . I have a few questions."

"Shoot."

"How are you making payments to this Care Less agency?"

"Cash App. It's all they accept."

"Do you have a record of invoices?"

"No, they just tell me what I owe."

"You'll need solid documentation to claim it as a medical expense, tax-wise. Get their tax ID number and whatnot."

"Hmm, might be a little problematic, they're a foreign business."

"Still, they need to provide documentation to operate here."

Carol, the waitress—a hardened warhorse, a codependent who peered into Akimbo's soul if she tried to order other than the Number 6—appeared and stood expectantly with pad and paper in hand.

"I'll have what she just had, please," Gia said.

Carol drifted away without comment, mute confirmation that Gia's order was preordained.

"The caregivers are aliens," Akimbo explained.

"Undocumented labor? Like illegals?"

"Yes, in a manner of speaking."

"Have the feds gotten wind of this?"

"I don't think so."

"Don't ignore the feds, that's all I'm saying. They're tough. They're all about jail time."

"Ha! Thanks, but they're the least of my worries."

"Seriously, by the time you've exhausted appeals, Clagett won't be around and legal fees will have bankrupted you. Prison is a tough way to spend your final years."

Akimbo appreciated the thoroughness of Gia's advice but took it with a grain of salt. Gia's judgment was decidedly clouded by hunger and burger envy. Akimbo jumped to the heart of the matter. "Let's talk about my immediate problem: How do I pay for Clagett's care and keep the farm?"

"Alright, if you're ready. I wanted to ease you into it."

When a friend warns of dying penniless in federal prison as a way to ease you into a financial assessment, you've got problems. Akimbo saw the writing on the wall.

"Does Clagett have life insurance?"

Akimbo uncomfortably formed an answer. She had convinced Clagett many years ago that life insurance was a corporatized extortion scheme. "No," she said.

"Does Clagett's consulting business have any salable assets like client lists, physical equipment, or intellectual property? Did he create any software tools?"

"No, I don't think so. He survived on his own expertise," Akimbo replied.

Without breaking stride, Carol slid a burger in front of Gia, who smiled and hefted it to her lips, pausing to make lingering eye contact with Akimbo.

Akimbo excused herself to the restroom. Now *she* was envious of Gia and her cheeseburger, ridiculously so, beyond reasonable proportion. The high point of her day was in the past; her own burger was but a bolus in her GI tract. The money talk was certain to be a massive downer. She lingered over the sink, scrubbing away the grease that napkins alone had left behind.

She smiled at a thought: with her yet to be discussed money woes, she could reasonably expect Gia to pick up the lunch tab. Would ordering a burger to go, claiming it was for Clagett, be too conniving?

Passing by the cash register, she placed a covert order with Carol.

She slid across the plastic-covered bench to square off with a glassy-eyed Gia. During Akimbo's brief absence, Gia had powered through her burger, giving herself over to its seductions.

"Give it to me straight," Akimbo said. "What do you make of my situation?"

Now it was Gia's turn to languish over her fingertips. She made a show of it until Akimbo's expression said she needed to move on to business.

"You've looked at the numbers, so this won't come as a surprise: you have real trouble brewing." Gia attacked her hands with napkins dipped in her ice water. She picked up the stack of statements and flipped through them as she spoke. "Your property taxes, mortgage, and maintenance costs aren't covered by your income alone. Clagett's caregivers aren't covered by insurance, and the cost is staggeringly high because of the number of hours they work.

You're pulling from liquid savings, but that will only last you another few months. After that...you pull from retirement savings or you sell the farm. If you pull from retirement, eventually you'll have nothing left for yourself. If you sell the farm, you'll have to buy a condo or something, eating up your net profit. It's a lovely property, but it's not going to command the kind of money you need."

"How much would I need to come up with to keep the farm?"

"Like, keep it until you retire? How long will that be?"

"Let's say another ten or fifteen years."

"I'll have to calculate that answer. It's a big number. Millions."

Akimbo felt her future slipping through her fingers. Gia sat back and turned her attention to the parking lot. Glints of sunlight bounced off chrome and glass and forced her to turn back to Akimbo.

Carol slapped the bill on the table, off-center, biased toward Gia.

"I've got this, don't worry," Gia said.

"Thank you, and thank you for your advice."

"Anytime. I wish things were different for you."

"As do I, but only if it didn't change all the healthy years Clagett and I had together. It's not all bad, you know? We still have each other. We still laugh together."

"That's more than most," Gia said. "Listen, give my best to Clagett."

"I'm going to sit here for a few minutes and think. I'm not ready to go home yet."

"There are three cheeseburgers on this bill, aren't there?"

Akimbo acted confused by the question.

"It's alright. Life has dealt you a bad hand. You deserve it...the burger to go, that is."

"It's for Clagett."

"Right. Stay in touch. Let me know how I can help."

———————————

Akimbo returned home and worked toward livid as Clagett explained how he came to be alone. He glossed over the nose-blowing lead-up and jumped right to an action-packed description of the caregivers' sortie into the barn and subsequent panicked retreat.

"Did this just happen?" she asked.

"A little while ago," he said nonchalantly, "while you were *having coffee with a friend*."

They engaged in a momentary stare-down, each maintaining a neutral expression.

Clagett saw guilt. "You got the Number 6, didn't you?" he accused. "I can see it in your eyes."

"What?" she said innocently.

"Don't lie to me. I wondered why you barely brushed my lips with your kiss. I tasted secret sauce!"

"I talked money with Gia, but I don't want to talk about it right now. I'm tired."

"The Number 6. Damn. Some things are harder than others to let go of."

She shook her head. "Am I a terrible person?"

"For cuckolding me with a cheeseburger?"

"No. Should it have occurred to us to tell the caregivers that the barn is a literal breeding ground for spiders?"

"We can only go so far to accommodate them," he said.

That the caregivers also abided by that rule went unsaid.

"Let's enjoy the moment. We're alone for a change."

They sat on the back porch, holding hands, catching whiffs of the lavender planted in the old claw-foot tub. A thunder shower moved through, and they listened to the rain pound on the metal roof. They watched the leaves sparkle in the dying sunlight.

Clagett and Akimbo were unsurprised to find affection so easily accessible; their bond was always present, even when blanketed by immediate concerns. They both wondered if they would experience the same depth of feeling were he healthy.

He felt unexpectedly and perversely thankful for having been pushed down the staircase of life. He was freed from distractions—the temptation to flip through the magazine that sat before him or root through the refrigerator—and surrendered to the perfection of loving his wife. The universe spoke to him of gratitude.

She lightly squeezed his limp hand to acknowledge she felt the love too. Rarely did she allow herself to glory in the passage of time. She distilled the essence of the moment to a few apropos words: *Sit down and shut up.*

"The world would be a better place if everyone would sit down and shut up," she whispered.

"I'm doing my part," he said.

Daylight faded, a light breeze continued long after the storm passed, bird calls filled the quiet.

Geldine showed up and found them sitting in silence. "Everything okay here?" she asked.

"Everything is good," he said.

She came up the porch steps and rested her skinny haunches against the railing.

"There's something I've been meaning to tell you, Geldine," Clagett said.

She squinted her eyes at the two of them, bracing herself for complaint.

"Having you available to help me has been our saving

grace," Clagett said with sincerity. "We're thankful for your help."

Akimbo nodded in agreement. "I wish we could have you here all the time," she said.

"Well, thank you, I appreciate that. This is a difficult transition for families and I try to be there for them. Transition to caregivers, not the afterlife," Geldine said.

"Geldine, you should start your own agency," he half seriously suggested. "You could name it *We'll Show Up* to promote the feature people most want."

"As long as we don't say that I'll always be on time, I guess that would work," Geldine said.

"What kind of name is Care Less anyway?" Akimbo asked. "It sounds cautionary, like We Could Care Less!"

"It's supposed to sound like they're inexpensive," Geldine said.

"I'm curious: Where did you learn to be such a good caregiver?" Clagett wasn't sure that *good* was a complete description, more like *capable but morally opportunistic*, but he went with the compliment.

"Taking care of my sisters and grandmother," she answered. "Granny watched after us until she got the cancer in her throat, then I took care of her until she went home to Jesus.

"Back then I wanted to be a medical examiner looking inside the victim to make sure they were killed the way they were supposed to be. Like that lady on TV. I think I would be good at that, figuring out crimes and how to commit them.

"But after Granny passed, I missed taking care of people and the feeling of helping. It's a calling and I kept getting called by bill collectors. I needed to get a job or a new phone number."

"That's rough," Clagett whispered sympathetically.

Akimbo didn't like the somber turn in the conversation. "Here's a name for an agency, how about *We Won't Kill Your Mother*?" She laughed.

"Funny, but it happens. Seen it a few times." Geldine scowled seriously. "Prescription mix-ups. You didn't hear that from me."

"I'm not surprised, given what we've seen here," Akimbo said.

"What goes on here is the same as everywhere. It's not just this agency or these reticular…vehicular caregivers. *Particular.*"

"Why are my caregivers inexperienced?" Clagett wanted to know. "We had the impression the staff has worked the area for a while."

"True enough, but you're a difficult full-service case. A lot of their other jobs are overnight shifts. They don't do much other than sneak around the house in the dark. *Maybe* they help somebody use the bathroom or chase them down the street if they wander off. With you, they do everything because you're awake and can't help yourself. That's new. Most people don't need so much help being sick."

"I guess that helps explain it," Akimbo said.

They heard a rustling noise beneath the porch.

"You're creating a hostile workplace!" a muffled voice called out.

Akimbo jumped up, poised for action. "Who was that?"

"Oh yeah, the two caregivers are still down there," he said. "I guess I should have mentioned, but…out of sight, out of mind."

His urge to shrug indifferently was referred up to his eyebrows, which in response danced up and down. The net effect was regrettably suggestive that he was pleased to have two women hidden in the basement.

"Why?" Akimbo asked.

"I guess they're waiting for a ride home," he said cautiously, worried the situation was reflecting badly on him.

"I'm proud of you, Clagett," Akimbo said gently. "I know how hard it is for both of us to forget about caregivers and lead our lives unimpeded. Sitting here together has been sublime."

"Thank you for saying that. This *has* been wonderful."

They smoochy-faced at one another.

"You'll be paying for our time, you ingrates!" came a muted outburst.

"Your time *hiding*?" Akimbo yelled at the floor.

From below, softer: "*Ingrates*…Can I get a kudo?"

"You don't get kudos for insults!"

Barely audible: "Oh."

"I tell people looking for a job that there are two kinds of caregivers: ones who do it because they like helping others and ones who do it for a paycheck," Geldine said. "If you're just looking for a paycheck," she said in a louder voice directed downward, "you should do everybody a favor and do something else."

"Which type are you?" Akimbo asked, too hastily, she realized once the words left her mouth.

Geldine was taken aback by the blunt question. She frowned and looked dangerously close to cursing at Akimbo. "I like helping people," she said defensively, "but I need money."

"That's probably true for most caregivers, except for nuns," Akimbo agreed, not wanting to prickle Geldine. She smiled disarmingly.

"I'm not keen on the idea of being in business for myself," Geldine said. "Work has always been something I could walk away from." She said it like a jewel thief who was willing to abandon a robbery at the slightest hint of trouble, acknowledging there was something inherently dangerous about entering people's lives. "Sometimes it's just too much when clients start attacking you, or cursing," she explained. "Sometimes the family blames the caregiver for every problem. Sometimes the family drinks or steals the patient's drugs and fights among themselves. Sometimes it's just too painful to watch a person slip away."

"Hopefully we're not that bad," Akimbo said.

"Even if you aren't a drinker like most of them, I warn these caregivers that they need to handle you with kid boxing gloves like every other client's angry spouse. They'd best be nice or they'll get popped upside the head," Geldine divulged to Akimbo. "They think you're a guardian angel for the way you killed that spider. I tell them I've never seen an angel, but you're not one of them."

"I don't believe in angels," Akimbo said.

"If you *were* an angel, you'd think differently."

Clagett rolled into the bathroom to begin his nightly getting-into-bed ritual. Geldine wordlessly followed. She placed his toothbrush, flosser, and mouthwash on a meticulously folded paper towel. Her movements were practiced and deliberate. She brushed, he spat, and they repeated the cycle three more times. He flossed, guiding the flosser tool with his tongue. He sucked up mouthwash with a straw, swished vigorously, and spat into the plastic cup she pressed to his lower lip. He thought of the ritual as a Japanese tea ceremony of sorts. It's what would follow a tea ceremony if they didn't want their teeth to stain.

In the morning, caregivers ripped off the covers and pillows and towels that propped him. They tossed them aside, rudely discarding his comfort as well. Nighttime preparations, on the other hand, demanded attentive reassembly of his blanket fortress. The smallest of misplacements had the potential to fester into sleep-killing pain. Bend an ear against a pillow and hold for six hours—a recipe for agony. Apply pressure to the bony elbow knob for hours—sharp pain torturing a dull ache.

His other caregivers struggled to maintain focus on his bedtime needs. They failed to appreciate the detail and exactness he needed to get through the night. His helpful instructions were received as annoyances that slowed them from completing their day's work. After all, what happened after they left was hardly their concern.

"Why don't you try lying in one position for twelve hours so you'll stop calling me obsessive!" he had blurted out at Wobbegong one evening. She had looked around the room and eyed the couch. "I don't mean right now," he said angrily.

Geldine capably worked from memory, arranging each pillow and pad around him and under him as she gently manipulated his joints into relaxed positions. He closely monitored her craftsmanship and estimated whether he was comfortable enough to make it through the night, providing feedback as needed.

They heard the metallic groans of the space van settling onto the driveway. He imagined Smaragdine and Belva sprinting out from under the porch, making a bid for freedom. The van's ruckus faded into the sky.

He broke protocol and stirred up conversation. "Listen, Akimbo and I talked about your play to take the aliens' savings."

"Langford said you've got preservations."

"Reservations, yes. We don't want to be involved."

She laughed. "It doesn't matter nohow. I asked around and heard something interesting about our alien friends."

"What's that?" he asked mid-yawn.

"They're broke," she said. "They don't have any money after all their trying. They racked up big credit card debt on these Earth inhibitions…exhibitions…expeditions. Now they're hard up to make payments. Their higher-ups aren't happy and they might get recalled home. That's what I heard."

"Who told you that?"

"I hear the scuttlebutt. Ariola talks, she's no fan of Adnoydd."

"It seems like it would take an awful lot of caregiving hours to cover the costs of living in space."

"I reckon so," she said. "Somehow they got the idea they would make a fortune on caregiving." She gently tucked pillows and pads under his heels and knees and elbows. She hung her head. "Can I ask your advice? Let's say you were abducted and you made promises about the money they'd make from caregiving. To save your own hide. Let's say they're disappointed. What would you do if you were me?"

"Uh. Is that what's going on here?"

"No, I'm just asking."

"Okay. I'll have to think about that one."

"Yes," she admitted. "Yes, it *is* what's happening."

"Jesus," he said.

"That's my answer too. I've filled Him in. I've been praying on it. He'll protect me like He has with those COVID vaccines I never got."

"Well, that's good. That might do the trick."

"Amen," she said.

She put the finishing touches on his elbow placement and foot angle. Their conversation digressed into a collaboration over the appropriate blanket layering. Like a caddy conferring with a golfer, she checked the weather and suggested a combination to keep him in the sweet spot between too cold and too warm. When they settled on a plan—which is to say when he finally agreed with her advice—she unfurled, smoothed, and tucked each blanket into wrinkle-free perfection.

15

ADNOYDD HIMSELF APPEARED AT their doorstep the following morning. He tried valiantly to project authority and outrage, fettered though he was by gravity, his lean build distorted into a hobbling Quasimodo. An unfamiliar paunch around his waist strained his scrub tunic, creating starbursts of shadows at each button.

Akimbo spied Ariola and Wobbegong peering out the space van's grimy back window.

"I need a word with both of you," he told Akimbo at the door. "It's about the treatment of his caregivers yesterday."

At bedside, Adnoydd looked down at Clagett with disapproval. This was a rare opportunity for Adnoydd. Historically, he was the accused in situations of cultural insensitivity.

Adnoydd had long nursed resentment for human attitudes toward aliens, in some small part because of the *Alien* franchise, which he encountered during his cultural acclimatization. What shocked him most about the movies was the utter insensitivity to alien life; wholesale slaughter was the human solution to every encounter. Never mind the movies' demeaning depictions of aliens. None of the alien characters were played by indigenous creatures; instead they were portrayed with animatronics, puppets, and graphics. With his people's history of robotic oppressors, the representation was beyond offensive.

"Is this about the *Alien* joke I made yesterday?" Clagett wondered aloud.

"What joke?" Akimbo asked with a frown, beginning to suspect she hadn't been fully briefed on the situation.

"I was blowing my nose and they looked scared, so I thought—"

"Don't repeat it!" Adnoydd bellowed. "Do you have any idea how vulgar you were?"

"None whatsoever."

"Those movies slander one of the most pleasant, fun-loving, sensitive species you will ever encounter."

"I was joking! It's science fiction!" Clagett insisted.

Adnoydd was uncomfortably aware that Clagett was looking up at his wobbling jowls. He took a step away from the bed and tilted his head forward to conceal the loose flesh. Regrettably, the change in posture added slack. He tipped his head back to tighten the flesh and found himself looking at the ceiling. He acted as if he couldn't bear to look at Clagett, so appalled was he.

"Well, in this case your fiction is, in fact, science," Adnoydd declared. "Smaragdine's college roommate hatched as a face-hugger! Huggie, she called them. Real sweethearts, she said."

"Really?" Clagett asked.

Adnoydd had expressed his honest indignation without limiting himself with facts. He was indignant, make no mistake, but there were no colleges in outer space. He knew of no species that incubated in other animals' stomachs, though after seeing *Alien* he stayed vigilant.

"Are you calling me a liar?" Adnoydd challenged.

(A tiresome expression oft heard with at least one *fucking*. His favorite variation: Once, mid-interrogation, an attorney got tongue-tied denying a bald-faced lie and retorted, "Are you calling me a *lawyer*?" Adnoydd loved the irony. Attorney-flavored jerky was a big seller.)

"Maybe it's time for an apology," Akimbo suggested. She raised her eyebrows at Clagett. "I don't think he meant to cause offense. His jokes miss their target sometimes."

"We don't do apologies," Adnoydd said. "Spite is more to our liking. 'It's like a flavor that lingers delightfully on the palate.' A priest I abducted once said that to me about prayer. He didn't use any profanity, but I'm sure he thought it."

"Well, how can we resolve this amicably?" Akimbo asked.

"I have a couple of thoughts on the matter. Demands, really."

"Go on."

"Item one: we're raising your hourly rate to cover this administrative hand-holding stuff."

"What? We had an agreement!" Akimbo spat out.

"Did we?"

"You know we did," she growled.

He would have preferred a richer response, at least a *cocksucker* or a *shithead* as the centerpiece with some *fucking* embellishments.

"Item two: I'll put it simply. The caregivers will no longer pretend to enjoy your company."

"They never acted like they enjoyed our company," Akimbo responded.

"Really? Maybe I have it backward."

He looked up at the fire in Akimbo's eyes and realized she was *significantly* taller than he was, considering she was taller to begin with and his body was hunched over and squished down by gravity. He recognized her expression from the ship, when she'd sworn to hunt him down, slice him in half, and infect his wounds with spiders or some such. Her exposed sternum had been a powerful distraction at the time, but he remembered the gist of her threat. It was only then it occurred to him that she might not take the rate increase in stride.

———————————

Akimbo gave up any semblance of politeness, any vestige of treating caregivers as guests, any notion that caregivers would lighten her workload or her mental burden. They had burned through what little generosity and compassion she had left. It didn't matter that the disease was behind everything, that the disease was nobody's fault. Adnoydd took their money and, in return, delivered more anguish than help.

She screamed at Adnoydd to leave, that they should all go home, that they were unwanted, that they were making a horrible situation worse.

Clagett clenched up and divorced himself from everything around him, retreating into himself. He was scared Adnoydd would refuse to be fired and seek revenge—if not a single boiled-into-flavor-extract act of revenge, then a death-by-a-thousand-cuts stream of micro-mistreatments by his caregiver henchmen. If they succeeded at dumping Adnoydd's crew, he was scared to saddle Akimbo with his care until they hired replacements. When they found replacements, he was scared of an entirely new set of problems.

"Can you hold on a minute?" Adnoydd abruptly turned heel and hurried back to the van to consult with Ariola. Seeing him approach, Ariola and Wobbegong dragged themselves out to meet him.

"Raise our rate! We should fire them, hire a different agency!" Akimbo spat out. "Where does he get off lying to us? A roommate named Huggie…my ass."

She paced the room with long strides, seething, breathing, settling herself. She checked the window to recon Adnoydd's next move.

"He's talking to Ariola and that young girl," she reported. "The orange-and-black tabby. The one with the phone problem. I guess she couldn't stand being apart…from the phone, not you."

"The one with the fingernails?" Clagett perked up. "Wobbegong."

"They're not going anywhere. They need money as much as you need help. I didn't think he'd let us go easily."

"Let's see how it goes today, since Wobbegong is already here," he pleaded. "Maybe everything is fine."

As much as he complained about caregiver behavior, he was surprised to hear himself advocate for their return. To himself he conceded the simple truth: he was physically reliant on them, even as they extracted their emotional toll. He was willing to tolerate their behavior and unwilling to go without care.

"We can't give in to fear," she said.

"Too late."

"I can't deal with any of this," she said. "We can't afford a rate increase. If he forces it, you'll have to die sooner or go without care. I don't know what else *I* can do."

She wounded Clagett with her comment.

"We'll figure it out," she said to make amends, though her voice lacked conviction.

Wobbegong made her way toward the house. She struggled to lift her feet off the ground, like she was fighting a stiff headwind, like she was a toddler sent to their room as punishment. She scrunched up her face into the most exaggerated frown they had ever witnessed. She communicated reluctance with every aspect of her appearance.

"We didn't expect to see you again," Akimbo said. "This is our lucky day."

"Adnoydd gave me a message," Wobbegong wheezed, setting foot inside the house. "Can you bring me some of that lemonade from the fridge? It's not flavored enough but it will do. Add a little tequila."

"No. Not happening. What's the message?" Akimbo demanded.

"First, tell them not to kill the fucking messenger. Second, tell them to act like they enjoy our caregivers' help! Or else!" she cried out. "That's just how he said it."

"But what if we don't?" Clagett asked.

"He didn't say. If I were you, I wouldn't test him. In other words, if I were you, I'd bring me some lemonade."

***

While Wobbegong readied Clagett for the day, Akimbo hacked weeds along the back fence line, deep in thought. When she frowned and swung sharp tools, he knew to give her space. Really, he had no choice—his chair couldn't drive to the back fence. Properly speaking, he knew to respect the space she took.

Akimbo embodied a contradiction: respect her gentle approach to life or face truly frightening aggression. Adnoydd had crossed her line, and Clagett believed the battle had just begun.

On occasion, naginata sparring partners had the audacity to joke about Akimbo's slapstick appearance in battle. Or worse, they heedlessly attacked her, thinking they could overpower and cow her into retreat. Those miscalculations usually ended in a barrage of blows from head to toes with Akimbo's screams ringing in their ears. She punctuated her counterattack with a final indignity: carefree laughter.

"What are you thinking?" he asked on her return to the house.

She scrubbed her hands in the kitchen sink. "Where's Wobbegong?"

"Off canoodling with her phone. Their separation was traumatic for both of them."

"Great," she muttered. Satisfied they were alone, she said, "Raising our rate? *Raising our rate?* I've never disliked anyone more than him," she said. "Or else! *Or else what?*"

She aggressively whipped her hands, flinging off water.

"I'll tell you what I think," Akimbo said. "*This isn't my problem,* that's what I think. Every little bit of this caregiving BS has been piled on me disguised as obligation." She drew an angry breath and growled, "Screw it, I'm done."

On better days, he would have pressed her for what she meant by *done*, especially considering it sounded like she was ready to move on...so he should die already. Clagett was hamstrung by the married man's paradox: he believed that her emotional outpouring did not completely reflect her inner truth (unless it did). Even though she hinted she wanted him to die, he didn't think she meant it, but, out of an abundance of caution, he kept his mouth shut. Briefly.

"I have a thought," he said.

"Oh Jesus, what now?"

"True enlightenment...satori," he said. "See, monks sat in meditation for a long time—"

"I know what satori is! I don't need a mansplanation! Especially right now!"

"Finally some *truly* enlightened monk jumped up and

said, 'Jesus, my butt is sore from all this sitting. I know we're peaceable folk, but—real talk—roving bandits keep slaughtering us. We oughta embrace the martial arts and kick them out of town!'"

"I question whether that's historically accurate."

Clagett felt her ease into their accustomed patter.

"I'm saying that we need to go on the offensive against Adnoydd," he said.

"I *just* said that."

"You did?"

"I just said I'm done with Adnoydd. He's got to go."

"Oh right, you did say that. We're on the same wavelength," he said agreeably, thankful to have cleared up his uncertainty. "Wait, we're talking about sending him away, right? You're not thinking of killing him, are you?"

"Are you?"

"No, I mean…maybe."

"I'm not, but I *am* rethinking Langford's plan to investment-fraud back the money they charged us…Plus a massive penalty for *my* pain and suffering," she said. "We need the money, God knows."

"Um…I'm afraid that plan is off the table."

"How so?"

"Breaking news: they don't *have* any money," he said. "Geldine told me the aliens are in debt and can't pay off the interest. She's inextricably tangled in this mess and thinks Adnoydd blames her. She's worried for herself."

"Why would she think that?"

"Under duress she made promises about the profitability of a caregiving business, maybe even gave them financial advice."

"'Aliens Bankrupted by Local Caregiver, Planet Saved'—I can see the headlines," she said.

"Or how about this," he said. "'Aliens Angered by Local Caregiver, Planet Destroyed.'"

"If the planet is destroyed, who writes your headline?" she questioned. "That's a fundamental flaw in your fear. Maybe dial it back to 'Local Farm Destroyed.'"

"I like your first headline better. Let's go with that."

———————————

Late that evening, Ariola called Akimbo to twist the Care Less knife. She said that the space van was out of service and repairs were expected to take a week or more. She told Akimbo to house and feed Wobbegong for the duration. They would charge for round-the-clock care, but she promised they wouldn't charge time-and-a-half for overtime hours, "...but we *will* be charging the higher rate Adnoydd negotiated with you this morning."

"Negotiated! I don't know the new rate!" Akimbo snapped back, but Ariola had wisely disconnected after delivering her message.

Akimbo moved in front of the TV to collect Clagett's attention. Wobbegong leaned sideways from her seat at the back of the den to see the screen around Akimbo. One glance at his wife's enraged face and Clagett shut down his movie.

She relayed the situation, accusing Adnoydd of deliberately fabricating a breakdown story simply to torment them and extract money. She began to sob.

"Oh, baby," Clagett said softly. "Come here."

She leaned over his arm and pressed her cheek to his chest. With one arm wrapped behind his backrest and one lying across his lap, she embraced him and his wheelchair.

He nuzzled his chin against the back of her head, burrowing into her hair.

"This will be fun!" Wobbegong clapped her hands.

"I can't take it anymore," Akimbo moaned.

"Not yet," Clagett whispered into her hair, not wanting the moment to end.

Akimbo pulled away from Clagett and raised her arms in resignation. "God forbid we forget you're here, Wobbegong. Sleep on the couch. A blanket and towels are around here somewhere." She left the room.

"She's supposed to act glad I'm here," Wobbegong whispered to herself.

Wobbegong readied him for the night. Clagett aimed comforting thoughts at Akimbo.

With Wobbegong temporarily stranded on the farm, Clagett and Akimbo were freed from the worry of caregiver arrival. Akimbo slept soundly knowing Wobbegong rested mere feet away from Clagett. For the same reason, Clagett slept poorly.

"Wobbegong, are you asleep?"

He knew she wasn't, because of her phone's glow.

"Yes." She exasperated loudly at Clagett's interruption, seemingly to ward off additional questions.

"Tell me about your home planet."

"Like what?"

"Like what's its name?"

"Why would we name a rock?" She snorted from her gills at his question's stupidity.

"Well, what do you call it?" He wasn't going to let her derail him with her disdain.

"In our language we call it *our planet*," she said.

"Okay... How about this, what's life like on your planet? Or should I call it 'our planet'?"

His words were lost in the void of her inattention.

"Life's a bitch no matter where you are," she announced matter-of-factly. "Sha'nona told me that. She also says you're *my* bitch. When she calls me *Bitch!* I like it. Is that weird?"

"I lost my ability to gauge what's weird."

"Sha'nona is the only one who *gets* me. *You* sure don't."

"Ouch," he grumbled. The truth hurt. He aspired to be understanding, that should count for something.

"Hey, Wobbegong," he said softly. "Wobbegong, remember when you talked about beef jerky flavored by a shoe salesman?"

He waited for an answer.

"Wobbegong?"

"What?"

"You weren't kidding?"

"No."

"How do you get flavor out of a shoe salesman?"

"Same as everyone else: a long, slow boil."

"How many people did you 'flavor extract'?"

"Lots," she said. "That was before I came on board. Adnoydd was part of that program. Ask him."

Clagett was horrified by the indifference with which she answered.

He heard her get up and go into the kitchen. She pulled something out of a cabinet and crunched loudly for a while. She returned to the couch and tapped on her phone. Neither the noise nor the glow were overly bothersome, but the imposition of the annoyances made him seethe.

"Hey, Wobbegong," he whispered.

"What now?"

"Turn off the phone, would you please."

"In a minute. It doesn't bother you."

Deep in the night, frustrated by Wobbegong's disparaging attitude, Clagett devised a counterattack. Inspired by the thought of Wobbegong's nails on his scalp, he premeditated exploring pleasures from a body that offered next to none. The body in question was his own, of course—Wobbegong's body was strictly her business. There was nothing unseemly going on; the pleasures he pursued existed at the foot-rub end of the gratification spectrum. To be precise, he meant therapeutic reflexology foot-rubs—no tongue involved—but he should probably omit that last qualifier. These were the arguments he prepared to defend his actions to Akimbo if Wobbegong ratted him out. He anticipated disapproval from Akimbo, as with his previous scalp-scratching scheme.

To a degree he felt foolish preparing a defense; asking for simple pleasures was ridiculously prurient compared to Wobbegong scrubbing and dressing his naked self. Akimbo would no doubt rebut his defense and reinforce that he must limit his requests to caregiving. She wasn't concerned about impropriety, she would say—although he was fairly sure Akimbo was concerned; he was a man and hence corruptible.

She's my surrogate, he would argue. *We pay her by the hour. Anything related to health or grooming is fair game, including swabbing ears and rubbing ointment on irritated skin!* He made a mental note to avoid the word *grooming*, with its media connection to underage girls, should he actually need to defend his actions.

Oh, so that's what you're up to, he imagined she would say. *Give it up. Tell me what went on this morning.*

———————————————————

His scheme began with the seemingly off-hand remark he had prepared during the night. "My ears are really filled with water today," he said to set the stage. He recommended Wobbegong probe into the depths and crevices of his ears with towel-wrapped index fingers. He told her it was the most efficient approach and minimizing her labor was foremost on his mind.

"Can you dry a little more, please? I have a problem with itchy ears if they aren't dried thoroughly," he then encouraged, as if itchy ears was a legitimate syndrome. "Dagnabbit, there's still something tickling my ears," he told Wobbegong. He asked her to circle his ear canals with a cotton swab, claiming there was water, that his wax was especially sticky, that it was building up, that it was clear and invisible to the eye, that he couldn't hear—anything to prolong the delicious swabbing.

Ear swabbing was more than an outrageously delightful sensation; for Clagett it was rich with taboo. The act embodied danger (*Don't stick anything in your ears!* his mother's voice still echoed) and thrillingly rebelled against his instinct for safety. It embodied guilt for allowing someone other than Akimbo to penetrate his ears—ears were demarked as partner-only erogenous zones, although they agreed that a tongue applied to an ear was louder and moister than they cared for.

Wobbegong didn't buy his inducements. She expressed skepticism that his ears needed such pressure and repetition to get them completely dry. She half-heartedly poked swabs in his ears to represent obeyance while falling short of his sensual goal.

With ear swabbing shut down, he moved to Plan B. An area at the base of his spine had become inflamed because of Belva's one carelessly forceful tug of his Hoyer sling. At the site of the injury, he nursed a fleshly delight: the intense sensitivity of mildly irritated skin.

Once abraded, the base of his spine became painful to the touch, and yet, if he wiggled his hips weakly, the friction against his seat cushion was heavenly. He complained of discomfort in the region. Once he was on the bed, Wobbegong dutifully rolled him onto his side to investigate. A circle of discolored skin caught her attention.

"You have a red mark here," Wobbegong said and pressed vigorously on the spot. "Does that hurt?"

"Yes! That's where the sling scratched me."

"I don't know where it came from."

"The sling!" he repeated.

"I doubt it," she said.

"What does it look like? Does it look infected?"

"It looks red. But not a bad red, more like a pink red. It's not *red* red."

"So it's not infected?"

"It looks like the skin was braised."

"Brazed?" he asked.

"Rubbed hard."

"Abraded?"

"Bruised, but it's just red."

With his complaint corroborated by visual evidence, she agreed to salve the area. When he moaned with delight, she asked if he was in pain.

"Yes, it's tender," he claimed, "but keep rubbing. I can tough it out." He told her to expect a lengthy rehabilitation program for the area. "We'll need to massage the area to encourage blood flow," he said. "Let's be sure to put lotion on that spot every day. We don't want a pressure sore to develop."

When all was said and done, he got away scot-free—Wobbegong did not squeal on him. Nonetheless, at first opportunity he guiltily confessed his manipulations to Akimbo.

"Why are you telling me this?" she asked.

"For a moment, life was supremely worthwhile," he guessed. "It didn't seem right."

She bent down to his level and looked into his eyes. "That makes me sad. You deserve pleasure just like everyone. You're not condemned to misery."

"Thank you," he whispered.

Contrary to his expectations, she admitted, "I probably would do the same thing. You enjoy having your head scratched, so ask if she'll do that for you too."

"Yes!" he cried out. In his mind he saw himself clenching his fist.

"Wobbegong, come here, please!" Akimbo called.

Her shuffling footsteps approached.

"Wobbegong, if my husband asks for his head scratched or his ears cleaned or his wounds lotioned, do what he asks for as long as he asks. It's not for you to decide what he needs."

"It's boring," she explained.

"Do your job," Akimbo snarled. Her order was guttural, pitched to a lower register like a blustering samurai. Plainly, there was no room for debate.

"Yes, Akimbo," she mumbled.

To hasten Wobbegong's exit, Akimbo emphatically pointed the way out of the room.

"Dispense with the imagined subterfuge. Tell them straight up what you want," she said to Clagett. "We're on offense now."

16

AKIMBO BEGAN CLASS AS she always did, silently waiting while her students gathered brooms and arrayed themselves in a line. There were more whispers and giggles than usual, but it was summer, the sun still shone, and spirits were high, like the carpool father toking up outside.

Starting the sweep was the duty of the senior student, Sha'nona, who had loitered around the house with Wobbegong all afternoon but was curiously absent from class.

"Alright, let's begin," Akimbo instructed.

Her students didn't move.

"Hajime!" she barked.

A great squeal of excitement reverberated through the loft. The children broke ranks and rushed the stairs. She watched with amazement and in an instant she was alone. She heard their delighted screeching move toward the house. Sha'nona held open the front door, waving the class inside.

Mystified, she made her way to the house, wondering—fearing—what she was to find.

Wobbegong waited at the front door and escorted her to the dining room. There, Clagett sat with a wide smile. Wobbegong showed her to a chair beside her husband and served her fresh lemonade with a sprig of mint and a straw for her to share with Clagett.

"Did you plan this?" she asked.

"Me?" he answered evasively.

With her hostess duties fulfilled, Wobbegong hustled to the kitchen and marshaled a clutch of sweepers in an attack on the corners, along the cabinet kickplates, and beneath the table and chairs. "Akimbo likes it super clean!" she was heard to say over the yelps of the counter-wipers who sang out when the sweepers raked brooms across their bare feet.

From the upstairs they heard Sha'nona driving her charges through each room and closet. She peeked over the banister, spying on downstairs progress. Akimbo sensed there was a competition afoot.

One of the youngest girls swept her way down the hall, conspicuously separated from the herd. The care she took to collect the dust bunnies huddled along the baseboards filled Akimbo with pride. Attention to detail was a cornerstone of her teaching.

"Ginny, come give me a hug." She forced a smile though she hovered on the verge of tears for gratitude that felt unmistakably sad.

Ginny was caught by surprise to find herself near her teacher. She rested her broom against the wall and approached Akimbo's open arms. They embraced for longer than the girl felt necessary; Akimbo released her when her squirming challenged her grip.

"Have you met my husband?" Akimbo asked sweetly.

"No."

"His name is Clagett."

"Does he pee sitting down?" Ginny asked.

Inappropriate questions were the parents' doing. Akimbo wasn't running a charm school.

"He goes like all boys do," she said. Hopefully her parents covered that lesson.

"Like a fireman?"

Akimbo looked to Clagett as if he was going to weigh in. He appeared amused and aghast and dead set against answering, for which she was thankful. She pictured him beginning a devilish explanation with *Imagine, if you will, a condom with a spout...*

"Why don't you ask your mom? She can explain it to you. We need to respect Clagett's privacy, okay?"

The downstairs sweeping apparatus rumbled down the hall, absorbing Ginny into the herd. Akimbo elevated her feet to escape broom swipes. In the throng Akimbo heard one of the older girls ask, "What did he say? Does he wear a diaper?" She hoped Clagett hadn't heard. He would be dispirited to have his lifetime of experiences and his intimate perspective on death bypassed for interest in peeing.

Clagett was unfazed by Ginny. "Did you see that pile of dust?" he said. He was appalled by the collected mass the girls ushered past them.

"Honestly, I don't know how you live like this," Akimbo said, hoping he picked up on her self-effacing humor and didn't take her barb as criticism, though he could try harder to get his caregivers to sweep where he ate in the kitchen and where his wheelchair tracked dirt into the house. But mainly she was joking.

He didn't appear to hear her, as he was lost in thought. "Geldine told me something interesting. Your little friend Ginny reminded me of it." Clagett evidenced a non sequitur spasm amid the mayhem. The quickest way to the other side was to let him ride out his impulse. "Geldine worked for an ancient woman—well over a hundred—who was lingering on her deathbed. The woman told Geldine she was ready to die. Do you know why?"

"Why?"

"The woman said she was tired of going to the bathroom."

"Interesting. How do you interpret that?"

"I don't know, but I know what she meant. It's an unrelenting hassle."

Above them, the sweepers converged at the top of the stairs. The downstairs crew panicked, realizing they were behind. A cry went up to sweep faster and the brooms became a blur of motion kicking dust into the air.

Clagett watched with amusement, laughing and cheering as they raced to the finish.

A standoff developed between the top and bottom of the stairs. In unison, the girls at the head of their packs flipped their brooms up and held them poised like naginata.

"Girls—" Akimbo felt the need to exert control.

Later, Akimbo would question Clagett about his next action and the potential consequences. His defense: it wasn't like he put the idea in their heads; he simply pulled the trigger.

"Attack!" Clagett choked out.

A shrill battle cry crescendoed as the two factions pressed forward.

"Whoa! Girls! Girls!" Akimbo stopped them in their tracks, halting the upstairs versus downstairs battle before they collided mid-staircase. "Back to class!" she instructed.

Sha'nona ushered the boisterous girls outside and held the door for Akimbo.

"Thank you, Sha'nona! This was a wonderful surprise," Akimbo said. "Sincerely, thank you."

"You're welcome." She bowed to her teacher. "It was his idea, you know." She waved her hand toward Clagett. "I just organized the girls."

———————————

Sweeping the house had worked the girls into a mood for

combat. Back in the loft, they clamored to don protective gear and go at one another.

Akimbo walked among the sparring matches in progress. The fighting was raucous but friendly, with more laughter and celebratory dancing than death matches usually called for. Sparring was the time for the girls to express themselves outside the boundaries of discipline.

"Change up your attack, keep them guessing," she coached.

In her experience, the challenge of sparring was letting go of the exercises and drills, the choreographed footwork, the numerically itemized attacks, the prescribed defenses, the whole *system*, and…winging it. That is, winging it while adhering to the fundamentals she taught them. To clarify: use the system, just don't use it *literally*.

She once attempted to articulate this thought for the benefit of a parent, and they responded, "I get you, it's like jazz music. Improvisation. Interplay. Conflict and cooperation." She nodded politely and let the parent picture their daughter making beautiful music. Sparring was nothing like jazz. For starters, the point of jazz isn't to kill the other musicians.

The two art forms did overlap in one regard: adaptation. When she actively competed in tournaments, her knack for fluidly changing tactics was routinely underestimated. She confounded her opponents, but they perceived her as erratic and untraditional.

She lost herself in her teaching until once again she was alone, bracing herself for an onslaught of reality, feeling tendrils of stress find purchase in her thoughts. In her tenuous state of clarity, she focused on smoothing the path for herself and Clagett.

They *had* to adapt. They had to find a better agency.

Bringing on a new agency *might* swap one set of problems for another. But swapping one set of problems for another at least maintained the status quo.

With the change, they *had* to address their looming financial crisis. Gia had worked out she needed around five million dollars to lead her lifestyle to the grave. The number was preposterous, like everything else around her. She felt corrupted just thinking it.

It went without saying that, during the agency change, they couldn't let Adnoydd abduct and kill them.

———————————

With each day Wobbegong was stuck on the farm, she moved a little slower and less helpfully. She became forgetful of simple tasks ("I wear clothes during the day," Clagett had reminded). She sighed heavily at each request for help. She moaned while helping. Akimbo coined a special name for her raspy sounds of gill respiration: *exaspiration*.

They didn't know enough about her to judge whether Earth's environment was sapping her strength. If she were human, her symptoms might mean she was burned out, depressed, or adolescent.

Clagett's insecurity fomented a bitterly suspicious opinion that she intentionally compromised her performance to aggravate him. This was revenge for his ear-swab ploy, he conjectured, part of her long game. As he further analyzed her every action, he found more evidence. Her toothbrushing, for instance, was primarily front to back, not little circles per dentists' recommendations, and she refused to comply.

Imagining that Wobbegong needed rest and deserved a night in a real bed, Akimbo suggested she sleep upstairs in the guest room. Once Wobbegong went upstairs, Akimbo came to Clagett and stretched her lanky self next to him. She rested her arm across his chest to maintain balance on the bed's edge. Her fingertips slid along the hollows between his ribs.

"Let's hope she feels better tomorrow," Akimbo whispered into his ear.

"She hates being marooned here," Clagett confided.

"She's probably burned out from taking care of you day after day. It's also possible her behavior has nothing to do with you."

"Whatever the reason, she pisses me off," he said.

"Tell me. Don't hold back," she implored.

"She started with a measure of commitment and a hint of compassion, but quickly burned through both. Now her attitude is 'Why bother?' I feel very susceptible to her influence, I don't know why. My defenses are weak or something. She makes me wonder too…Why bother?"

"Get it out of your system now, don't let your bitterness fester," she encouraged.

"Caring for me is futile. It will get harder. Eventually it will be inadequate. Ergo, I'm a waste of everyone's fucking time."

"That's better," she said. "You really stuck the landing."

Venting riled him up. He panted and coughed and rolled phlegm around with his tongue. She massaged his chest, feeling the gravelly percussion of each cough. She bided her time, waiting for him to settle down before restarting the discussion.

When his breathing normalized, she said, "Hey—"

"Hey, want to know something interesting about my backside?" he asked. Non sequitur time. He was like a cat sensing a vet appointment. He picked up the scent of a difficult discussion and took evasive action.

Reluctantly, she played along. "What?"

"See, I have this sensitive spot at the base of my spine, where Belva injured me. Aggressive massage—the only kind my caregivers know—perpetuates a balance between complete recovery and further injury. The slightest touch on the area feels awesome. I've been hovering in a state of blissful sensitivity for weeks."

No one had made her aware of an injury. She was alarmed that he spoke about the injury and prolonged recovery so excitedly, as if his caregivers had convinced him to enjoy the pain.

"The sensation is incredible!" he gushed. "I suspect that I'm growing a clitoris on my backside. I'm evolving! It's recompense for all the muscle nerves I've lost." He laughed at his joke.

"Lucky you," she deadpanned, hoping to shut down his diversion from the conversation…and propriety.

Akimbo took a deep breath before she moved to the difficult topic—she knew it would generate anxiety—but she wanted to give him hope.

"I've been thinking…There *are* people who want to make you comfortable and who find the work personally rewarding. I know I do…or did, before it was too much for me. You deserve that. We need to find more people like Geldine, caregivers you're comfortable with."

"You're talking about changing the agency?"

"Yes."

"I want that too. But…I have to admit—again—that the idea scares me. I feel…vulnerable and…dependent on my caregivers even though they frustrate me to no end. They have a hold on me."

"I understand how you feel, but I wonder if your dependency isn't somewhat the result of emotionally abusive behavior on their part. You shouldn't feel threatened, you should feel supported."

He grew agitated at the mention of mistreatment. "Do you really think they're abusive? That's a strong word. They do take care of me."

She anticipated that he would question her characterization and vouch for the caregivers. "There's more to caregiving than taking care of your body. I know we can agree on that."

"What does it say about me? I didn't complain enough?" he asked. "Am I a sucker, a patsy, a wimp?"

"Not at all. You're in a vulnerable position. Partly I think you're trying to protect me from your problems, which I appreciate."

"I want you to be right. It's just that..."

She waited for his next counterargument. He was still sharp, capable of matching wits, but he was raddled by the emotional and interpersonal and extra-galactic angles to his illness. In his topsy-turvy reasoning, he argued against his best interests.

"Change makes everything so unpredictable," he said.

"We can't accept poor service just because it's predictably poor. You deserve better."

"I'm not sure I *do*."

"*I'm* sure." She let his comment slide past without further assurances, though it hurt to hear him devalue himself. "What would you think about Geldine and Langford taking care of you?" she asked. "They seem to do a good job."

"She didn't seem open to the idea."

"Are you okay if I talk with her about it? Let me try. I think she and Langford have grown to care for you."

"Sure. Thank you."

"Trust me. We'll get through this together, just like we always do. I'll look out for you." She squeezed his arm and kissed him on the lips.

17

FOR A VARIETY OF eco-economic reasons, Akimbo was not a supporter of the *Free Shipping! Next-Day Delivery! Subscribe to Auto-Ship and Save!* lifestyle. Clagett, ever the supportive husband, supported her nonsupport of home delivery. However, when he weakened and was unable to lift a loaf of bread from the store shelf, or rein in his anxiety while out in public, he surrendered to the allure of internet shopping. Akimbo understood that he gave in to spare her the trouble of shopping, but he also reneged on his obligation to preserve the Earth, which put her in the bind of appreciating his consideration while not approving of it.

Nearly every afternoon, Akimbo suffered watching a delivery truck pull down their long driveway—trailing a plume of dust like a harbinger from a postapocalyptic wasteland—to drop off a single tube of eye gel or whatever other necessity Clagett needed on demand. The task of retrieving packages from the porch, opening them, and questioning Clagett's justification for same-day delivery fell to Akimbo. Consequently, Akimbo was the first to notice when packages started arriving damaged. The eco-impact of the initial shipment was bad enough, but she couldn't live with return shipments and replacement shipments on her conscience too. She duly investigated.

Jan Nurb, the culprit behind the mishandling, was surprisingly easy to identify. Exhibit 1: Someone claiming to be Jan sent threatening messages to Wobbegong's Space Hotel phone. Exhibit 2: Jan owned the company from which Clagett ordered. Exhibit 3, the most damning of all: Each package had an enclosed gift message reading, *Suck on this! —Jan*

Clagett and Akimbo theorized that Jan's minions tracked the location of Wobbegong's Space Hotel phone to the farm. When they compared the phone's location against company shipping records, they turned up Clagett's name. Conclusion: Jan established that she was *the* Jan Nurb by blindly lashing out at Clagett.

Clagett proclaimed that for Jan—one of the world's wealthiest people—to bully them, on top of all their other worries, was biblical in scope, like Job himself—*Job* Job, not Steve Job who was plagued by John Sculley, he explained. It's Steve *Jobs*, she told him, he's plural. Anyway, he maintained the universe spoke to them through Jan's vexation and they'd best pay attention. She didn't buy into his assertion; in Jan's vexation Akimbo found nothing *but* vexation. But if Clagett found meaning in a caring, chatty universe, who was she to question it?

———————————

His wife, that's who. Akimbo listened for herself, but the universe mumbled and frustrated interpretation. For the universe to barely exert itself on their behalf, to use such lazy diction in important matters, confirmed in her mind that it was just an incoherent, curious *thing*, albeit an impressively large one.

Jan made her message unequivocally clear: *Suck on this!* Technically, she left some ambiguity as to what they should be sucking on, but the tenor of her message was unmistakable. Her shipping interference and threatening messages, her boorish approach to intimidation, provoked Akimbo into a counteroffensive.

Akimbo called Jan's phone.

"Is this Jan Nurb?"

"Who is this?"

"I'm calling in regards to the Space Hotel. My name is Akimbo."

"What is that? Is that like an Asian name? Where are you calling from?"

"That's neither here nor there. It's just my name."

"This Space Hotel isn't a Chinese spy setup, is it?"

"No."

"North Korean?"

"No."

"Okay. But your name *sounds* Asian."

"It's not."

"If you say so."

"I do."

"If you're not Chinese, then what are you?"

"Jan, that's all beside the point. I want to discuss business, but first, I must insist you stop meddling with my husband, Clagett's, package deliveries."

"Husband, huh? So you got my messages?"

"*Suck on this!* Was that really necessary? Doesn't that strike you as childish?"

"*Childish?* You do know who you're talking to?"

"Yes. We've established that you're Jan, the bitch pestering me and my husband."

The phone went quiet and Akimbo imagined Jan seething, foaming at the mouth over her stinging matter-of-fact delivery.

Jan rebounded with a personal attack: "Your husband is a terrible orderer! He should bundle his shipments! I can feel the earth dying every time his name pops up! Sending a same-day truck to deliver one bottle of laxatives just isn't sustainable! That's not the best example since popping the cork *does* feel urgent, but you get what I mean."

"Actually, we're on the same page there."

"Oh…good."

"So you'll dial back your childish attacks?" Akimbo asked. Really, it was a demand lightly cloaked as a question.

Jan said, "I guess I'm open to the idea. Being childish is how I learned to manage, and I've done spectacularly well with it. I must say though, it stings to actually be *called* childish. You've got nerve and I respect that."

"Good. So, to get to the point, I'd like to facilitate business discussions with the Space Hotel," Akimbo explained. "I have a piece of information that will interest you greatly."

"I doubt it."

"The hotel is operated by an alien civilization."

"Like the Central American variety?"

Jan seemed to be losing interest in the conversation. Akimbo pictured her flipping through a word-of-the-day calendar.

"No, I mean *alien* alien. Outer-space alien."

"So basically this is a hoax."

Though acting skeptical, Akimbo could tell her interest was piqued.

"No hoax. Real aliens."

"Seriously?"

"Yes."

"Bullshit."

"No BS. Ask yourself: If someone from Earth built a hotel in space, wouldn't everyone know who it was?"

"Fair point, but hardly proof. Are you claiming to be one of them?"

"No, but I can make introductions...for a price."

Broaching the subject of payment made Akimbo feel sullied by capitalism. No doubt Jan detected her discomfort and realized she was dealing with yokels.

"So this is a shakedown, a scam or something," Jan said.

"No, come to my home and we can discuss further. I'll introduce you to an alien and the rest is up to you."

"What do you get out of this arrangement?"

"Just a finder's fee."

"How much?"

"Five million. Dollars." Akimbo grimaced, scarcely believing that number came out of her mouth.

"Whoa! The girl swings for the fences! You've got moxie, I'll say that much."

"That's how much I need."

"I'll think about it. If I agree to come, I'm not paying any fee unless I close a deal with them."

After the call, Akimbo took a few minutes to decompress, then found Clagett in the kitchen eating lunch with Wobbegong. Akimbo confessed that she had called Jan out of frustration and had ended up inviting her to their home.

"I'm new to the business game but I think I did okay," she said. "I implied I could facilitate negotiations with the Space Hotel."

Clagett was mid-chew and unable to comment, but he opened his eyes wide to compliment her for her clever initiative.

Akimbo continued, "I'm going to text her and suggest she join us for dinner later this week. What do you think about asking Geldine and Langford to join us? Maybe they'll have some thoughts on how to profit from this venture. I'm embarrassed that it comes down to money, but we need to look out for ourselves—no one else will."

Clagett nodded in agreement.

"Tentatively, I asked for a finder's fee to introduce her to an alien…which would be you, Wobbegong."

Wobbegong was caught off guard by her involvement in the plan. "What am I supposed to do? I don't know anything."

"It's nothing to worry about," Akimbo assured. "I'll introduce you. That's it. Nothing to it. This is just to set bigger things in motion."

Wobbegong didn't know what to make of Akimbo's disclosure. Following the afternoon class, she caught up with Sha'nona, explained how she was being pulled into a scheme with that lady Jan from her phone, and sought advice.

"Jan Nurb is coming here to meet you?" Sha'nona questioned.

"That's what she said."

"Wow, that's unbelievable. *Jan Nurb?* She's, like, mega rich."

"Akimbo wants money for it," Wobbegong added.

"Really? How much do you get? What's your cut?"

"Nothing? She didn't say anything about that."

"That's not right," Sha'nona declared. "You deserve something. You're the feature attraction."

"I'm not going to argue with Akimbo."

Sha'nona agreed that approaching Akimbo was risky. "How about we ask for our own payment? I mean payment for you—I'm just here to help."

"Can I do that?"

"It can't hurt to try. You've got the phone, after all." Sha'nona grew excited. "What do you want? Jan can get you practically anything. No, hold on! I know exactly what you want. I saw this picture of an actress wearing super-cool sunglasses and they would look amazing on you. Let me see your phone." She found the picture and showed it to Wobbegong. "Designer, luxury expensive, we'd be styling!"

"Sure. Okay."

Sha'nona pasted the picture into a message to Jan and added: *Bring two pairs of these sunglasses or you will PO the emperor of space.*

Days later, Sha'nona appeared at the house as Wobbegong situated Clagett on the back porch with his coffee. Wobbegong, unlike Clagett, anticipated her arrival. The two young women dove headlong into selecting a color palette for Wobbegong's nails, followed by the actual application of the nails, followed by a spell of admiration.

"Let's see what we can do with your toenails." Sha'nona watched eagerly while Wobbegong undressed a foot. "Yikes!" Sha'nona screeched. "Tell you what…Closed toe is the fashion move for you."

Clagett by no means had a foot kink, but he did feel inappropriately interested as he tried, and failed, to glimpse the nude foot.

Sha'nona numbly shuffled her way to Clagett, eyebrows pinched together as if one brow, neck muscles taut, muttering, "She's *not* like the other girls."

Sha'nona filed the corners of his toes in silence as she processed. He politely asked if she had progressed with her plan to study mortuary science, and she acted as if she had never heard such a lame idea. "I'm joining the military," she scoffed. "I'll be an MP so I can become a homicide detective when I get out."

He nodded supportively. "Homicide. Nice."

She expressed concern for his big toes and took him to task for letting them carry the weight of his nighttime bedding. She called over Wobbegong to examine the redness and instructed her to add a support pillow under the bed covers to alleviate pressure on his toes. Her explanation seemed straightforward to Clagett, but Wobbegong struggled with the message.

"His foot is sensitive here, at the corner where the nail meets the skin," Sha'nona patiently explained. Her willingness to discuss feet appeared to signal she was open to anatomical diversity in their friendship.

Without his approval, the two women disappeared to the living room and he heard Sha'nona climb into his bed. From what he could suss listening to their laughter and the hum of the bed's motors, Wobbegong gave Sha'nona a ride on his hospital bed and demonstrated the extreme positions it afforded.

When they tired of playing with the bed, Sha'nona realigned them to her mission and they devised a toe support structure out of two rolled-up sweatshirts, as he came to learn at bedtime.

On one of her passes through the house, Akimbo made a point to tell the women that their food had arrived while they were busy doing nails. She had put the bag on the kitchen counter.

"I ordered it for us," Sha'nona explained. She glanced sweetly at Wobbegong.

"Well, the food sure isn't mine," Akimbo shot back. She was strictly against food delivery—carbon emissions to satisfy one person's appetite, and all that. She was against plastic packaging. She was against marketing cheap, unhealthy food at people who didn't have better options.

Not catching the socio-economic angle to Akimbo's answer, they were left with the impression that Akimbo was disgusted by their food, which she didn't mean to imply, though she was.

The mention of food brought on a rush to the kitchen and hasty preparation of Clagett's lunch. They excitedly pulled items from the delivery bag and tore through the wrappers like children at Christmas. Over burritos, chips, drinks, and brownies, the women began a running repartee over the latest Space Hotel text messages delivered to Wobbegong's phone. Feeding Clagett was assigned a low priority. So enthralled were they by text messages, Wobbegong fed him his leftover sandwich at a pace agreeable to breaks in their conversation.

NASA pestered her with messages about a technology-exchange program and intimated they had boatloads of government money to offer as their part of the exchange.

Send cash now! Sha'nona replied.

The joint military communications officer questioned whether the Space Hotel was a foreign threat and, as such, wanted them to weigh in on their intentions before nukes were launched in either direction, but especially in the direction of Earth, unless they targeted, for the sake of argument, North Korea.

"I have no idea what all those words mean," Sha'nona said. "Don't they speak emoji?"

They replied with a peace-fingers emoji to emphasize their war-is-bad position to the war mongrels—their words.

Jan, to their delight, had received their previous message and simply replied: *Looking forward to meeting you this evening, Space Emperor.*

Likewise, Sha'nona responded. *Don't forget the gifts.*

Distracted as she was, Wobbegong occasionally bypassed Clagett entirely with the fork and fed herself. After the first time, he requested a clean utensil, after the second he knew better than to interrupt and face the repercussions.

They vindictively turned their attention to his sandwich, a Reuben, and discussed the noxious ingredients. The sauerkraut was aptly judged as "coleslaw from Planet Hell." The meat, a delightfully tender fat-marbled pastrami, was guessed to have come from a pig judging by "…an odor so foul that I can smell the way it was killed," according to Wobbegong.

"Some people eat every part of the pig, right down to the hooves," Sha'nona said and made a gagging face. Sha'nona lowered herself to Wobbegong's level and they formed a tag-team alliance to better mock him.

"Do you eat lobsters? They're just bugs. Scavenger bugs. Bottom-feeders," Wobbegong chimed in.

He smiled as he chewed, as if to laugh along with their jests. He loved lobster tails and pork belly and other parts of their bodies too.

"Squid. Do you eat squid?" Wobbegong asked. She grinned, insinuating that she knew he did and was already revolted.

Until seeing a news report that pig rectum was sometimes sold as a cheap substitute for squid, in fact, he *had* squeamishly tolerated calamari. He admired the capitalist creativity of upselling flesh even more loathsome than squid as loathsome squid, but his support stopped short of eating it.

What he refused to eat was fast-food burritos or any recombination of ingredients disguised by a tortilla layer, like their lunch, which the women had stuffed into their gullets without so much as pausing to taste the regret.

"It's pastrami—seasoned beef," he said, returning to their question about pigs. "Have you tried beef?"

The two women looked at one another and seemed to agree the answer was "Duh!" which Wobbegong finally verbalized. He appreciated her succinct response. Ask an adult human about food and you get a medical/medicinal/lifestyle screed revealing of a pathological need to bare their digestive peculiarities. *Duh!* had real conversation-stopping firepower.

———————————

Sha'nona changed into her uniform and joined Akimbo for the afternoon's class. Clagett assumed his window position to watch the students arrive and depart. Wobbegong was effectively chained to an outlet in the kitchen, looking still at her phone as it recharged.

A straggler SUV showed up well after class started and parked dead in front of the house. A professionally attired middle-aged woman climbed out with her purse held in a white-knuckle grip. She drank in the surroundings, coming to terms with the manner of backwoods cesspool in which she found herself. Gnats swarmed around her head. She whipped off her sunglasses and clawed at the bugs in her eyes.

With tears streaming down her face, she stalked to a waiting carpool parent, the divorced husband who got stoned as soon as the kids' car doors closed. He pointed the woman to the barn. As she walked off, he shook his head in disbelief.

"Wobbee!" Clagett clamored. Wobbegong was spurred to look in on him because of the urgency in his offensive infantilization of her name. He didn't need anything but company; the events needed witnesses.

The woman yelled through the open barn door rather than set foot in unknown territory. Shortly thereafter, Akimbo appeared outside, naginata in hand. The woman began to express herself passionately, seemingly unflustered by Akimbo's attire and weapon.

"As I live and breathe, that's Jan Nurb standing in my yard," Clagett swore.

Akimbo emerged from the barn decked out in her fighting regalia, from helmet down to shin guards. Waiting impatiently for her was a well-appointed stranger, who Akimbo quickly recognized as none other than Jan Nurb.

Jan began a self-introduction that amounted to a testimonial of her greatness and godlike business acumen that none could surpass. She spoke boldly as if she was operating under the misguided notion that she was introducing herself to a royal court.

Akimbo listened, keenly aware that *the Jan Nurb* was being watched by students, parents, and her husband alike. She had half a mind to whack Jan in the noggin and be done with her arrogance, but suppressed that instinct to teach the way of peace, as wordy as it might be.

Jan's delivery sounded overwrought, a bit community-theater Shakespearian, and Akimbo felt certain her staff had prepared her introduction. She waited politely for Jan to wind down so she could introduce herself, but Jan continued to spout accolades, culminating with the shout, "I offer tokens of peace!" With that, she made an aggressive reach toward her purse.

The oddity of Jan's public display had put Akimbo on edge, which triggered a violent reaction when Jan made a sudden move. She sharply rapped Jan on the ear, used the naginata's bamboo tip to snag a purse strap, and lifted it out of reach. The purse slid down the weapon's haft into the hands of Akimbo. She peeked inside the purse and saw a handgun with the clip sitting next to it. Not wanting to alarm everyone, she closed the purse without remark.

Her students thundered out of the barn amid squawks as the chickens fled the scene. They formed a kill box around Jan and posed threateningly. Akimbo had never been prouder.

Carpool dad cheered for his daughter to "Get some!"

Akimbo pulled off her helmet and gloves. She wiped her face with her sleeve and puzzled over Jan, who rubbed her ear and winced in pain. Akimbo had no memory of striking her there, but since she had just contemplated a noggin whacking, she assumed she had.

"Sorry, I should have introduced myself sooner. I'm Akimbo," she said, breaking the moment's tension. "We spoke on the phone. We weren't expecting you until this evening."

"I came early to evade your ambush," she said. "By the way, my ear is fine, thanks for your concern. I anticipated this meeting would be unusual, but I never imagined getting conked on the head with a stick."

"It's a naginata," Akimbo said.

"Is that like a low-end lightsaber?"

"It's Japanese."

"Whatever you say. Listen, can I have my purse back? I brought the peace offerings for the space emperor. There's two pairs of sunglasses in there, in those velour cases. Nice choice, too, he or she or they or it has taste."

Akimbo pulled out the two cloth bags and checked that they held sunglasses.

Sha'nona, who stood nearby guarding Akimbo, stepped

forward and relieved her of the glasses. She bowed to Jan and said, "The emperor is most pleased."

"There's some weird shit going on here," Jan observed.

Akimbo agreed, saying, "You don't know the half of it."

"I have the feeling I've been pranked out of expensive sunglasses after making an ass of myself with an overblown introduction. By the look of things, there's no emperor here. My PR team said to impress them. Were you impressed?"

"Oh yes. Very memorable," Akimbo promised. She waved at the window to let Clagett know she was fine. She knew he sat worrying for her.

"Staking out the high ground with a sniper? Am I already painted with a laser? Was that the kill shot signal?"

"No. Why would you think that?"

"Because that's where my security people are stationed," she said, as if stating the obvious. "This is one of those nut-job UFO compounds, isn't it? Like the FBI burns down. What kind of cult do you have going on here?"

"Satanic," Akimbo couldn't resist saying. Her students murmured with excitement at the revelation. "I'm joking," she added for the benefit of the few parents. "It's strictly atheistic." Akimbo told her class to go back inside and she would join them shortly. "Let's talk in private," she said. She strolled toward Jan's SUV and Jan followed. She removed the ammo clip and tucked it inside her gi before passing the purse back to Jan. "Don't ever come here with a gun. I'll poke your eye out next time."

Jan apologized for the firearm but insisted it was for personal protection. Her security detail was concerned about her walking into a nest of aliens and their fanatical worshipers. She wasn't aware there were children on the premises.

"I don't really have snipers on the high ground. I came alone. You can't imagine how tiresome it is to be married to a security detail. Zero privacy. I'd never hear the end of it if this alien thing is a put-on. They love busting my chops."

"It's for real."

"We'll see," Jan said. "Where's your husband? I have a package for him. It's the food thickener he ordered this morning, not our top-rated brand and a little pricier too."

"He's inside with his caregiver. I'm sure he's confused by the spectacle of your early arrival."

"Caregiver?" Jan asked respectfully. "Is he ill?"

"Why? Are you looking for a wound to salt?"

"No. I just got through a stint with caregivers. My mother. Parkinson's. Nine years. Now my father is starting to go." Jan studied clouds in the distance.

"Oh, I'm so sorry."

"Your husband, his name is Clagett, isn't it?"

"Yes, Clagett. He has ALS."

"Brutal. Illness explains the strange vibe permeating this place. I should have recognized it sooner. My order analysis team wrongly figured that more fiber in his diet would straighten him out."

"Brutal. Yeah."

"Make sure you take good care of yourself. Don't go down with the ship. How are the caregivers working out?"

"Not great. They're…difficult. Not uplifting."

"That's tough. We went through a lot of caregivers for Mom. Eventually we found a few she would tolerate, and then I paid an arm and a leg to keep them. Even when you're incredibly rich, that stings. I did right by her. I guess that means something. To someone."

Akimbo felt the need to clear the air. "I'm sorry I called you the *b* word on the phone the other day."

"You're not wrong. I'm somewhere between the *b* word and the *c* word, a *B minus* you could say. I'll put a stop to your husband's package mishandling. I'm certain you don't deserve that hassle on top of everything else you're dealing with."

Akimbo thanked her for that consideration.

"Please take what I'm about to say as a sign of respect," Jan said. "You're one scary badass."

"That's generous of you. Thank you."

"I tell you what," Jan said. "I'll skip out of here and return later, like I was supposed to. I'm eager to meet your alien, but I ought to be polite about it."

"I'm running behind on preparations," Akimbo said. "Would you mind bringing a few bottles of wine and some noshes? The emperor will be most grateful for a peace offering."

"You're messing with me, I see that now," Jan said. "But yes, I'll bring food and drinks."

18

WHEN SHE RETURNED TO the farm that evening, Jan sought out Clagett and apologized for messing with his shipments. At the same time, she more or less suggested Clagett deserved it because of his environmentally unconscious ordering habits.

"I can't imagine what you're going through, but remember the earth is suffering too," she admonished.

Clagett was unsure how to respond to criticism from an unrepentant mogul. Caution seemed prudent, so he told her, "That's okay," even though it wasn't.

Jan's use of the expression *I can't imagine what you're going through, but…* annoyed him. He had heard that qualifying comment many times, often before well-intended advice on how he might better cope. Contrary to her statement, he believed physical disability for the most part *could* be imagined. In fact, in many instances disability can be experienced. Want to know why a parent won't cooperate with caregivers? Submit to their care. Want to know what end-stage ALS is like? Don't move. Breathe through a straw. By his reckoning, her actual meaning was: *I could imagine or experience your situation but choose not to because it must really suck.* He didn't appreciate the reminder.

Geldine, Langford, and Jan arrayed themselves around the dinner table while Akimbo fetched glassware. Clagett had parked his wheelchair at the roomy end of the table, and Wobbegong moved toward a chair near him. She wore her new sunglasses, which did look killer, but they also impaired her vision. She groped her way around, moving so painfully slow that the crowd went silent to fully appreciate her performance.

Jan kept her eyes on Wobbegong, clearly deciding she was the alien among them. She kept her suspicions to herself, either out of politeness or because the table of eccentrics left room for uncertainty.

"So you're the famous lady," Geldine said to Jan.

Jan glanced at the others, feigning surprise to find herself at the center of attention. "I'm sorry about my behavior earlier," she said. "I try to make a point of not looking foolish."

"You brought a much-needed diversion to the day." Akimbo placed bottles of beer and wine and assorted glasses on the table. The wine had barely touched the table before Jan snatched up a bottle and filled a glass.

"It's been a rough week, on top of coming all the way here," Jan let escape with a sigh. She continued with the confidence of someone accustomed to rapt audiences: "My brother came to help sort through our mother's belongings—she passed away last year—but he sits around nagging our father without lifting a finger to actually help. His complaints seem personal, like he's intentionally driving me nuts."

"That's family for you," Geldine assessed.

"Is your father in good health?" Akimbo asked politely.

"He's gone downhill without my mother around—mainly vision issues. His right eye is in a coma and it dreams all the time. It's one of those rare disease syndromes that insurance companies don't believe in. He gets disoriented, as you can imagine.

"We have caregivers arranged...but he's so obstinate

and unpleasant they may not last long. My mother was docile with her caregivers, an angel. He's either withdrawn and uncooperative or angry and overly instructive. I just don't understand what's going on in his head. He *needs* the help."

"I've seen this a thousand times when people don't want to let go of control," Geldine said. "He'll get used to it if you give him time and apply pressure. That's how diamonds do it. That might sound insensitive because it is."

"But it's the truth," Langford contributed.

"Amen," Geldine said.

Clagett had noticed that his presence sometimes triggered a spontaneous support group, as if looking at the statuary ravages of ALS felt uncomfortably intimate, obliging people to reciprocate with personal stories. Consequently, Jan's story of family hardship did not come as a surprise. That the entire story led up to the easily solvable mystery of why her father was not graciously accepting care...now that irked him.

"How are *you* adapting to caregivers?" Jan clearly addressed her question across the table to Akimbo, intently looking past Clagett to do so. "I've been down this road before, so I have an idea what to expect. Are they working out?"

"Um—" Clagett cleared his throat, and Akimbo reacted like it was a lead-in to criticism that might devalue her finder's fee.

"Yes, they tell us we are." Akimbo gestured in Wobbegong's direction. "Wobbegong here is one of a handful of caregivers who have darkened our doorstep," she said.

"It's nice to meet you," Jan said. "I love your hair! Where are you from?"

"The Care Less agency."

"Yes, but where did you grow up?"

"In a cave," Wobbegong specified.

"Just to bring you up to speed, she's from another planet," Akimbo explained. "We don't know much about it."

"So *you're* one of the aliens? Fascinating! Is it okay if I say the *a* word? You're my first other-planeted being and I have no problem with that," Jan said. "Unless you plan to eat us, ha ha!"

"Too salty," Wobbegong said.

Jan guffawed. "And you're here with the Space Hotel? What a fabulous business idea! I mean, the space tourists have to stay somewhere, am I right?" Jan looked around the table for consensus. She slid her chair closer to Wobbegong. "I have to tell you, I've been hoping for a long time that one day I would come across an alien," she confided. "You're something of a longstanding fascination to me." She studied Wobbegong intently and went so far as to reach out and tentatively stroke a finger along a stripe of black hair. "What's it like?" Jan asked with interest. "Being an alien?"

"It's just different," Wobbegong said.

Jan sustained uncomfortably long eye contact with Wobbegong's sunglasses. "You poor thing," Jan whispered. "A beautiful creature like you stuck as a caretaker."

Clagett cleared his throat. "I have a thought about understanding your father's reaction to caregivers," he said.

"Do tell." Jan smirked, annoyed to have her attention pulled from Wobbegong.

"Try it for yourself."

"Believe me, I've tried to keep him happy."

"No, I mean let someone take care of you. You seem given to reckless abandon...Get showered. It's the real litmus test if you're comparing caregivers."

"Your husband has certainly kept his sense of humor

intact!" Jan laughed and hoisted her drink in a toast to Clagett.

"I don't think he's joking," Akimbo said.

"It's impossible to tell," Wobbegong mumbled without moving her lips.

Jan caught up to the conversation. "Wait…Are you actually suggesting that I ask my father's caregivers for a shower?"

Geldine jumped in with an opinion. "There's nothing wrong with it. They give showers to women all the time. Naturally, you'd have to pay them, but that doesn't make them a ho, if that's what bothers you."

"To begin with, I don't need help bathing. I'm not comfortable getting naked in front of some chatty old ladies. I'm nearly fifty years old for God's sake."

"Nobody is going to gossip about your body," Geldine promised. "Caregivers are trained to respect your privacy unless you have something interesting like webbed toes. Or are famous."

"She once saw a birthmark like the face of Jesus," Langford said.

Clagett interrupted, "Excuse me, but I'm suggesting that a caregiver give you a shower *right now*. We have Wobbegong and Geldine here. Perhaps one of them is willing to assist. Though, to make it gender comparable to your father's experience, you should get a male caregiver. Which would have to be Langford."

"I guess I could do that," Langford said.

"Like hell," Geldine said.

Langford playacted outrage. "Why not? You give showers to *men* all the time."

"Those men are old and wrinkled and barely know what's

going on. No disrespect, Clagett," Geldine responded. "Jan here is…Well, she's taken pretty good care of herself all these years…for the most part."

All eyes swung toward Jan and appraised her looks, extrapolating what was visible to what wasn't.

"Well, maybe it's okay," Geldine concluded.

"Why does it matter what she looks like?" Wobbegong wondered aloud.

"If she's got a great rack, it might pose an irresistible seductive threat," Langford said.

"Jesus!" Jan growled. "Like I don't have a say in who my body seduces? I've never been so offended."

"That *was* a painfully male comment, Langford," Akimbo admonished.

"I meant no offense," Langford apologized. "Jan, you have—"

Geldine jabbed her palm in front of Langford's face. "Don't you dare say something about her body."

"I was going to compliment her," Langford said.

"No."

Indignation radiated from Jan's flushed cheeks as she proclaimed, "I'm not letting a stranger bathe me. That's not why I'm here."

"Thinking about showering seems to have upset you." Clagett panted from the effort of speaking and grouped his words a few at a time. "Your father probably feels the same."

Jan scowled, unhappy to have been caught up in dialectics when there was an actual alien at the table.

"I like your thought experiment, Clagett. Very provocative," Akimbo said. "I think we see your point." Sensing that Jan wanted to get back to Wobbegong, Akimbo reached over and squeezed Clagett's thigh as if it were a handbrake to stop conversation.

"I didn't mean it as a hypothetical," he said softly, his words washed away by a conversational tide change.

"This is nice," Jan said. "To just sit around and drink and quarrel. I usually have to deal with polite, posh types."

"We're glad you feel welcome," Akimbo said.

"Forgive me for asking…No, never mind," Jan blurted, her voice trailing off to a whisper.

"What?" Akimbo asked.

"No."

"*What?*"

Jan's eyes danced around, avoiding eye contact, finally landing on Wobbegong's sunglasses. "Is it true about the rectal probes?" she spluttered.

Wobbegong looked at the ceiling and muttered, "Always they bring up probes."

"Not in my case," Geldine said.

"I don't recall it being mentioned to me. But, he threatened Clagett with an odyssey to his ileum," Akimbo said to blank expressions.

"Am I the only one who *hasn't* been abducted?" Jan asked.

Wobbegong rolled her eyes. "We don't abduct anymore," she said.

Jan said loudly, "What's a girl got to do to get swept off her feet around here?" The table chatter died at her outburst. She grew wistful and softly added, "I'm only joking…Unless there's a wait list or something."

Akimbo glanced at Clagett and led his eyes to Jan's empty wineglass. She had already pounded down at least two generous pours and was reaching for the bottle.

Akimbo tried to corral their guest, who seemed to be unraveling. "Tell us about your own space venture. Have you been in the spaceship?"

"Yes, let's talk about that. But, Wobbegong, I'd be willing to pay money for the real experience. When I was a kid, I was enthralled by abduction stories. I spent many a night pretending to lie helpless while strange creatures examined me. I think that's why I'm so interested in space exploration. My therapist tells me to confront these childhood obsessions, for my mental health, which is healthy I'm happy to say."

"I don't know," Wobbegong said. "Like I told you, we don't abduct anymore."

"Could you recommend me to your boss? I want to talk business, but, as you can tell, this is also a personal journey."

Wobbegong shrugged.

"What's the big picture here, Jan?" Langford asked. "Where's the money in this for you?" He cut straight to his area of interest.

"Well, I see many possibilities. Here's one, since we're talking about it...Imagine wealthy people who pay a small fortune to risk their lives climbing Everest or diving to the *Titanic* or flying into space. These are people for whom lavish vacations are no longer satisfying. You know the type, right? I give them...*The Abduction Experience*!"

"Why don't they cure a disease or something instead?" Clagett asked.

"Where's the risk, the adventure in that? What's their motivation?" Jan responded. "I mean, *I* get philanthropy."

"Why would people pay money to be abducted? We used to do it for free." Wobbegong couldn't wrap her head around the idea. "Maybe I'll mention it to Ariola. I doubt she'll be interested."

Jan was crestfallen. "I would pay a lot. Corporate expense, you know." She slugged back the dregs of her wineglass.

When the bottles emptied, Geldine and Langford headed home. Jan sought out the couch and made herself comfortable, knowing she shouldn't drive.

Clagett wanted to be put in bed, but Wobbegong had disappeared. Akimbo called for her and looked around the house. Noticing the bathroom door was closed, she gave it a gentle knock. She heard a guttural response and cracked the door to peek inside.

"I knew you'd come!" Wobbegong gushed. She sat on the toilet lid, elbows braced on her knees, looking unsteady. "You're my hero. My angel!"

Her intonation was sloppy and her lips were working to a different script than her gills. Akimbo had been caught up in the discussion with Jan and hadn't monitored what Wobbegong drank. She felt *too much alcohol* was a safe guess.

"I need to tell you something." Wobbegong was wild-eyed.

"What now?"

"It's very important."

"What?"

"I shouldn't tell you." She crossed her arms over her gills so she couldn't be compelled to talk.

"What!" Akimbo asked impatiently.

"The Space Hotel is returning home."

"How soon?"

"Days, they say."

Akimbo's mind raced to decide whether their leaving was good or bad. Her aim was to change agencies anyway, so that was good; but she didn't have a replacement lined up yet, so that was bad. Clearly, her well-meant resolve to solve their problems had failed to crystallize into a better understanding of their options—to say nothing of crystallizing into a well-conceived plan. In her sporadic free time, she worked to *forget* about their problems, which, come to think of it, was regrettably shortsighted.

She slowed her breathing and relaxed her shoulders. More than anything she wanted to be alone, released from the madness in which she was mired.

"I don't want to leave you without care for..." Wobbegong's voice trailed off.

"Clagett."

"Right, for Clagett. We've gotten to know each other so well and I'm sure he'll be hurt when I leave. That's why I've decided to stay on Earth and live with you. It's just all so perfect. You have extra bedrooms and won't charge me rent and I can take care of...your husband three days or maybe two days—at least one day—a week and Sha'nona will visit me and sometimes spend the night."

"Wait! Hold on," Akimbo demanded. "You can't just dump this stuff on me!" The situation was unbearable. She turned her back to Wobbegong, tilted back her head, and let out a silent howl.

"I told Ariola to leave me behind!" Wobbegong slurred. "I'll be like a daughter to you."

"Let's get out of the bathroom for now. We can discuss this tomorrow. I can't take all this in at the moment."

"I don't want to get rebirthed! Please! Let me stay!" She went to her knees and then toppled sideways into a sloppy-drunk fetal position. "I want to get old. Please..." she pleaded through sobbing jags. "Sha'nona!" she cried out.

"Not now!" Akimbo insisted. She fled upstairs to her sanctuary and flopped on the bed, burying her face in a pillow.

Ariola's banging on the front door was Clagett's first indication that the space van repairs were complete. "It's me, Ariola!" she hacked through phlegm to announce herself.

Clagett yelled, as best he could, to come in. He was reclined, waiting for someone to help him into bed, listening to Jan's drunken murmurs and Wobbegong's mewls. Wherever Akimbo had escaped to, he wished he was there with her.

"Where's Wobbegong?" Ariola said brusquely. "I'm in something of a hurry."

"Are we back on schedule?" he asked.

Ariola ignored him and frantically swiveled her head, looking for her lost lamb. "What have you done with her? How do you explain her text message?"

Clagett didn't know what she was on about. He was in a place beyond explanations, a thoughtful place where his wine played especially well with his other medications. Explanations seemed like an outdated, passé, inadequate notion. Things just *were*, he thought.

"Check the bathroom there," he said. "I've been hearing noises in that direction."

Which is how Ariola came to find Wobbegong lying on the floor, sobbing.

"I won't go!" she cried out as Ariola pulled her upright. "Help me! Help me!"

"I am helping you, what do you think I'm doing, you poor girl?" Ariola glared at Clagett. "What did you do to her?" she accused. "What kind of creatures are you?"

"I admit this looks bad, but it's not what you think. Not that *I* pretend to know what *you* think. I guess my point is, can Wobbegong get me in bed before you take her, and will she be back tomorrow?"

"She's in no condition to help you!"

"That's never stopped her from trying." He laughed. "Little joke. Poorly timed."

Jan came stumbling out of the living room. She couldn't help but overhear the exchange and reasoned that Ariola was taking Wobbegong back to the Space Hotel.

"Take me with you!" Jan spluttered. "Please, take me to your leader! Abduct me!" she pleaded.

Ariola recoiled. "Who are you?"

"It's me! Jan! *Jan Nurb!*"

"I'm tired and I'm running behind, if you don't mind," Ariola wheezed from her gills.

"I could be valuable to you. I know stuff. Lots of stuff about business and trade and money! Contacts! Interrogate me, please. I'll spill everything." Jan brimmed with excitement as she argued to be taken captive.

"I'll mention you to my boss, but that's the most I can do." Ariola supported Wobbegong out the front. Jan desperately trailed them, begging to go along. Clagett trailed Jan and watched from the porch.

"Let me meet your boss. I promise he'll want me!" Jan shouted as they teetered toward the van. Ariola tried to shoo her away as if she were a pestering insect.

Akimbo, at some point, had come downstairs to see the show. She stood behind Clagett, framed by the doorway, watching with detachment. "Show her your sternum!" she shouted.

Jan looked back to make sure she heard correctly. Akimbo imitated Superman ripping open his Clark Kent civvies. So desperate was Jan, and so confused was she by

Akimbo's shouts, she ripped open her shirt and undergarments to display her bare chest.

Akimbo was right, that did the trick. Jan clambered into the back of the van and helped Ariola sprawl Wobbegong on the floor. Ariola sealed them both inside.

"She went overboard with the exposure, but good for her," Akimbo declared.

"Yeah, a shame about the exposure." Clagett looked forward to telling Langford he'd been right about the persuasive power of Jan's rack. "I have to say, Jan has a bad case of the poor impulse control."

"To say the least," Akimbo agreed. "Should we have tried to stop her?"

"This is what she wanted—risk and adventure. Plus some kinky stuff, too, but to each their own. Besides, no finder's fee unless she makes a deal."

"That's where I worry my judgment is clouded."

"What's the worst that can happen?" Clagett asked, in an effort to reassure Akimbo.

"Jan Nurb disappears from our property and we explain to the FBI that aliens abducted her."

Clagett thought that over. "She's tough. I'm sure she'll be fine."

19

ADNOYDD GLUMLY WAITED FOR Ariola. She had called ahead on her return trip to say she had a surprise for him, said it would make him happy. Fat chance. He scraped frost from the interrogation room window to better see a crescent of Earth. *What a shit hole,* he thought. *What a place to flush away a career.*

Make them slaves, they said, colonize them, prey on the weak. High-minded sentiments he agreed with, to be sure, but *they* weren't the boots on the ground swatting away black flies and gnats, struggling for breath, fearing bullets both intended and stray. They might as well have ordered his crew to colonize the gnats and squeeze them of their riches—same level of difficulty, same outcome.

They were the high muckety-mucks who dreamed of space expeditions. They drooled at the idea of extraterrestrial income, mooned over the pricey space vessels at the dealership. *He* had no influence, making him a perfect scapegoat for the whole Earth fiasco.

They promoted him before sending them off on this run at caregiving. Caregiving! *Genius idea you've got there, Director,* they said, probably winking behind his back. They foresaw the need for an officer to take the fall, whereas he was blinded by prestige.

He had time before he reached the age of mandatory rebirth, time he had planned to spend at home. They'd probably take it all away, claim he broke a leg—or maybe they'd break his leg—and say rebirth was the only thing for it. Which begged the question: Why return? To escape Earth, that's why. Staying here was the proverbial fate worse than death.

One thing was for certain: he wasn't going down alone. He'd see to Geldine, with her pipe-dream visions of money trees as far as the eye could see. She was a clever saboteur—not classically clever and certainly not up to the standards of cleverness of his kind, but he'd give her credit for unwitting cleverness. She had misdirected their exploitation plans, he could see that now. What had Geldine promised? Borrow money to make money, money would tell him how to get it home, money was its own answer, or some such nonsense.

If he learned one lesson on Earth, it was this: their money was worthless. Chasing after money was like earning a salary in hell; no amount made the agony worthwhile.

Ariola shoved a human into the room. She left, saying, "This is Jan, have fun," on her way out the door.

Jan took a few wobbly, unsure steps forward. She clutched at her blouse, but he caught a glimpse of thorax with tan lines teasing the edges. His day might yet finish on a high note.

"And who might you be?" he asked.

"Hi, I'm Jan Nurb, and I would just like to say that it's an absolute thrill to be here. I'm loving the decor, your whole retro-future vibe is really working for me. If I may, I was a little disappointed that my 'abduction,' if you can even call it that, was more voluntary than I imagined. I really think a more physical approach—assertive, not abusive—was more what I had in mind. This has been a dream of mine for a long time, and I want every last detail perfect. I've been a deserving candidate since childhood, so I do wonder what took you so long—not that I'm complaining, the buildup has been stellar and now I'm all atingle for my interrogation. Listen to me! What a terrible guest I am, not letting you get a word in edgewise. Okay, enough about me. Go ahead, do your thing."

Adnoydd heard the unmistakably arrogant undertones of an old-school crackpot.

It was late, and his mission was a failure; he felt faint stirrings to strap her down like the old days, but he couldn't summon the mojo to bother.

"I'm sorry, I'm just not in the mood to interrogate right now. It's been a difficult week. We're heading home soon and I've been occupied with provisions and whatnot. Going home stirs up such mixed emotions, you know." He looked to her for commiseration. "I'll get to push the deadwood out the airlock soon, so I'm looking forward to that."

"You have to focus on the little things. I enjoy a good employee purge myself," Jan sympathized. "But I have to say, I'm disappointed you don't want to question me. I was planning to stay silent until you applied enough pressure and then I was going to spill the beans on business ideas for intergalactic banking and trade. I'm all about creating marketplace infrastructure. You can't imagine all the cheap, pointless crap Earthlings could consume. You'll have to work hard to get all the details out. I won't make it easy for you."

"I do appreciate your offer. Perhaps we can resume tomorrow when we're fresh? We can offer you a suite or you can make yourself uncomfortable here. The exam table is cold metal. I don't recommend it even for a short nap."

Jan sat on the exam table and turned on the interrogation lamp. "I'll just wait here," she said.

Her attitude cheered him—he enjoyed the prospect of

someone else's misery…which gave him pause. He found Ariola in her quarters and gave instructions for the next morning.

"You know the fellow on the farm? We need to send a message that Wobbegong's treatment was unacceptable. Let's give him a little parting gift. Tomorrow, send him Goostapher."

She gasped.

"It's time for the rough stuff."

———————————

Akimbo paced the hallway, fuming that no caregiver showed up. She unsuccessfully tried to reach Ariola for an update. She called Geldine, but she was working until the afternoon.

Clagett cajoled her into bringing him food and coffee, but remained in bed, listening to the outbursts of frustration echoing around the house, sometimes from the direction of the barn, where the livestock suffered along with him and Akimbo.

A few hours later, a new caregiver knocked on the door. Judging by the pace he moved and his struggle to draw a breath, his lateness could almost be explained by the time he took to mount the front steps and cross the porch. He said his name was Goostapher.

Funny story, Goostapher had worked a shift the night prior and was getting off work when Ariola called. She described how to catch a bus into town and then take a taxi out to the farm. He misremembered the bus number and sat at the stop for at least an hour.

"Was anyone there, where you waited?" Clagett asked him. "Anyone you could have asked about the bus?"

"People came and went all the time. Busy place," he said.

His voice was difficult to understand because of his labored breathing, his accent, and the gelatinous layer of mucoid slime that leaked from his gills, wetting the front of his scrubs.

He didn't cotton well to Clagett's implication of incompetence and he shifted from defensive to indignant. "I asked a woman for her phone number," he said, implying that by some stretch the number related to bus schedules. "She was carrying some weight, do you know what I'm saying? Thick. She said, 'Fuck off, buddy.' What else was I supposed to do?"

Akimbo watched the interaction from the hallway and looked ready to throw her bran muffin at Goostapher, which was more of a threat than you would expect from a muffin. Clagett was known to refer to them as brick bread when quietly warning house guests off their dental and digestive dangers.

"Maybe check you have the right bus number?" Akimbo suggested. "There's only, like, five buses in the whole county. Or call us? Call anybody?"

"The buses all look the same!" He threw up his arms, insulted she questioned his actions.

"Except for the bus numbers, I imagine," Akimbo said.

In all likelihood, Clagett's care wouldn't have gone any smoother if Akimbo had withheld her last comment, but it seemed possible Goostapher's patronizing attitude toward women would have been less on display.

As it were, Goostapher groused that he didn't need Akimbo's help or Clagett's training tips to give a shower. "I know a man's body better than any woman would," he declared. While technically true, his opinion ignored the detail that he was accustomed to interacting with men's bodies, and his own, with a rough-and-tumble disregard for comfort, as would come to light.

Goostapher took swiping blows at Clagett's body with the washcloth to demonstrate how little cleanliness mattered to men, which was largely accurate, but Clagett had grown accustomed to comprehensive showers and wouldn't stand for slapdash.

"Scrub under my arms, please," Clagett asked after the swipes had connected with his chest in a few random spots and then moved on to his thigh.

Goostapher jammed his soapy fingers into an armpit and jackhammered them forward and back a few times as if he were removing plaster from a brick wall.

"The other arm too," Clagett said. "And could you lift my arm first? And could you use the washcloth? Gently?"

"Beauty is pain," Goostapher counseled, persisting with impetuous sighs and forceful scrubbing.

In a mockery of contrition, Goostapher turned solicitous, asking repeatedly if Clagett was comfortable. Goostapher grinned with each question, making sport of Clagett's delicacy. Unfortunately, Clagett was *not* comfortable and he used the questions as an opportunity to present instructions, to which Goostapher took offense and became aggressively impatient, which, in turn, made Clagett's instructions more frequent and more uncompromising.

Faced with these mounting irritations in the heat of the shower, Goostapher sweated profusely. Drops of perspiration rolled off his face and onto his shirt, where they collected above the shelf of his paunch. Each wheezy exhale of his laboring gills blew a spray of sweat over Clagett, who kept his eyes clenched and tried to rein in his disgust.

Afterward, Goostapher hoisted him out of the shower

chair and moved him to the bed with all the tenderness a mechanic shows a blown engine as it is extracted from a car. He applied lotion with brisk inefficiency, leaving some areas untouched and others nearly bruised.

Once Clagett was buckled into his wheelchair, Goostapher plopped onto the shower chair and mopped at his face with a cold washcloth.

"Are you okay there?" Clagett asked Goostapher. Any answer would have been fine. *No* more so than *yes*.

"I just need to cool down," he said. "You make the shower too hot." He struggled through the explanation with rapid panting and gave up on lip-synching entirely.

"You're not going to have a heart attack, are you? I'm lousy at CPR."

"I'm fine. There's nothing wrong with me."

He polished the sweat off of his nose and talked about all the women he bedded during his time on board. (Thirteen in thirteen days was his streak, and boy was he tired!) He felt it important to inform Clagett that a strain of men on his planet had enormous stalks that dragged the ground when they squatted, though he made no claim to be related. He did not elaborate on what he meant by *stalks* or why men squatted without clothing on.

His stories seemed designed to assure Clagett that he was attracted to women—and women were even more so attracted to him. He acted apologetic for being unavailable, as if he believed that Clagett was irresistibly drawn to him too. With his overbearing masculinity established, he meandered the short distance to the kitchen, steadying himself with a hand sliding along the wall. He abruptly collapsed onto a kitchen chair to again catch his breath. Clagett parked close by, eager for lunch.

Goostapher stood up and staggered to the kitchen counter, keeping balance first with a hand on the table and then with a grip on Clagett's headrest.

"My belly hurts," he said. "Did you do this to me?"

Vastly misreading the situation, Clagett needled Goostapher, "I'm thinking out loud, but you look about ready for rebirth. You must be excited!" Clagett smiled.

"I'll be fine. I ignore pain," he said with bravado, his last words before he collapsed.

———————————+————

Goostapher leaned against the kitchen counter, vomited into the sink, rolled his eyes upward, and collapsed. Prostrate on the floor, he moaned softly, breathed shallowly, grinned through his discomfort as if this sort of thing happened all the time.

"I don't feel good," he said.

Clagett watched him out of the corner of his eye. He couldn't turn his chair for fear of running him over. "Are you okay?" he asked.

"No."

"You want me to call someone?"

"No. I'm okay."

"I think I ought to call someone to help you," Clagett said with insistence. "Should I call 911?"

"Ha! What would a doctor know about me?"

"What are we going to do? I can't go long without needing help."

"I'll be fine. No problem," Goostapher said, his voice pinched by a spasm of pain.

"This isn't right," Clagett declared. He eye-gaze dialed Akimbo.

"What's up?" she answered.

"I've got a situation. Goostapher isn't feeling well—for real, I think—and collapsed on the kitchen floor."

"Can you call Ariola?" she prompted.

"Goostapher doesn't want me to call anyone. He's confused."

"Confused is a good reason to call someone, as if his lying on the floor wasn't reason enough. Call Ariola. I'll get there when I'm done with my groceries."

She disconnected.

———————————————

Clagett managed to reach Ariola somewhere in the ozone layer, making her return run to the mother ship. She expressed skepticism that Goostapher was completely unable to work and opted to call his bluff—to leave him on Earth to come to his senses. "Tell him he can't leave until a replacement shows up," she instructed.

"Are you bringing a replacement?" he asked.

"I'll try to find someone," she replied, which he understood to mean *no*. The layered deception of her lie on top of what she saw as Goostapher's lie was simply the care business in action.

He took it upon himself to call Geldine and ask for advice.

She said she was at the nursing home and had told Akimbo so earlier that morning. Irritated by the agency's unwillingness to deal with a sick caregiver, she muttered that she never should have fallen in with out-of-towners, that they weren't trustworthy and lacked commitment. Since childhood, she had mistrusted greenish animals like tobacco grasshoppers and the snakes that got into the house when the floodwaters rose.

"This is bad," Clagett whined.

"Let me call Langford," she said. "Lord knows he's got nothing better to do if he's awake."

"Langford?" Clagett asked. Geldine was already off the call, spurred to action.

He tried to soothe Goostapher with assurances that he would be fine and there was nothing to worry about. In his agitated state, Goostapher lashed out at his source of comfort and demanded to know why Clagett had done this to him. He then went silent.

Clagett sat quietly for a long while, hoping Goostapher was alive, now and again deciding he wasn't.

Langford entered the house like it was his own. Goostapher gave a well-timed moan and Langford tracked their whereabouts to the kitchen.

Clagett extended a quick nod for greeting. Langford did not.

Langford studied the Goostapher situation. "What's this then?" he asked.

"I'm fine right here," Goostapher said. "Don't worry about me. He's got some pills that helped me this morning. I'll just take one of those. I don't need help."

"My pills?" Clagett asked with disbelief.

"The little round white ones, not the green capsules, they made me dizzy."

"Who is this anyhow?" Langford asked.

"He's supposed to be taking care of me," Clagett explained.

"He's worse off than you and that's saying something," Langford commented.

"You don't need to worry about me." Goostapher chuckled. "It's not contagious. Let me put your mind at ease… I've got problems with my pump. My pressure is low."

Langford looked at Goostapher with indifference. "Uh-huh."

Clagett felt far from at ease. Contagions hadn't even occurred to him. He looked for an exit strategy, but Goostapher had him pinned against the kitchen table.

"I could use a little assistance," Goostapher said. "I need to empty my bladder."

Langford gridlocked as he processed what was being asked of him. He adopted the slack expression of a teenage male when presented with a sink full of dirty dishes. He understood the expectation, but the unwanted responsibility prevented action.

"What are you wanting me to do?" Langford asked. His tone made it clear that he didn't want to do anything.

"Grab the urinal bottle from the bathroom and help me out," Goostapher said with some urgency.

Langford's cogs slowly meshed. Where Clagett worried Langford would sooner kick Goostapher than help, Langford took the request in stride.

Langford returned with the bottle. "My daddy had one of these for all-night poker games." He chuckled, handing the urinal to Goostapher.

From the floor, Goostapher offered commentary on the mechanics and perils of each step as he self-applied the bottle. He was nonplussed to have spectators, happy even for the teachable moment. Clagett and Langford averted their eyes and pretended to be absorbed in something over their shoulders. Clagett had no interest in learning what a stalk was.

"Just hold the bottle in place so I can relax, would you?" Goostapher asked.

Langford complied. He knelt motionless, gripping the handle.

When Langford decided that Goostapher's performance

was being hampered by stage fright, he told him to relax and ran sink water for inspiration. When that failed, he tried unbearable silence. Finally, he settled into distracting conversation to while away their wait.

"You wouldn't surprise me if you died," he said. "You look like a gut-shot opossum."

"Reborn," Goostapher said with a note of panic.

"So some people say, never the ones that deserve it. It happened to my uncle, a prayerful sinner who went straight to perdition. He deserved it too. Terrible man. One foot missing, one eye blind from superglue he thought was eye drops. He was smart but partial to stupidity. Us kids called him Blackbeard."

"What happened to his foot?" Goostapher asked. Clagett was wondering the same thing.

"The doctors took it. They found the diabetes in it after the accident."

"Once I had a one-legged woman chase me down the street," Goostapher volunteered. He divulged his story in pieces separated by gulps of air, his tone rising and falling in time with his discomfort. "I drove people here and there for a while. I was supposed to pick her up. She screamed at me to park closer so she didn't have to hike to the car. I pulled up real close and then left her behind. I don't put up with disrespectful treatment from a woman."

"Uh-huh."

"The woman reported me, claiming I had driven over her foot, the fancy artificial one. She could have jumped out of the way."

"And how bad would that hurt anyway?" Langford asked knowingly.

"She put on quite the sprint. Guess that foot worked alright after all," Goostapher said.

"My wife says it's human nature to attack the people

helping them. That's a caregiver's life. Heard her say it a thousand times."

"Exactly," Goostapher agreed.

A trickle issued forth as Goostapher's attention wandered. Langford checked his grip and positioning of the urinal's spout. They lapsed into a hopeful silence until the flow quieted.

"Let's have a look," Goostapher requested.

There was a lot to be said for the shame-free attitude of a caregiver, Clagett thought. Not since childhood had he witnessed such sharing during a personal act.

Langford held the bottle for Goostapher to evaluate the dark-orange color.

"I need to be better about hydration," Goostapher acknowledged.

———

Akimbo charged into the house, found Langford holding the bottle aloft, and aborted her rush into the kitchen. "What the…?" she said.

"Ma'am," Langford said politely.

"I'm fine. Just leave me be. You won't even know I'm here," Goostapher assured through gritted teeth as he clutched his abdomen.

Langford plainly offered his assessment. "He's dying." He exited for the bathroom with urinal bottle in hand.

"I'm thirsty, that's all," Goostapher said. "Grab some water for me," he instructed Akimbo, more insistently than she cared for.

Akimbo ran tepid water into a coffee mug. Her expression and bearing quickly caught up to the circumstances. She wasn't going to put up with this shit. She handed the cup of water to Goostapher. "You're the agency's problem," she fumed.

"I just need a little time," Goostapher mumbled.

She whispered to her husband, "Are you okay for now?"

"I need to get out of here." When Langford returned, still drying his hands on the seat of his pants, Clagett begged, "Langford, I'm trapped. Can you drag him out of the way, please?"

Langford obliged by roughly grabbing Goostapher under the armpits and dragging him with an urgency befitting a burning building rescue.

"Christ, he's sweaty." Langford scrubbed his hands again, using the vegetable-designated brush for his fingernails.

Clagett and Akimbo beat a retreat from the kitchen, Langford lumbering behind them.

"Thank you for pitching in, Langford," Akimbo said.

"Anything for my friend here." He scratched Clagett on the top of his head like how people express affection to a dog. But for it feeling delightful, Clagett might have been offended. As it were, Clagett immersed himself in the role and barked softly, which mystified Akimbo and Langford, in light of the overall situation's dire qualities.

Wanting to reestablish his standing as an adult, Clagett grew serious. "I called Geldine after trying Ariola. We can't count on Ariola to send a replacement."

"Will she at least pick him up tonight?"

"Unclear."

Goostapher's cries of pain echoed through the house. They exchanged worried glances.

"I think he's getting better," Clagett said.

Akimbo snorted in laughter. Langford smiled. Goostapher moaned.

"This isn't funny. I can't take it," Akimbo declared.

"Forgive me, but there's something I need to bring up," Clagett said.

"Oh Lord, what now?" Akimbo braced herself for more bad news.

"What if his stomachache *is* something contagious? Or... what if his stomachache is, you know, like, carnivorous? Like something is gestating in his body. That could look really bad for us, for example, through the lens of history."

Langford cupped his chin in one hand and nodded with understanding, bending at the waist to put his body behind his wholehearted agreement. "Your man's got a good point," he declared. "This isn't just about doing what's best for the sick fellow. You need to think about what's best for you... and the whole world. If this were a sick animal and the vet was unavailable—off shagging away the day with that doctor's wife like he's known to do—you'd best be served by quarantining the creature."

Leaving them to provide end-of-life care to the caregiver assigned to help Clagett was a special torment foisted on them by Care Less. For that reason alone, Akimbo, for one, had no intention of helping with Goostapher and favored the idea of quarantine. Even so, she felt obligated to at least mention charity, though she didn't subscribe to it in this situation.

"You don't think we should at least *try* to take care of him?" she asked. The question was rhetorical; Clagett was in no position to take care of Goostapher, and Langford—in her view—was in no position to offer a sound answer. The question wasn't for naught; she felt righteous for having voiced it, and at the very least, it might absolve them should ever a federal prosecutor or alien inquisitor ask, *Did it even* occur *to you to come to his aid?*

"I'll take him out to your barn," Langford said. "You got an empty pen? Some sawdust or hay for bedding, in case things get messy?"

Akimbo and Clagett nodded to one another to confirm agreement with the direction events were moving.

Not wanting to slow the action or cause Akimbo alarm, Clagett refrained from mentioning that, should Goostapher's stomach contents be...alive and hungry, the goats were going to take one for the team.

"Where's your wheelbarrow?" Langford asked.

"I'll grab it." Akimbo jumped at the opportunity to get out of the house.

"I'll let Goose know what's happening," Clagett volunteered.

He parked his chair a safe distance from Goostapher's prostrate form. Gravity flattened him against the floor, like pudding held in shape by his scrubs.

"Um, hey there, you awake?"

"I'm fine. Don't tell Adnoydd, okay? I'm still young. I just need to rest."

"Sure, sure. Listen, we're going to move you out to the barn where you can...have privacy. How does that sound?"

"Fine," Goostapher whispered, his gills laboring. "Can you do one thing for me?"

"Perhaps."

"It's very important. I don't have much time left."

"What? Tell me."

"A bucket."

"A bucket?"

"A trash can, whatever. Something waterproof," he wheezed. "My stomach hurts."

Clagett spun his chair around and called, "He needs a bucket, stat!"

20

ARIOLA CAME TO ADNOYDD in a dither. Goostapher had fallen ill and was unable to carry out his duties. The client and his wife were bugging her with messages, demanding a replacement.

"How do you want to handle this?" she asked.

Adnoydd held up one finger in front of Jan, who lay face down on the exam table. "Hold on one second," he said to her. "I've got more important business to deal with."

Ariola's timing was fortuitous—he'd had enough of Jan.

"I'll just wait right here," Jan said through her gag.

In Adnoydd's estimation, Goostapher was a twat near the top of his "ballast" list, crew he planned to jettison on the trip home. He had predicted that Goostapher's twatness alone would rile up the natives, but sickness and a complete inability to discharge his duties was an unexpectedly delicious twist.

"Let's milk this. Leave him there until tomorrow," he commanded.

"Okey dokey, artichokey," she replied.

She looked expectant, wanting a kudo for her folksy turn of phrase. He didn't hand out kudos indiscriminately and certainly not without a *fuck*. He dismissed her with a flick of his fingers.

"Wait," he ordered.

She stepped back into the interrogation room.

"Tell them that I will personally retrieve Goostapher

tomorrow. Make it sound like I'm deeply concerned for him. Paint a heroic picture."

"Heroic. Got it."

"Next, tell Geldine I want to personally thank her for her service. Tell her I'm bringing her a bonus," he instructed. "Make sure she's there."

And then I'll get her! he thought with glee.

"One last thing, we'll dump this one while we're down there. She's of no use."

"At least ask for ransom," Jan said through her gag. "I'll pay a lot. I'd feel valued if you did that much for me."

"What did she say?" Adnoydd asked.

Ariola shrugged.

Jan had really put on a show with her screaming and writhing, bless her heart. He had lingered over her sternum exam, savoring the feel of each bump of cartilage, playing his tongue on her clavicle's mole. The experience was bittersweet. Sadly, the knowledge that she was probably his last…client…blocked a wholly rapturous inspection.

She asked for the probe and he told her, "I'm feeling a touch melancholy. I don't have it in me."

"At least have the courtesy to threaten me with the probe," she said. "I didn't come all this way for some half-assed experience."

She was an uncompromising freak—he liked that much about her.

He pulled a probe from the supply cabinet and waved it in front of her.

Unimpressed, she said, "That's it? That's what all the fuss is about? Do you think we could make it more…alien?"

He didn't know what to say to a question like that.

She chastised him. "When we get *The Abduction Experience* up and running, you'll need to have a handle on your mood swings. High-roller adventure seekers want genuine pain and suffering, not wussy excuses!"

After her physical, he'd sipped his drink and relaxed in his chair, barely needing to interject questions during her interrogation.

She hammered him over the head with the idea that rich people would pay to get abducted.

"Let it go!" he finally yelled at her.

To regain his trust, she took it upon herself to confess all manner of sins and to reveal corporate secrets ad nauseum. From there she circled back to big ideas of interplanetary banking and trade.

He appreciated her performance, but everything she said resonated of Geldine's lies and he refused to again be taken by empty promises. Her plans all revolved around money, and he got fed up. He gagged her. Couldn't take another word of her chatter. When Ariola showed up, he saw his escape—dump Jan back on Earth, where she belonged.

Adnoydd wouldn't miss this final visit for anything; payback was in the air—the stifling, humid, barely breathable air smothering this wretched planet.

———————————

With Goostapher installed in the barn, Akimbo and Clagett met Langford on the back porch to reassess the situation.

"Ariola finally messaged me," Akimbo said. "She said they'll take him off our hands tomorrow. She said Adnoydd himself is coming to save the day. He wants to meet with Geldine too."

"The man himself," Langford said. "Seem odd to you, him showing up?"

"I guess, except there's nothing that's not odd with them," Akimbo said.

"That's the gospel truth."

"Any mention of Jan?" Clagett asked.

"None."

"What about the Goose?" Clagett asked out of genuine concern. "Is his food still coming up? He's not pulling a full-on double-ender, is he?"

"He's lying down. The heaving has slowed. I can't speak for the other end," Langford reported. "Your goats are worked up and making a racket."

"Could we please give him something to make him 'comfortable'?" In Goostapher's suffering, Clagett felt vibrations from his own future. "Like painkillers?"

Akimbo and Clagett unconsciously looked to Langford for an answer, as if they expected him to have access to such products.

"Sorry, that isn't me," Langford apologized. "One of my relations is a hobbyist…semi-pro really. He's on track to ruin his life ahead of family expectations. I'll see if he's awake."

Langford sat on the back porch with Clagett, whiling away the afternoon in thought, talking little. Periodically Langford strolled out to check on Goostapher. He refilled his water bottle and offered him food, which was always declined.

In the early evening, an unfamiliar vehicle crept down the driveway and stopped by the sourwood trees, well short of the house. Langford was unsurprised by the arrival and strode out to greet the driver. They confabbed for a short while and made a hand-to-hand exchange.

Akimbo looked up from her weed pulling to see who had shown up. "Drug deal?" she called to Clagett.

"Strictly a delivery, I think," Clagett answered. "What's the world coming to when junkies don't have to spend their days desperately searching for a fix? I thought that was their job description."

"Killing people faster with convenience," she said.

The car peeled down the driveway, spitting gravel and dust.

Langford stopped by the barn to administer medication. When he returned to sit with Clagett, he reported that Goostapher now rested comfortably and his horrifying moans had diminished to a whisper.

"Was that car someone you know?" Clagett asked cautiously.

"My nephew."

"A twin?"

"In the flesh."

"His car?"

"No idea. He don't have a license yet. I don't get involved in my family's dark doings. I'm too old for that. Let me tell you something about that lifestyle—it's deathly stressful. Geldine's on me to mind my blood pressure."

———————————

Geldine arrived after her shift, bearing two pizza boxes. Langford updated her on the situation and gave her a glimpse inside the barn. Akimbo and Clagett waited nervously for Geldine's reality check.

"He's dying alright. Isn't nothing for it," she said, delivering the final verdict.

"But there's a chance he'll survive, right?" Clagett asked hopefully. "I mean, we know so little about them."

Geldine wasn't keen on having her judgment questioned and tersely explained, "It's the look in his eyes. There's no mistaking it."

"What do we do?" Akimbo's question carried the weight of Clagett's desperation as well. "What would you do if he were your patient?"

"Sit with him. Tell him to let go. I wouldn't promise heaven unless he was a believer in Jesus, because that would be a lie I couldn't live with. Morphine staycation... sedation helps a lot. For him, not me, though caregivers differ on that point."

"I gave him a 'sedative' earlier," Langford freely admitted with a flourish of air-quotes. "I didn't know how you'd feel, considering its source and the possibility of overdose. He asked me if I wanted painkillers heavy on the pain part or heavy on the killing part. Let's get this over with, I told him."

"The nephew?"

"Yep," Langford acceded.

"Good. We can relax. The worst that can happen is what's already happening."

Over dinner, without prompting, Langford gracefully delivered spoonfuls of pureed pizza to Clagett's lips. Langford's own table manners broke conventions of politeness but he understood spoon mechanics, for which Clagett was grateful.

Geldine and Langford lingered after dinner to provide companionship, rightly surmising that Akimbo and Clagett were unsettled by the alien dying in their barn.

Geldine expressed the turmoil they were all enduring: "It's a strange world we live in."

"Amen," said Langford.

"How did it come to this? Waiting around for a caregiver to die. It's supposed to be the other way around." Akimbo genuinely wanted a concise answer to explain it all away.

"Adnoydd is behind everything," Geldine acidly sniped.

"He'll get what he deserves. They always do," Langford promised. "There's no forgiving for what he did to you."

"What's he coming here for? To get Goostapher? I don't like it," Geldine spat out. "Ariola tells me to watch out. He thinks he can abduct me again? He's playing me for a damn fool, saying he's bringing a bonus right before they shoot home."

"At least with their leaving our problems will be over," Akimbo said, stretching positivity to absurd lengths, Clagett believed.

Clagett allowed for the possibility that *their* problems were near an end. He was certain that *his* problems were still in play.

"How about we take care of Adnoydd while the getting is good?" Langford suggested. "We'll bushwhack him and make him disappear. Problem solved."

No one wanted to second his idea—not that they disagreed, it just seemed inappropriate to be convinced of killing so easily. Agreeing also seemed like an unnecessary formality since Langford was poised to deal with Adnoydd regardless of anyone's opinion.

"I'm on board with that," Geldine said. "He gets what he gives."

"I'll take care of it. Y'all don't have to lift a finger. Especially you, Clagett," Langford offered.

"Up yours," Clagett responded.

"Sounds like another *yes*," Langford decided.

"I can agree to punishment, but does he deserve to be killed?" Akimbo squirmed.

Clagett said, "There's the matter of him participating in the abduction and flavor-extraction scheme. That's Nuremberg-level atrocity."

"I guess that's true, but I don't know the details. I'd prefer a nonlethal option," Akimbo said.

Langford smiled, showing off his tooth implant to attractive effect. "Unanimously in favor of punishment and I'll determine the severity. Good, that's settled then."

Clagett bit his tongue through the discussion but he could no longer suppress his unavoidably selfish concern. "Once they're gone...I wonder, Who will take care of me? That probably sounds petty. I mean, I know we're all struggling here."

Akimbo jumped in to reassure him. "I think it's safe to say we're all concerned about your care. You're *my* top concern. I've avoided weighing you down with details, but you know I've been discussing options with Geldine. We've come to an agreement."

Langford explained, "She...We could use steady work and mean to propose that between the two of us we could tend to your needs. I can pitch in with the farm work too. If you will have us. We can bridge you to another agency if that's what you want."

"We want to do right by you. This one here needs to associate with other than his family." Geldine jabbed her thumb toward Langford. "It's a win-win."

"And if you could be so kind, we'd prefer this were a cash-like agreement," Langford said, politely suggesting tax evasion. "Off the books, so to say."

Akimbo placed a hand over her heart. "That's generous of you both. I'm touched by your willingness to help us. We can work out payment later."

"Yes, truly generous," Clagett said with sincerity.

Miraculously, he wasn't troubled by Langford's willingness to "take care of Adnoydd" and then take care of him.

———————————————

When Clagett wheeled bedward, Langford looked to Akimbo to see if she'd like him to stay and talk. He saw otherwise. He accompanied Geldine and the two of them readied Clagett harmoniously, without competition or complaint, with Geldine offering very little by way of instructions.

From his bed, Clagett overheard a brief exchange as Geldine and Langford headed out the door. Akimbo asked Langford to return in the morning to deal with Goostapher because she didn't have the stomach for it.

"No problem," Langford said.

Clagett never imagined he would be grateful to have a "friend" for whom disposing of a dead alien was not a problem. But, having arrived at that point in his life, he couldn't imagine a better expression of friendship.

The three of them went outside and talked a while longer in conspiratorial whispers, with Clagett staying blissfully ignorant of their plan.

Akimbo couldn't tolerate sleeping upstairs, alone. She pulled blankets and pillows to the couch and cocooned herself to fend off thoughts of the barn.

"They'll both be back in the morning," Akimbo said, her only concession to keeping him informed. "You must find this upsetting to see us scramble helplessly around death. You'd think we'd be better prepared. I'm upset thinking you're upset."

"I don't like this waiting. My long goodbye must be torture for you."

"No, not at all. Just knowing you're here, in the house, brings me comfort."

"I feel the same."

Their simple expression of love overflowed with emotion. They stopped talking and cried quietly, each listening to the other. When the tears slowed and the sniffling was managed, they laughed together.

"A fucking alien dying in our barn," Clagett said.

"A *fucking* alien."

"So weird."

"I'm worried about the goats." Her face was turned toward the cushions, muffling her words. "This must be terrible for them. PTSD will probably sour their milk."

Clagett pictured the goings-on in the barn.

Gracie: Zoey, try to get his attention.

Zoey: Hey, buddy! Thirsty? Take a look at these tatas!

Gracie: First hooters, now tatas? Honestly, have some self-respect!

Zoey: I knew it would work! He opened his eyes! Hey, don't nod off. Open our gate, would you?

Goostapher: "Where am I?"

Gracie: Welcome to the gulag, comrade!

Zoey: He looks green around the gills.

Gracie: Good one!

Goostapher: "Have I been reborn?"

Zoey: Excuse us, but we're talking here! Jesus! If you're not helping with the gate, then pipe down.

Clagett promised, "The goats will be fine. They're resilient. They'll take this in stride, maybe even take pleasure in his comeuppance."

"I like your optimism."

———————————

As agreed, Langford appeared early in the morning to look in on Goostapher. Akimbo awoke to the squeak of the barn door. Clagett slept on as she pulled the blanket around her shoulders and crept around his bed.

Langford didn't spend long inside. He emerged to lean his backside against the barn, shaking his head in dismay.

Akimbo stumbled outside and headed toward him, but he waved her back to the house like he was returning a runner to first base. He shoved himself upright with a snap of his hips and made his way to Akimbo.

"Spiders," he said simply.

Akimbo had no response.

"Spiders ate him."

She mulled over his words, hoping sense would come with time. "A spider ate him? Was he still alive or dead at the time?"

He shrugged. "He's gone now, that's all there is to say about it."

"A spider?"

"Not just one. All of them. All of the spiders."

"They ate him?"

"Yes, ma'am. Trussed him up in webs and ate him. They scampered off when I went in, but their work was mostly done anyway."

"Are the goats and chickens okay?"

"Happy as can be. The spiders only had it out for that fellow. Never heard of such a thing."

"What do we do now?"

"Well, there are the remains—the hard parts and a bunch of soupy mush."

"Stop! I don't want to know."

"Not wanting to know is the sensible thing. I've field dressed plenty of animals, but I've never seen nothing to rival this. Turned my stomach at first glance. Soup, I tell you."

Akimbo put a hand over her mouth.

"I'm of a mind to let the spiders finish their work."

Akimbo nodded in agreement, hand still covering her mouth. "Let's not mention this to Adnoydd," she choked out.

Clagett woke to find Akimbo scratching his head. He heard conversation in the kitchen that sounded like Geldine and Langford.

"You'll never guess what happened to Goostapher," she said with such horrified incredulity that he wasn't inclined to even try guessing. "He was eaten!"

He was unaccustomed to beginning his morning with painfully impenetrable news. He felt consciousness make a hesitant approach and waited for its arrival.

"Eaten by *spiders*!"

Consciousness disengaged and retreated with that detail—man-eating spiders were allied with nightmares more than reality. He couldn't process a rational response to the idea that he had played a part in a barely acquainted subpar-alien-caregiver's consumption by spiders. He felt guilty for not feeling guilty, unsettled for feeling relieved that Goose's situation resolved quickly.

She tried again to engage him. "No wonder they are so scared of spiders, it's with good reason!" She latched on to the only comprehensible cause-and-effect connection in sight and, like Clagett, necessarily steered clear of interpreting Goostapher's weirdly unfortunate end.

"Are we excited because something finally makes sense or because Goose was eaten?" he ventured to ask.

"What do you *think*?"

"Something making sense. Being excited about spiders eating Goose seems in poor taste."

"Is that a joke? Let's try this again later, after you've had coffee. Geldine is going to get you ready for the big day."

———————————————

A large fellow met the space van. He said his name was Langford in a way that implied Adnoydd might know of him. He looked affable with his big smile and wave of a meaty hand. He wore boots made for shit-kicking. Adnoydd felt overdressed in the black block-heeled pumps he picked to compete in stature with Akimbo.

Ariola trundled around the van and opened the cargo door. Jan spilled out in a snit and marched toward the house, grumbling all the while about her disappointing abduction experience. Akimbo ushered her inside and disappeared from sight.

Adnoydd looked over Langford, but nothing about him jogged his memory.

Meeting a former abductee out in the wild was a recurring concern for Adnoydd. To randomly encounter someone after sharing the intimacy of an interrogation was... inappropriate. It was like "encountering your therapist at an orgy," as awkwardness was once described to him. (The original quote, "encountering your *fucking* therapist at a *fucking* orgy," was notable for its literal use of *fucking*.) He would remember a specimen of this size, but he didn't, so he ignored the man's familiarity.

"And you must be the mighty Adnoydd," the fellow said. Name recognition: part and parcel of rolling into town with superior intelligence.

"Too right," he said. "Have we met?"

"No, no. I've heard about you. From caregivers."

"You're very kind."

"You're here for Goose?"

"Goostapher, yes. But it's important I see Geldine too. Is she here?"

"They're waiting in the barn."

"In the barn?"

Langford gave him a quick rundown on the chain of decisions that landed Goostapher in the barn.

"So he was sick and you took him to the *barn* in case his illness was contagious?"

"That about sums it up."

"This is unacceptable!" Adnoydd tried to pull off energetic outrage over Goostapher's handling but was fairly sure it came across as hemorrhoidal irritability. If anything, he should thank them.

"Quarantine was his idea," Langford improvised. "He put the health of his client first."

"Enough said. On to other matters, it's important I speak with Geldine. I have something for her in the van."

"She's right this way. She's tending to the Goose."

"In the barn?" He wasn't keen on going in the barn, nor was he keen on collecting Goostapher. He was keen on collecting Geldine.

The fellow just stood there—slack jawed, bovine, dimly comprehending.

"Hello?" Adnoydd prompted.

"She's in the barn with your man." Langford turned and trudged in that direction. "She's waiting there for you."

21

AKIMBO AND CLAGETT AND Geldine peeped through the window blind, watching the space van settle onto the driveway. As promised, Adnoydd himself slid out, looking more pancaked by gravity than on his last visit—his face bunched into horizontal wrinkles, his torso compressed until his scrub's shirttail reached halfway down his thighs.

Unexpectedly, Ariola released Jan from the cargo hold. They worried Jan would get in her car and flee before settling the question of their fee, but she had other designs and joined them in the house.

"My God, do I need to use the bathroom!" she declared and proceeded without invitation down the hall.

They turned back to the window to watch Langford and Adnoydd chat. Langford, on his part, looked as relaxed as he always did. Adnoydd yanked his head around, looking furtively for who knew what. The physical difference between hulking Langford and squashed Adnoydd was so pronounced that Adnoydd was justifiably on guard.

"What did he think he was going to do?" Geldine spat out. "Ask politely if I'd go for a ride? How stupid does he think I am?"

"I don't think he thinks you're stupid," Clagett said. "He thinks he's smarter than everyone on Earth."

"If he was smart, he would've brought a gun," Geldine said.

Langford led Adnoydd to the barn as if it was the most

natural thing in the world. He called back to Ariola that they would just be a minute and said she should relax and take a load off. They slipped inside, the goats bleated, the door closed.

"What's going on?" Jan came up behind them and bobbed her head to peer out the window.

"Nothing, just keeping an eye on Adnoydd," Akimbo said smoothly.

"Watch out for yourself, Geldine," Jan counseled. "He's got it in for you, I heard him say as much."

"Ha! We'll see about that!" Geldine chortled.

They waited in silence until Langford stepped out of the barn alone and gave a subtle *okay* gesture.

"It's your turn, Geldine," Akimbo directed. She motioned Geldine out the door.

Geldine touched base with Langford by the barn, then wandered over to the space van, saying howdy to Ariola, appearing sociable. She led Ariola to a shady spot away from the van and they talked for a spell. Ariola looked shocked and then distinctly pleased by what was said. She sealed up the van and departed.

"What do you think Geldine told her?" Jan asked. Clagett was equally curious.

"She said Adnoydd defected and wasn't returning to the ship," Akimbo said. "She said he loved Earth and Earthlings more than his own kind. She also said Goostapher disappeared during the night and wouldn't be making the return voyage."

"No kidding." Jan chuckled. "Is that for real? Who's Goostapher?"

Akimbo didn't answer and Clagett followed suit. With nothing more to see outside, they appraised Jan, who looked haggard but still filled with manic energy.

"Sooo…how was the abduction?" Clagett asked.

Jan let out a sigh. "Disappointing. Slipshod."

"Did you at least get probed?" he asked.

"Ha!" Jan blurted. "Don't even get me started. I could abduct better than them. Grade-A aliens they are *not*."

"How did they like your business ideas?" Akimbo asked.

"No interest whatsoever."

"Not even *The Abduction Experience*?" Akimbo asked hopefully. "That seemed like a sure thing—get paid for something you're already doing for free."

"Thank you!" Jan exclaimed. "But Adnoydd didn't even bite at that one."

"That sucks for us," Akimbo said. "So I guess no finder's fee?" Tension in her voice belied the importance she placed on the question.

"Sorry. I imagine you really need the money for your husband's care, but I'm the opposite of a charity. I'll throw some store credit your way just for brokering my abduction, such as it was."

Akimbo was shaken to see their money problems looming still. Clagett read her disappointment and suffered a debilitating resurgence of guilt for getting sick in the first place. All of the madness swirling around them originated from that one inescapable development. Technically, ALS wasn't his fault, it wasn't a deliberate act to sabotage their lives, but he *had* made consequential decisions, like marrying Akimbo, that put her in the line of fire. He should have lived as an ascetic in a cave. He should have killed himself when he was first diagnosed. He should *not* have passively trusted the universe to have even an iota of interest in his welfare.

"This changes things," Akimbo said. In her distant tone,

Clagett recognized she was recalculating on a subconscious level. Unlike his surrender to hopelessness, she kept fighting.

Later, when Akimbo and Clagett rehashed the day, they disagreed about Akimbo's next words. Clagett claimed she started with "Six million dollars." Akimbo had no recollection of saying anything, but crassly jumping straight to a dollar amount sounded unlike her.

"Six million," Akimbo said in a grave samurai's baritone.

Clagett paused his self-flagellation to refocus on Akimbo. She was giggling, which made him believe someone was about to get taken down.

"Excuse me?" Jan said.

"Six million dollars ransom."

"You're kidnapping me?" Jan asked. She sounded incredulous, but there was a hint of pride for the recognition of her value.

"No, no," Akimbo quickly corrected. "Six million dollars for Adnoydd. After taxes."

Jan cocked her head to better hear. She seemed immediately interested, but her brain hadn't caught up to why.

"That's our price for letting *you* abduct *him*."

Clagett watched the exchange and knew better than to speak. Akimbo bedeviled Jan with a proposition that flowed counter to Jan's expectations—and his.

"He's got access to all sorts of intergalactic know-how," Akimbo elaborated, impatient now for Jan to catch up. "You can take the reins of interplanetary trade, banking, or whatever. He can tell you how to make your delivery vans fly. There's no telling what you might get out of him."

"I feel like you're joking," Jan suspicioned.

"I'm not."

Jan looked to Clagett for signs that she was being pranked. If anything, he relayed signs of being clueless, because he was.

"Are you even in a position to sell him?" Jan asked.

"Langford has him captive in the barn. Ariola isn't coming back. You don't have much time to decide."

Jan weighed the offer. "And if I don't pay?"

"Langford will feed him to the spiders."

Jan was listening intently but now looked confused. "Sorry, I'm not familiar with that euphemism, is that like 'sleeping with the fishes'?"

"It's fact, not an expression, and I would prefer it didn't play out like that." Akimbo gave Jan her stare of death to prod along the proceedings.

"It's not much money, and it *is* a unique connection."

"This is the opportunity of a lifetime."

Jan considered the options. "Sorry, I need to ask," she apologized. "What's your return policy?"

"Seriously? You get him as is with no take-backs," Akimbo said with disbelief.

Jan pondered a bit longer. "What do you know about the resale market for used aliens?"

Akimbo and Clagett's eyes met. Akimbo took the lead. "That's a great question, Jan, but it's something we know nothing about. If you do choose to go that route, we'd appreciate it if you left our names off the chain of custody."

Clagett grew uneasy. "I'm uncomfortable treating this transaction as a 'sale.' Could we come up with something else? *Ransom* as a source of income might draw IRS scrutiny. Handling fee? Intellectual property exchange?"

"I'll consult with Gia on the particulars if we reach an agreement," Akimbo said.

"Adnoydd didn't strike me as all that bright, but there

must be some way to monetize what he knows," Jan declared. "It's a question of whether I can recoup my investment."

"It's a risk," Akimbo said. "But if nothing else, you could keep him as a plaything or trot him out at cocktail parties to show your friends."

Jan waved a hand for Akimbo to stop speculating. "Give me a minute," she implored.

She walked onto the front porch and paced off its length a few times. She came back inside.

"Alright, I'll take a chance," she said.

———————————————

With Gia's assistance they worked out a plan for Clagett to sell his consulting company and all its "intellectual assets," meaning Adnoydd, to Jan's business for six million dollars, after taxes. The entire payment was due up front. They kept Adnoydd tied to a chair in the guest bedroom for the day it took to transfer the money.

Jan insisted that Adnoydd had to come willingly, so Langford politely asked if he'd prefer to go with Jan or face the spiders. Not surprisingly, Adnoydd chose Jan. When they last saw Adnoydd, Langford was slinging him into the back of Jan's SUV. His hands and feet were bound—at his request. He accepted he was deserving of abduction and wanted to do a respectable job of it.

"He might act like he doesn't know much," Geldine counseled. "You'll need to question him *hard* to get it out of him. Long and hard."

Jan nodded at her advice and took to the road.

Akimbo offered substantial payment to Geldine and Langford for their support. They said they didn't want a big chunk of money because they would waste it. Akimbo bought them new cars, paid for every kind of insurance, paid off their debt, and funded retirement accounts for each of them. Within a month, one of the nephews totaled Langford's new car.

In the chaos of Clagett's final months, Gracie and Zoey made a bid for freedom through a tunnel they painstakingly dug under the pasture fence. They headed away from their pen and came hard against the barbed wire and snarling dogs bordering the Shiflett wasteland. There they decided that Akimbo had been protecting them all this time and returned of their own accord.

Langford spent afternoons sitting with Clagett and on one occasion unburdened himself with a confession, making Clagett promise he would take it to his grave. Before Ariola's final departure, he had wrapped up a whole mess of spider egg sacs on a stick and wiped them inside the space van. He didn't know the fate of the homeward voyage, but he hoped they didn't make it and hoped they'd never return.

Geldine and Langford took excellent care of Clagett. When his needs increased and hospice care was unavoidable, Sha'nona pitched in and for a few months lived out of the guest room. When he and his needs disappeared, she stayed for a few months to look after Akimbo.

Akimbo and Geldine were at Clagett's side when he passed into the sweet hereafter. Geldine broke precedent and told him he would be going to heaven, even though he didn't believe in Jesus, because she hoped he might have a last-minute change of heart during his stopover in purgatory.

Akimbo told him she loved him, knowing that was all that needed to be said, that it held everything they shared. She held his hand, scratched the top of his head, and rubbed the tender spot on his tailbone, which seemed to bring a smile to his face, through the morphine, as his breathing slowed.

———————

Akimbo survived.

Acknowledgments

THIS NOVEL WAS INSPIRED by the caregivers I came to know as ALS progressively debilitated me. Their willingness to help me through the most mundane aspects of my life is a gift I cannot repay, despite paying—a lot—for their services.

I would like to thank Sheena, Dan, Tisha, Thomas, Faith, Sheila, Tyrell, and Laura for their long service and sensitivity to my needs. I am grateful for their assistance and companionship.

Many other caregivers helped for short periods of time. Five minutes was all it took before one woman jumped ship. More times than I can count, a caregiver visited to get to know my routine and, once they saw the labor involved, didn't return. My experiences with the caregivers who did show up, and the agencies that arranged them, formed my thankful-yet-chafed attitude toward caregiving.

I couldn't have survived without the love, support, and care of my wife, Helen, and my children, Conor and Bridget. They, too, had to adapt to the constant presence of caregivers in their home, and they did so with understanding and a sense of humor.

Though twisted into a science fiction tale of alien abductions, I tried to capture the real feeling of surrendering yourself to someone else's care. A caregiver's work is physically and emotionally invasive. The patient and caregiver are near strangers, forced on each other out of necessity, at a difficult point in the patient's life—or end of life. When done well, a caregiver's help is a miraculous relief. When done poorly, their presence can seem more vexing than the patient's health problems.

I do not represent myself as broadly knowledgeable about the many forms of disability and caregiving. I'm not. The socioeconomic pressures that produce low wages for caregivers and crippling costs for patients is also beyond my expertise. This is a story based on my limited experience.

Many of the story's elements are true. Transportation problems leading to chronic lateness and absenteeism, language and cultural differences complicating communication, inexperience with quadriplegic care, emotional breakdowns (mine and caregivers'), and ongoing caregiver health issues are all very real. I, in fact, *did* have a caregiver collapse with stomach pain one morning. Kneeling on the floor at the foot of my bed, with his head resting next to my feet, he asked if I had made him sick with black magic. He died that night at a hospital.

This novel was written by eye-gaze control using Tobii Dynavox software on a Microsoft Surface computer. Typing by eye is slow, but so is my ability to form sentences, so all in all the experience was surprisingly workable.

9 7 9 8 9 8 5 9 2 6 4 3 9